CREATIVE TEXTS PUBLISHERS
PO Box 50, Barto, PA 19504

Creative Texts Publishers products are available at special discounts for bulk purchase for sale promotions, premiums., fund-raising, and educational needs. For details, write Creative Texts Publishers, PO Box 50, Barto, PA 19504, or visit www.creativetexts.com

BLACKBEARD: A PAGE FROM THE COLONIAL HISTORY OF PHILADELPHIA
by MATHILDA DOUGLAS
Published by Creative Texts Publishers
PO Box 50
Barto, PA 19504
www.creativetexts.com

Creative Texts Edition, *Modern English Version*
First Printing
Copyright 2016 by Creative Texts Publishers, LLC
All rights reserved
Cover photos modified and used by license. Design by Daniel Edwards
Copyright 2016 Creative Texts Publishers, LLC

The following is a work of fiction. Any resemblance to actual names, persons, businesses, and incidents is strictly coincidental. Locations are used only in the general sense and do not represent the real place in actuality.

ISBN: 9780692769263

BLACKBEARD.

A PAGE FROM THE COLONIAL HISTORY OF PHILADELPHIA.

VOLUME I

THIS MANUSCRIPT WAS ORIGINALLY
PUBLISHED IN NEW-YORK:
BY
HARPER & BROTHERS,
NO. 82 CLIFFSTREET.

1835.

"Full well I wot, most mighty sovereign,
That all this famous antique history,
Of some the abundance of an idle brain,
Will judged be, and palsied forgery."

Spenser.

To J. F. WATSON, Esq.

Respected Sir,

As an individual, I claim not the privilege of a friend to inscribe to you the following pages; but, in common with others, an admirer of your disinterested labors in rescuing from oblivion the primitive records of our beloved city, I venture to hope that the liberty taken with your name may be deemed neither impertinent nor inappropriate; insomuch that an attempt has been made to delineate incidentally the manners and domestic habits of our ancestors. To such anachronisms as I may happen to be charged with (as they will doubtless be supported by sufficient proof) I plead guilty, to save further trouble; these apart, I have executed an historical sketch — not a fanciful romance.

Pure fiction, indeed, is the prerogative of genius alone; oral tradition, and in especial the written records of times past, crave a humbler pen.

That the author of the "Annals of Philadelphia" may long live to raise still higher the trophy which he has already reared to his indefatigable and enthusiastic labors, is the sincere prayer of one who, like him, takes pleasure in looking back, not only upon the years, but the days of olden time.

BLACKBEARD

BLACKBEARD.

CHAPTER I.

"But how the subject theme may gang,
Let time and chance determine;
Perhaps it may turn out a sang,
Perhaps turn out a sermon."—Burns.

On the fourth day of July, 1732, the ship *Santa Claus*, with Heinrich Oster master, left the port of Amsterdam, with a fair wind, bound for the Quaker settlements on the Delaware; where, under the peaceful administration of William Penn and his successors, had grown up a fair and flourishing town, called Philadelphia.

Towards the end of August, the sun rising as usual, one morning far out at sea there might have been seen the aforesaid ship slumbering peacefully on the sluggish mass of waters, that, as far as the eye could reach, presented that state of repose termed by sailors as "a dead calm." Built on the most approved model, the *Santa Claus* was exceedingly short from stem to stern; but, by way of compensating for deficiency in length, she was endowed with a marvelous breadth of beam.

The characteristic expression of jollity visible in the carved figure-head indicated that St. Nicolas had been selected to preside over the destiny of the beautiful fabric; and seven ports on a side, garnished with huge wooden guns, gave her a warlike appearance, well calculated to keep at a distance the bold buccaneer. The sails flapped at times lazily against the masts, and sundry sailors, modelled, as to breadth of beam, much after the fashion of the ship, smoked their short pipes with a phlegm savoring much of Dutch philosophy.

MATHILDA DOUGLAS

Captain Oster, a middle-aged man, of most portly dimensions, wore a small but very rubicund nose, which but barely projected beyond the line of his rosy cheeks, and bore indubitable evidence that he was one much conversant with cups and flagons. His eyelids nearly closed upon a pair of small blue eyes, of a lusterless and rather solemn expression. A flaxen wig, that had seen service, curled around his ample visage, surmounted by a steeple-crowned hat, the brim of which overshadowed his features. The upper portion of his person was enveloped in a waistcoat of bright scarlet cloth, garnished with a row of immense silver buttons; his outermost pair of breeches had been originally of black velvet, but, by dint of long exposure to the action of salt-water, and habitual retention of such unctuous and resinous material as vessels generally abound in, the color became somewhat difficult to describe. Woolen hose, displaying a muscular leg, and heavy shoes, with huge steel buckles, completed his investment. Leaning over the side of the vessel, Heinrich seemed absorbed in solemn meditation, puffing the while volumes of smoke, and unconsciously toying with a beard of five days' growth.

Near him stood his mate, by name Jeptha Dobbs, lank and loosely framed, inclining his head and shoulders with a view of reducing himself to a conversational level, — his stature being precisely six feet and a half, at his utmost elongation: straight sandy hair fell on either side of a remarkably small head, whence issued at times a voice peculiarly shrill and clear.

"Any sign of wind?" demanded the captain, looking directly up into the sunburnt visage of Mr. Dobbs.

"Not about these parts," responded the mate, shifting his head to several quarters as he spoke.

The captain mechanically refreshed his pipe, gazed out upon the sea, and set about digesting the information thus afforded. Jeptha raised himself on tiptoe, and took a deliberate survey of the horizon: not a single breath ruffled the surface of the water; for five days had it been, and still remained, a glittering mirror, reflecting a burning sun in a cloudless sky. Muttering somewhat touching the proper employment of time, he accordingly coiled his long form under shade of the longboat, and proceeded to adapt a new piece of twine to the circumference of an ancient hat, whistling the while something intended for a tune.

The two cabin passengers on board were an old man and his niece, who, carried along by the tide so strongly setting in for the New World, and urged by the representations of many who had preceded them, had left their fatherland for the green banks of the Delaware.

Major Scheveling had served under Prince Eugene: although now, by reason of age and wounds, incapacitated for military duty, he still bore the commanding air and upright carriage of a veteran officer. His principal amusement during the calm had been playing chess with his niece Barbara, who, under his instruction, was no mean proficient in that scientific game.

The light, that entered the cabin from the stern windows, fell full upon the features of the lady, considering with deep attention every move of the enemy, and at times lighted up with a smile of anticipated triumph. Directly opposite sat the major; his cogitations equally profound, but, to judge from his countenance, not of so pleasing a nature. His case indeed was nearly desperate— his sole remaining castle guarded the king against the furious attack of two rooks and a knight. His brow grew darker as the foe hemmed in his slender garrison — "Check to king and castle, uncle!" said Barbara, and at the next move her knight swept his rook from the board: the king moved out of check, but the foe pressed on: soon the silver voice of Barbara uttered the exulting "checkmate!" and the veteran acknowledged his defeat with a grim smile.

"The third game this morning, uncle! you should compliment me on my rapid improvement; even the curate of Oppelstein would fear me now."

"Fear *thee*, child! — tush! I have barely looked at the game, else wouldst thou have found the result far different: and I assure thee that the curate plays a game which I find it rather difficult to excel."

"I should think so, good uncle; for I have heard him boast, that in playing with you he could safely calculate on four games out of five, though he did admit that you played an excellent game."

Here the major gravely took from his left waistcoat pocket a snuff-box of agate set in gold, and accommodating himself to a liberal portion of the stimulant, he hemmed twice, and invited his niece to walk on deck. Issuing together from the companion-way, the first object that met their view was the ingenious mate, in the occupation and position sometime described. Jeptha raised his eyes, and without discontinuing his whistling, returned the military courtesy of the major, and the good-humored salutation of Barbara, with an oblique nod to the one, and a gaze of admiration at the other.

In good sooth, Barbara was a damsel well to look upon; fair-haired as her Saxon ancestors, an azure eye, and a countenance expressing a vigor of health almost destructive of feminine delicacy, were it not softened by the dimple that played around a very pretty mouth, enclosing a row of teeth which ever, when she spoke or laughed, exhibited their perfect regularity and exquisite whiteness. Add to this, a figure rather inclined to embonpoint; a step firm but elastic; a well-turned ankle, fully displayed by the shortness of a dark-colored and comfortable woolen skirt; and a foot, the diminutive size and symmetry of which were set forth by a little slipper, adorned, according to the fashion of the day, with an enormous rosette of orange-colored band.

Jeptha had never been in love, his cool and equable temperament being in nowise adapted to the development of such a fiery passion. He was aware that his forefathers, during many generations, had not deemed it unbecoming to take unto them ribs, therein following the ensample of the early settlers; and, generally speaking, his ideas concerning the duties and accomplishments of the fairer portion of creation were, for lack of personal knowledge, rather crude and peculiar. The term "wife" conveyed to him the mixed idea of scolding, children, and pumpkin pies: he fancied that his peculiar knack at whistling would counteract the feminine tendency to objurgation; children fall under the denomination of necessary evils; and the bare possibility of pumpkin pie made his mouth water. To a mind thus prepared, matrimony bears a more feasible aspect than to those highly susceptible imaginations which blaze up with the slightest spark from the eye of beauty, reaming of fancied bliss, and reflecting not that marriage, like riches, is calculated to give us many advantages in prosecuting our search after happiness, and both may result in disappointment if we consider them anything further than the means of enhancing virtuous enjoyments.

Jeptha looked hard at Barbara, and whistled, and looked again, and thought much, and whispered to himself, "Mrs. Dobbs," and almost jumped at the sound of his own whisper; then smoothed down his sandy locks, and proceeding, with a delicate smirk upon his visage, to the object of his cogitations, he addressed her as follows: —

"This here calm is not so remarkable agreeable, though I shouldn't like to bet that, as being a female, you mightn't naturally prefer squally weather."

"Nay, Mr. Dobbs, I am well-nigh tired of this part of the ocean; pray, when do you expect to see land?"

"Some time before we touch it," answered Mr. Dobbs, breaking into a low chuckle, partly repressed through respect for the lady, yet sufficiently indicative of the delight he experienced from his own quaint jest. Strengthened by this happy introduction of the conversation, Jeptha was on the point of expounding his matrimonial views, when the brightening prospects of the fair damsel were suddenly overcast by a small cloud making its appearance on the edge of the water, directly in the east, to which the attention of all on board was speedily directed. Slowly it grew larger, and its masses became darker, as they rose one after another from the watery level. The captain and mate held a brief consultation, and sundry directions being given in pursuance of the same, the little Dutch sailors were set to work, and all sail which were considered likely to endanger a vessel during a heavy blow, were gradually and carefully taken in. Barely sufficient canvass was left for the proper management of the vessel, and every one became busy in making observations on the threatening appearance of the heavens.

"All snug, Mr. Dobbs?" inquired the captain, as a matter of course. Mr. Dobbs leisurely inserted a long slim portion of pigtail into his nether jaw, ere he answered, in his usual shrill and monotonous manner. "Everything but the little brown pig, that Flemish Peter has been catching all the morning."

Fully satisfied, Captain Oster turned to the placid enjoyment of his pipe, being persuaded in his own mind that, under St. Nicolas, the safety of the good ship *Santa Claus* depended upon the seamanship and watchfulness of his mate Jeptha; and reflecting, that when everything which prudence can suggest, and skill perform, has been duly accomplished, we should trust to the merits of our patron saint for the issue, he buttoned a coarse pea-jacket of bearskin over his scarlet waistcoat, and abided the coming storm.

The cloud, which had been scarcely visible at first, low in the horizon, had risen with threatening rapidity, and, swelling as it approached to the most gigantic proportions, now covered one-third of the heavens. The low sound of distant thunder was distinctly heard, and sudden gleams of lightning traversed the black clouds that hung in gloomy folds over the edge of the waters. The gentle and almost imperceptible heaving of the ocean gave way to long and regular swells, denoting afar off the war of angry elements; and the ship itself, that for so many days had lain almost motionless upon the glassy waters, began to pitch violently in the rolling sea.

Barbara gazed upon the gathering gloom with feelings in which admiration of the sublimity of the scene before her was powerfully blended with vague and undefined apprehensions of coming danger. Large heavy drops of rain soon warned her of the propriety of repairing to the cabin; and as she descended, assisted by her uncle, a vivid stream of lightning flashed through the murky atmosphere, blinding the eye for a moment with intolerable brightness, followed by a crash of thunder that shook the heavens.

On came the wind, beating down the waves to a level surface of angry foam — no sound but the deep and fearful rushing of the tempest; and the ship, head before the wind, dashed madly onward, her tall masts bending, and her strong frame trembling before the fury of the storm. For some time, the gale increased in violence, and the more aged and experienced mariners exchanged looks expressive of doubt and anxiety. The gentle Barbara, kneeling before her Maker, prayed in the fervor of a pure heart, imploring protection against the fierce power of the tempest; and besought Him who formed the waves, and lets loose the sweeping blast, to still them, lest all should perish. While she yet kneeled, as if Heaven regarded the pleading voice of innocence, the fury of the gale evidently abated, the darkness of the heavens diminished, and the rain, that but now poured down in overwhelming cataracts, subsided to a gentle shower. Jeptha regarded the sudden change with an observant eye, and approaching the captain, who was leisurely unlashing himself from the mainmast, made some remarks touching their narrow escape, without alluding, however, to any providential interference.

"Ah! Mr. Dobbs," observed the captain, with an air of as much solemnity as his features could command, "it were well that you put your trust in the blessed St. Nicolas; sinner as I am, I did but breathe a devout prayer to that worthy saint, and the wind immediately fell." This being a much longer speech than Heinrich Oster was in the habit of making at any one time, Jeptha paid particular attention to it; at the conclusion, observing in return that he doubted whether St. Nicolas himself actually quelled the storm, inasmuch as he probably might have been otherwise engaged at the time, and, it may be, heard not the pious invocation, to which Captain Oster would fain attribute such marvelous efficacy. Heinrich gravely shook his head, as if much shocked by the heretical opinion promulgated by the mate; and suddenly assuming a bustling air of command, turned to among his sturdy little crew to inspect the ship and repair damages.

The squall had disappeared as rapidly as it had approached: again the blue vault of heaven appeared in all its beauty — the bright sunbeams danced merrily on the waves — the short seas, that dashed the spray over the bow and against the sides of the vessel, alone bore witness that a gale had sometime swept the deep; and far as the eye could reach, the glittering waves curled their white crests in the sun. Pleasant weather and favorable winds now sped the *Santa Claus* on her voyage — nothing occurred to retard her regular and gentle course; prudently kept under such canvass as would not be dangerous in case of a sudden squall, she entered the Capes of

Delaware early on a Saturday morning, all hands well, save a sailor named Hans Gobleick, who had eaten too much codfish the evening before.

On the first annunciation of land, Major Scheveing had hurried his niece on deck, and they both gazed on the low shores of the bay with mixed and varying emotions. There is a feeling of delight peculiar to such a situation, of which, unless once experienced, one can scarcely form an adequate conception. The simple words, "land on the lee-bow," had a singularly thrilling effect. Barbara felt that joyful excitement usually produced in a young and ardent mind by the near approach to new scenes and anticipated wonders. There was the city of Penn, reared among the wild forests of the Delaware, a monument of the peaceful virtues and revered integrity of its amiable founder. There roamed the painted savage, darting across the waters in his light canoe, or striking down the fleet deer in its rapid coarse; and there, it may be, the proud Indian chief, bound to the stake, bade stern defiance to the foes of his tribe, chanting his wild death-song, and smiling scornfully in extremest torture. An involuntary shudder accompanied the vivid picture of imagination — the maiden gladly turned to the realities of the scene before her. Her uncle stood near her, regarding the New World with a melancholy gaze — years had passed since his only son, a youth of twelve years, had fled the paternal home; certain particulars were gathered, which, added to the knowledge of his roving disposition, left no doubt that he had embarked for some distant country, and every inquiry had been set on foot, but in vain. Long abandoned as lost, and by others long forgotten, intrusive memory would oft-times sadden the father's heart; and still lingered that faint hope, that year after year yet awaited tidings from his lost child.

BLACKBEARD

CHAPTER II.

"But some love not the method of your first —
Romance they count it, throw't away as dust."
Bunyan.

A month had elapsed since the arrival of the *Santa Claus* at Philadelphia, and Major Scheveling began to feel somewhat at home in the pleasant and beautifully situated mansion in which, thanks to the kind superintendence of his niece, he had the gratification of being surrounded by comforts and conveniences which strongly reminded him of his house on the Wausport, near Amsterdam.

From the river Delaware a gradual ascent of about three hundred feet terminated at the level of Svenson Street. This street ran parallel to the river, and contained many handsome dwellings, being, in fact, the principal thoroughfare for the southern part of the city. From this street, a carriageway, beautifully shaded by tall and venerable sycamores, wound around the southern fence of the graveyard, and led to the residence of Major Scheveling, distant about a furlong from the church; beyond this a narrow path turned into the woods that skirted the place, and formed part of the forest that stretched along the wild banks of the Manaiunk.

The mansion itself was of a solid and massive structure — bricks, alternately red and glazed black, imported expressly from Holland by Cornelius Erigson, the late proprietor, had lost, in some degree, their pristine brilliancy; for that reason, it may be, according the more with the somber beauty of the adjoining forest The projecting eaves and penthouse over the first story were adorned with carved woodwork, somewhat fanciful in decoration, and of a heavy style of architecture, fashionable at that time, evincing the opulence, if not the taste, of the wealthy Cornelius.

Facing the south, a doorway opened into a porch of most ample dimensions; a light trellis supported the climbing vine and sweet-scented jasmine, mingling their verdant foliage in unchecked luxuriance, and embowering the entrance with cool and fragrant verdure. Beds of the rarest tulips lined the smooth gravel walks, that led to various parts of the garden; arbors, supporting heavy clusters of tempting grapes, gave promise of shelter and repose; and the warm air of the south, passing by, was perfumed with the blended fragrance of the wild locust and honeysuckle; around this cultivated spot arose a low paling — beyond lay the dense shadow of the forest.

A footpath through the woods north of Erigson House gave access to the domains of an old Swedish gentleman, who maintained the dignity of his noble race by a certain style of magnificence and luxury, as yet unprecedented in the colony. The Chevalier Oxenstiern, as he was universally denominated, was considerably beyond the prime of life, as could be satisfactorily proved by the testimony of contemporaneously aged men; and yet, singular as it may appear, his form and features bore not the slightest indication of old age. Time had passed, and, as if upheld by some unearthly influence, had left no trace on his unchanging lineaments.

Regarded by many as the possessor of some mysterious power, his deeds of benevolence excited among the credulous and uninformed even more of awe than affection. In the best society of the colony he moved with the ease and dignity of a well-bred gentleman; with the grave and reflecting, his profound acquaintance with every department of science, the mass of interesting information which he displayed on every important subject, and his familiar acquaintance with classic authors, entitled him to their highest respect and consideration; to the young and gay, his eloquent and animated conversation, his varied tales of other times, and his sparkling and playful wit, possessed an attractive influence, to which all yielded with delight.

On an elevated spot in the garden of Erigson House stood a large sundial, which, by reason of long-continued neglect, had become overgrown with the luxuriant tendrils of the ivy. Barbara had for some time contemplated restoring this instrument to its original service, and on a bright autumnal morning issued forth for this especial purpose. What was her surprise, however, on approaching the dial, to observe a stranger occupied in removing the parasitical plant! Her first impulse was to retire; but finding that the stranger was too earnestly engaged to notice her presence, curiosity induced her to take a survey of his appearance. In stature somewhat below the ordinary height of man, his muscular and well-knit frame was set off to much advantage by a dress of the most costly materials; his hair, turned back from a broad and noble forehead, was scrupulously powdered, after the manner of the age; large dark eyes, an aquiline nose, a handsomely curved mouth, and a well-set chin, formed the outlines of an aspect graceful and commanding — it was Oxenstiern.

She was about to retire, when, as if for some time conscious of her presence, the stranger slowly turned, and saluted her with an easy and unembarrassed air,

"Permit me to introduce myself, Miss Scheveling, — you probably have heard the name of Oxenstiern; as a neighbor I claim acquaintance and friendly intercourse with your father and yourself."

As Oxenstiern spake, his eyes read the countenance of Barbara with so much earnestness, and he pronounced the word father with such emphatic meaning, that Barbara almost blushed as she replied, with some hesitation, that her uncle would be happy to acknowledge his courtesy.

"You sought the dial," continued Oxenstiern, "for the sake of noting the flight of time. I have marked the hour and the moment in which we met, and should it be that the future links your fate to mine, doubt not that the stars shall be read aright."

Barbara felt no alarm, — she comprehended not the language nor the motives of the stranger. She listened to his deep rich voice as to the sound of music, — replied with a pleased glance at his benignant smile, — and proceeding to the house, gave him a formal introduction to her uncle. Major Scheveling.

CHAPTER III.

**"Sir knight and skilful clerk, and courtier vain,
Paid homage to this lovely suzerain —
While she, in careless guise and equal air,
Nor favored one, nor bade the rest despair."
Donne.**

Matters had proceeded for some time without any event worthy of particular notice having taken place; the winter had commenced with its usual rigor; several heavy falls of snow had whitened the housetops, and numberless fields of ice rendered the navigation of the river dangerous, if not altogether impossible.

The major found in Oxenstiern a companion well calculated to dispel the tedium of a winter evening: piquing himself on his own masterly game of chess, he was pleased with the shrewd and wary game of the chevalier: exceedingly well informed on the subject of military tactics, and somewhat proud of his many campaigns, the art of war was a theme on which his eloquence was not readily exhausted: but Oxenstiern met him on his vantage-ground; for battle he gave battle, siege followed siege, and towns were taken and cities sacked alternately. One circumstance perplexed Barbara, although it appeared in nowise to excite the surprise of her uncle, — the chevalier spoke of incidents which had occurred from fifty years to a century back. True, he might have heard of such things; but the familiar manner in which he gave many a minute detail of individual heroism, and his graphic sketches of famous scenes of carnage, irresistibly impressed her with the idea that they came from the lips of an eyewitness. To suppose such a thing involved an absurdity; and thus Barbara reasoned with herself: — she looked at Oxenstiern — he was "certainly not over forty-five years of age,"— he was extolling the personal valor of the great Gustavus Adolphus during the bombardment of Riga, and her glance met his eye, lighted with all the enthusiasm of recollection—a singular thrill passed through her, and the absurd impression was stronger than ever.

"By-the-by," continued Oxenstiern, "I have been duly commissioned by Madam Markham, of whose attractions you have doubtless heard, to bring captive Major Scheveling and his fair niece to her house this evening. Learning, wit, and beauty there unite to pay homage to the charms of the hostess. You, young lady, may there behold a woman beautiful without vanity; and the major is too gallant a soldier to decline so fair a challenge."

Although the major had not, Barbara had heard more than once of the beauty, the wealth, and the accomplishments of Madam Christine. She had lost her husband in the first year of her marriage; and though still young, remained faithful to his memory. Highly accomplished herself, she had the tact of drawing to her circle men of learning as well as the votaries of fashion. Perfectly independent in aught else, even *she* felt the influence and bowed before the undefined power of Oxenstiern.

The invitation was accepted, proper preparations were made, and the sleigh of Oxenstiern being already in waiting at the door, the party set out.

The moon was rising as they left Erigson House, glittering on the snow that lay around them, and lighting the smooth path over which the sleigh was whirled by four rapid steeds. Muffled up in warm furs, the travelers felt not the keen north-westers that poured their fury on the now leafless sycamores.

Passing over Dock Creek, the surface of which was a solid sheet of ice, where merry skaters were joyously disporting themselves in the clear moonlight, they turned into Second Street, and, but a short distance beyond Christ Church, stopped before the dwelling of Madam Christine Markham.

Disembarrassing themselves of cloaks, snowshoes, and so forth, the major and his niece followed Oxenstiern into the saloon. Upon their entrance Madam Markham advanced to receive them. Nothing could exceed the grace and delicacy which she manifested in a cordial welcome to her new guests: she saluted Barbara with the affectionate warmth of a sister, and extended her hand to the old soldier, evincing indeed some surprise, but by no means displeasure, as he respectfully pressed it to his lips, in due conformity with his ideas of military politeness.

The apartment in which Madam Christine received her guests was of moderate dimensions, and furnished with unusual elegance and taste: high backed chairs of mahogany, supplied with cushions of crimson velvet were ranged along the wainscot; an elbow chair of more ample capacity graced each side of the lofty mantel. Directly over the fireplace, whence a huge hickory fire shot its cheering glow over the dark mahogany, hung a portrait of the royal martyr Charles of England; on the right hand might be seen the calm and benignant features of the virtuous founder of Philadelphia; on the left frowned the stern-visaged, iron-handed Gustavus Adolphus. Madam Markham herself was of exquisite beauty: from her mother she inherited the deep yet rich complexion of a southern clime; from her, too, the large dark orbs, where passion needs must lie sleeping, though subdued to a downcast and bashful glance; her rosy lips pouted as if they disdained aught but each other; and if time had dealt with Madam Christine, it was but to ripen her lovely form to more voluptuous beauty.

Endowed with such natural perfections, the young widow was urged by early education and habit to neglect no art by which her dominion might be strengthened in every heart; and her bosom swelled in haughty triumph as she noted that her approach kindled unwonted fire in the eye of the sober sage, and affected not to perceive the timid yet passionate glance that betrayed the fears and hopes of modest youth.

Barbara had seated herself, and was observing the appearance and movements of her hostess with undisguised interest. The person with whom Madam Markham at that moment held converse was a gentleman of some fifty years, dressed with a fashionable gayety perhaps in some degree unseasonable at his time of life; the more especially as his features and person gave tokens of the unsparing hand of time. Beneath a full and handsomely curled wig lay almost hidden the small nose and angular chin appertaining to a wrinkled and sallow countenance; two little eyes, deeply imbedded in the head, shot their vivacious rays through a pair of spectacles handsomely framed in tortoise-shell. The remainder of his person was in keeping with his physiognomy, — lank, tottering, and powerless; yet the general impression was given, that he was attempting the demeanor of a devoted cavalier; and, somewhat to the surprise of Barbara, the fair widow appeared agreeably interested in the attentions of her antiquated admirer.

"That ancient lover," said Oxenstiern, who at this Moment joined Barbara, "is Sir William Keith; he has lost the form and features, not the follies, of youth; his adoration has outlived the belles of two successive generations, and Madam Christine charitably fans the dying flame."

Barbara looked up at the speaker, but his countenance wore that calm and polished affability from which naught may be divined: she almost thought a sarcastic glance accompanied his mention of Madam Christine. She knew not why, but a cloud seemed ready to obscure her conceptions of this fair and faultless being.

Thomas Hasell, a man whose countenance was strongly expressive of benevolence, exhibiting a form of excessive *embonpoint*, and clothed in a garb of Quaker-like simplicity and neatness, entered and shook hands with Madam Christine. At the approach of the mayor (for Thomas at this time filled that station in the city), Sir William Keith surveyed him from head to foot with evident displeasure; and moving from the center of the apartment, entered into conversation with a young man of most unpretending exterior, who had been hitherto a silent spectator.

"That young man," said the chevalier to Barbara, "with whom Sir William appears to be discussing an interesting subject, is a character with whom I wish you to become acquainted; he is a pupil of mine, shrewd and inquiring: however humble at present his name and appearance, something tells me that he will be remembered and admired long after his present master will be forgotten."

Barbara shook her head, as if doubting the correctness of this prediction: but a century has passed, and he who was only known as the protégé of Sir William Keith and a leading member of the Apron Club, is now the immortal Franklin.

The party passed as parties usually do. Madam Christine glided from one group to another, mingling in conversation with a readiness and grace that fully sustained her reputation for wit and intellect. Oxenstiern and Thomas Hasell were unanimous in thinking that the bridge in Chestnut Street, hard by Daniel Mason's tannery, was exceedingly in want of repair; and that the riotous conduct of the Indian servants in the upper part of the town, especially the preceding Sabbath on Mulberry common, called loudly for the authority of the council. The mayor further observed, that some persons, whom he would not name, were of opinion that the present council lacked somewhat of the zeal of their predecessors. Major Scheveling was complimented on his youthful appearance by Sir William Keith; but being too conscientious to return the compliment, was considered by Sir William as rather deficient in courtesy. Barbara in the meanwhile, was, perhaps, in some measure surprised to find that young Mr. Franklin was fluently entertaining her with a series of pithy and amusing observations.

Wine wad handed around by a negro servant, followed by an Indian boy bearing an ample silver salver filled with cakes and comfitures. This appeared to be the signal for departure, and the exit of Thomas Hasell set all in motion.

In a short time, all left the house: merry tinkling bells rang gayly before the porch; and the broad moonlight gave an enlivening appearance to the scene, as sleigh after sleigh rapidly left the residence of Madam Markham.

Upon the arrival of the chevalier at his own house, he proceeded directly to his sleeping apartment, a square chamber of moderate dimensions, less remarkable for rich and costly furniture than for the rare paintings that adorned the walls, and several statues of exquisite sculpture, selected by the somewhat singular taste of the owner to adorn his bedroom.

Having carefully locked the door of the chamber, he took down a painting of the largest size, behind which a massive oaken door, elevated about three feet from the floor of the bedroom, appeared as if imbedded in tbe solid wall.

BLACKBEARD

Applying a small but curiously fashioned key to this door, it opened inwardly on well-oiled hinges, and admitted the chevalier into a recess of considerable size, admirably adapted to all purposes of secrecy and concealment. A waxen taper faintly glimmered on an assemblage of dim and shadowy objects; among which a human skeleton of gigantic proportions reared its ghastly shape, its right arm extended in a menacing gesture. Oxenstiern approached the taper to a small and antique vase, which the figure held in its bony palm, and instantly a flame gushed forth and filled the room with a powerful and brilliant light.

A furnace occupied one corner, and sundry crucibles, vials of many-colored liquids, ingots of different metals, and other paraphernalia of an alchemist, denoted that Oxenstiern attempted the more occult chemical combinations. Few, indeed, at that time, indulged the hope of obtaining the philosopher's stone; but the transmutation of metals was not yet despaired of; and much laborious experiment, patient investigation, and multifarious research were directed to the means of prolonging human life.

On a table in another corner lay a telescope, a portable quadrant, a transit instrument and equatorial sector, an ivory circle containing the Chinese zodiac, and a tablet of the moon, divided, according to the computation of the early Arabian astronomers, into twenty-eight mansions; in addition to these, a multitude of papers, containing figures of triangles, spheres, and ellipses, calculations of solar and lunar eclipses, distances of certain planets, the sun's right ascension and declination, the moon's horizontal parallax, sizes and relative positions of the fixed stars, and observations on the distances and diameters of the known comets.

The third angle of the recess was occupied by numerous shelves, on which were gathered rare birds of gorgeous plumage, perfect skeletons of singularly small animals, and human skulls, differing in size and shape, and presenting every known variety in the race of man.

The skeleton that lighted the apartment stood in front of the remaining corner, before which hung, with an appearance of mysterious concealment, a curtain of blue silk.

The dawn of day found Oxenstiern profoundly absorbed in the perusal of an antique volume bound in crimson velvet; curious illuminations relieved the manuscript, which in deep black letter loaded the vellum page. His studies were, however, suddenly interrupted by the warning sound of a little bell, which hung directly over his head; and closing and securing the book by its silver clasps, he proceeded to his bedroom, and gave himself up to repose.

BLACKBEARD

CHAPTER IV.

"They swore by the Rood they were saylors good,
But rich merchants they could not bee —
To France nor Flanders dare we pass,
Nor Bordeaux voyage dare we fare;
And all for a Rover that lyes on the seas,
Who robs us of our merchant ware."
Romance of Sir Andrew Barton.

Much excitement prevailed in Philadelphia about this time touching sundry piracies lately committed in the bay. The famous Lowe, in a ship of thirty guns, called the "Merry Christmas," was said to be still cruising in the neighborhood of the capes, after having taken and plundered many vessels; eight or ten of Sprigg's men had, in an open boat, pillaged Grant's shallop, between Newcastle and Apoquiming, and carried off with them two valuable negro men; besides which, the brig May, having on board much choice wine for Jonathan Dickinson, as she lay in the stream off Marcus Hook, had been boarded at night, and the said wine taken out of her, as was thought at the time, by others of Sprigg's men. Other depredations of a similar, and some of a more daring character, had at times been committed by the aforesaid buccaneers, and sufficed in no small degree to annoy and perplex the peaceful citizens; but their alarm was much increased by a rumor which spread rapidly in all directions, that the notorious Captain Teach, commonly called Blackbeard, had threatened to visit Philadelphia, and only delayed this projected attack until the arrival of his consort, a vessel of twenty-six guns, then fitting out at Providence.

MATHILDA DOUGLAS

This Blackbeard had acquired a reputation for daring fearlessness and cruelty very little inferior to that of his predecessor Captain Kid. His name, and even his person, were familiarly known along the Delaware, and many persons in Philadelphia were suspected of having intercourse with him, although none openly acknowledged it; which, together with his known resolution and desperate contempt of life, added to the belief that his comrades were within reach of his summons, may readily account for the fact that he walked the streets of the town in broad daylight, at sundry times, with perfect nonchalance, touching his three-cocked beaver to the most substantial citizens, who in turn saluted him with that outward respect and inward aversion which one would be disposed to pay and feel towards a civil advance from his Satanic majesty in proper person, and wondered much among themselves at the marvelous hardihood of the man; some, indeed, going so far as to hint that private citizens were authorized to take hold of him: notwithstanding which alacrity of opinion, none seemed actually disposed to peril their individual persons by attempting the arrest of the bold buccaneer.

While the town lay in this state of gloom and despondency, the face of things was on a sudden entirely changed and enlivened by the arrival of the British man-of-war *Greyhound*, commanded by Captain Solgard, whose instructions were precise to bring in Blackbeard, dead or alive. The town, of course, rejoiced exceedingly, and the captain, being moreover young, handsome, and in nowise given to bashfulness, not only received distinguished attention from the municipal fathers, but speedily became a favorite with the daughters also; insomuch that bright eyes became yet brighter at the sight of his becoming uniform, and not a few parties were given, which would have been considered little worth without the presence of the handsome captain.

To the soirees of Madam Markham the captain, from his rank and official station, as well as by the influence of easy manners and an agreeable person, became a welcome and not infrequent visitor. As a natural result, he suddenly fell in love with Madam Christine — at least he thought so — and the fair dame, whose ruling passion was universal dominion over the hearts of the sterner sex, experienced more than ordinary gratification in receiving the homage of the gallant captain. Solgard imagined that her dark eye, as it met his glance, beamed with more than wonted fire, and fancied that her fascinating voice addressed him with unconscious tenderness: he accordingly wrote several passionate madrigals, looked as melancholy as his jovial nature would allow, and dreamed, among a variety of fantastic visions, that as he was leading the lovely lady to the altar the ferocious Blackbeard suddenly appeared and carried her off in triumph.

About half a mile below the Swedes' church, and on the river bank, stood a log-house, inhabited by a withered old crone, but little known by her neighbors, with whom she appeared to shun intercourse; and being sufficiently ugly, and withal as deaf as a post, she was, on this satisfactory evidence, pronounced a witch. This being established, it was conjectured that the tenement which she inhabited, being of no small extent, and utterly disproportioned to the sole accommodation of her diminutive person, most probably served as a nocturnal resort for other witches, who, being out from Salem and other parts, found this a central situation to dismount from their broomsticks and hold their diabolical orgies. Persons passing at midnight, and obliged to cross the run at no great distance from the house, had also made solemn oath that many lights were shining in the building, and testified to unearthly yells and bursts of fiendish merriment.

Reports of this nature had reached the ear of Solgard, and, acting on his skeptical and inquisitive nature, stimulated him to employ some means of ascertaining on what they were founded. One stormy evening, accordingly, having been, as he thought, very agreeable to Madam Christine, he was returning to his vessel in no little elation of spirits, and humming, as he passed along Water Street, an irregular stave of some fanciful love-ditty, his attention was arrested by certain sounds of a convivial nature, proceeding from the second story of Peg Mullen's beefsteak house; and having been previously initiated as an honorary member of the club, be forthwith entered without hesitation, hoping to acquire some information concerning the aforesaid witch, the idea of whom did certainly, in a most supernatural manner, persist in haunting his brain.

His entry into the room was quietly performed, and was not immediately noticed by the club, the respectable members thereof being one and all somewhat noisily engaged in convincing a reluctant individual that decorum, good fellowship, sobriety, and various other equally important considerations, imperatively required that he should quaff a very large bumper of Madeira.

"Nay, Nicolas! the wine is good, I will warrant me," said the president, in a smooth oily voice.

"By the wreath of Bacchus! but this cup shall be crushed! and thou, Nicolas Salomen, art the man!" shouted a young member.

"Most erudite Nicolas," observed Oxenstiern, who was evidently imbued with the merry spirit of the fraternity, "thy wisdom hath taught thee to search after truth; deny not then the genial goblet, as thou regardest him that said, 'in vino veritas.'"

The little man, to wit, Master Nicolas Salomen, to whom the foregoing exhortations were addressed, looked through his tortoise-shell spectacles with singular gravity at his advisers. His features and figure might speak for some sixty winters, but deep study and much learning had, as it were, incrusted him with an air of antiquity, heightened by unsuspecting and simple bearing.

The abstract nature of his intercourse with the world about him — confined to a few physical wants, and even those supplied for the most part with but partial interruption to his classical reveries— joined to a guileless and inoffensive deportment, rendered him almost always unconscious of the numerous jokes perpetrated on his simple nature, and a universal favorite with old and young.

His apparel for the last forty years had been invariably a coat, vest, and breeches of black velvet, adorned with black horn buttons; his gray hair was unpowdered, and terminated behind in a long queue; the pockets in the rear of his coat, being immeasurably capacious, contained, not only his favorite Greek and Latin authors, but fragments of tobacco-pipes, mineralogical treasures, and divers spoons belonging to his landlady, who, from long experience being well aware of the learned Salomen's eccentricities, instituted weekly a search after such articles as were missing about the house, invariably finding the same in said pockets,—at which Nicolas would marvel exceedingly.

It was the custom of the learned Nicolas to fold his hands behind him on these protuberant portions of his garment, and in this guise to traverse the highway without paying attention to any external object: collisions occasionally took place; in which case he would gravely beg pardon, a mode of expression finally so habitual that he had been known to apologize to a pump.

"Doubtless, my very good friends," said Nicolas, "the bowl is ample, and filled with veritable Falernian; yet I would fain —" reiterated clamors here interrupted his speech, and many voices were heard persuading him to do justice to the bumper. Still he struggled manfully, with sundry ejaculations, heard at intervals; such as, "good Master Hasell"— "three full goblets during the Symposium"— "ne quid nimis, most learned Oxenstiern"— "aliam otatem, alia decent."

"Hardly decent," echoed the president "Bear witness all ye, that Nicolas Salomen vituperateth our goodly fellowship; for this must he needs swallow another goblet.

"Prithee, Master Hasell! I would explain this matter: some things I would say are unbecoming — "

"He scandalizeth," said a member; "yet another forfeit" At this moment Oxenstiern whispered somewhat to the president, whose eyes twinkled at the new idea; the meeting was called to order, and Solgard for the first time became observable to the boisterous company. He was immediately accommodated with wine and a seat, and being put into a fair way of indemnifying himself for his late attendance, the president, with a mock solemnity, addressed "worthy Master Salomen" in the following manner: —

"It can hardly be unknown to thee, most profound sir, that it ever hath been the usage of this club, in regard to such members as have transgressed in a grievous manner, to inflict upon the same certain pains, penalties, or taxes, as the offence may manifestly require. In thy especial case, although there be who think that we have touched too lightly both thy non-conformity and thy dangerous words touching the deportment of this grave assembly, yet being moved by sundry considerations, we may, and hereby do, remit the vinous libations — the which, nevertheless, have been most justly adjudged to thee — provided thou dost, in consideration and in the lieu thereof, sing, recite, rehearse, or in some melodious guise set forth any quaint or merry ditty."

To this address Nicolas vouch-safed no immediate answer, pondering awhile on the feasibility of the change proposed; then, as if slowly recollecting some long-forgotten metre, he nodded his head to the imaginary inflections of the tune; this having continued for a few moments, he gathered himself up, and hemming at first at some length, and then briefly, he sang as follows: —

"Be it right or wrong, 'tis men among
On women to complain —
Answer me this, how that it is
A labor *spent in vain*
To love them well, for never a dele
They love a man again."

At the conclusion of this stanza, Master Salomen drew out his snuff-box, and proceeding to refresh himself from the same, ere he continued, he gave time to the audience, who were no little amazed at his choice of subject, to interchange various remarks, among which were intimations and hints from some of the older members, that certain unfortunate love passages had actually occurred to the learned man in the heyday of his youthful blood.

Master Salomon continued —
"For let a man do what he can
Their favor *to attain — Yet, if anew do them pursue,*
Their first true lover than
Labor*eth for naught — for from her thought*
He is a banished man."

This sentimental excerpt from the ancient ballad of the "Not-browne Maid," being sung in a cracked voice to the tune of Lilli-Burlero, was received with much approbation; and many merry catches, lively canzonets, and Bacchanalian glees followed.

Solgard had not as yet entirely lost sight of the object of his entrance into the club-room; he made direct inquiries, therefore, as to the grounds for the popular belief concerning the "old lady," as he politely denominated her, who was conjectured to be a witch. Some whom he addressed gave him dark and mysterious replies; others, whose intellects must have been in no slight degree subverted by persevering potations, winked knowingly, advised him to court the girl by all means, and took the liberty of recommending an early wedding. He finally applied to the chevalier; but his response was couched in terms equally unsatisfactory, and intimated that, if he required more particular information, he must apply to the witch herself.

In half an hour after this the captain of the *Greyhound* was in full chase, as he muttered to himself, of this suspicious craft: it was within half an hour of midnight, and he was alone, but in that peculiar state of vinous ferment that makes the timid bold and the brave foolhardy. He traversed the city rapidly, and soon became shrouded in the gloom of the forest that stretched below the dilapidated ruins of Schute's mansion.

At a turn in the path still farther on, Solgard beheld with distinctness many lights gleaming through the trees before him. This confirmation of common report further excited the curiosity of the captain, and he pressed onward.

A singular combination of sounds assailed his ear, as he made his way through the thick copse which almost obstructed a view of the log-house from the north; like Tam O'Shanter, he resolved to take a peep, and after cautiously groping his way close to the logs, he found a large chink, through which, by raising himself on tiptoe, he had a full view of the proceedings within.

CHAPTER V.

**Oh! for that gallant soul of old,
Who sang with heartfelt glee —
"My love it is my vessel bold,
My mistress is the sea."**

Old Ballad.

Around a low pine table, which extended the whole length of the apartment, sat some twelve or fifteen ruffian-looking men, carousing in most boisterous revel; some sending forth clouds of smoke from their long chiboques, others recounting amatory or belligerent adventures, the while twisting their well curled mustaches; and all ever and anon devoutly quaffing ample potations from beakers, flagons, and other vessels of various forms, but well adapted for deep and potent draughts.

"Just in time, captain; good wine needs no bush,"

uttered a gruff voice close to his elbow, accompanied with a familiar tap on the shoulder, which nearly destroyed Solgard's equilibrium.

Solgard looked around in no small surprise, and beheld close upon him a man of low stature, but otherwise of most Herculean conformation, in the garb of a sailor, and fully equipped with pistols, dirk, and cutlass; a three-cornered hat adhered to part of his enormous head, which, at the chin, was adorned, or rather disfigured, by a huge jet-black beard.

To the address of this formidable personage Solgard was uncertain how to frame a reply; when he was relieved of this embarrassment by a polite invitation from the stranger to join his merry mates within.

Under the peculiar circumstances of the case, as it may be supposed, this request was of course complied with; and the stranger, on entering the room where reveled the joyous band, introduced, in an audible voice, "Captain Solgard, of his British majesty's man-of-war *Greyhound.*"

All started at the word, but reading somewhat in the eye of their leader (for such evidently was the stranger), they reseated themselves, and filled their wine-cups to the brim.

The leader took the head of the table, and seating, with some appearance of ceremony, Solgard on his right-hand, he placed a silver cup before him, bade him fill up, and rising with an immense beaker in his own hand, proposed the health of "His majesty King George."

This loyal toast was hailed with enthusiasm, as was subsequently evidenced by the empty condition of the tankards. The "Free fishermen" followed; after doing justice to which, the leader informed his guest that the term explained the ordinary avocation of himself and messmates. To this candid information Solgard acquiescently bowed, inwardly substituting the word "pirates" for "fishermen".

This opinion he had not formed without show of reason: the men were all strong, of a daring and resolute aspect, and armed with offensive weapons; and Sir William Keith's Madeira, mellowed as it had been by voyage to an eastern clime, was hardly equal to the ruby juice which flowed in such reckless profusion around him.

The office of bringing in fresh supplies of wine was performed by the withered old crone herself, who acted in some measure as hostess: ever, as she appeared, the ear of the ancient Hebe was assailed in every direction.

"This way, if you please, Madam Sluysv — Here be four empty cups, old woman — Hilloa, Mother Sluys. Will ye be handy, ye old *creature*? — Be kind enough, Mistress Sluys — Stir up, Jezebel!"— and other ejaculations, at which the old woman frowned, smiled, or replied in exceeding wrath, as the nature of the address required.

Solgard more than once endeavored to reflect soberly on what was passing before him; but, in sooth, when he sallied forth from Peg Mullen's he was exceedingly "hot with the Tuscan grape"; and the good cheer he had since met with among the "free fishermen", entirely deranged the continuity of his ideas. In this disordered state of his imagination he detected the old witch, as he felt persuaded she was, scanning his features with a triumphant smile of fiendish malignancy; an involuntary thrill of an unpleasant nature passed over him, and rallying himself with the energy of despair, he slapped his right-hand man, a tall hard-favored sailor, on the shoulder, and called on him for a song.

The idea was happy; a simultaneous concert of gruff voices sung out, "No back out, Bill — give us good measure, Jones — go it, my old tarpaulin — a song from Bill Jones!" until Bill Jones, thus powerfully appealed to, succumbed to the wishes of his messmates, and in a voice about as gentle as a rough north-easter, complied, —

> *"I am none of your fresh-water sailors,*
> *But I am a real sea-dog;*
> *And all that I ask of my betters,*
> *Is plenty of 'bacco and grog.*
> *If it comes to a fight, why I'm ready*
> *To handle a pike or a gun;*
> *For whether they're cruisers or quakers*
> *To old Billy Jones it's all one.*
> *So pass on the bottle, my hearties —*
> *Dick Jenkins has got it, I spy;*
> *For as for your flummux of poetry,*
> *That ere thing is all in my eye."*

On finishing the concluding stave, Bill seized a full beaker that stood near him, and drank long and deep, with the air of one who had justly reaped the reward of his exertions.

Still the carousal went on, and still Captain Solgard quaffed the "blood-red wine;" and the room appeared to him to change into the deck of a vessel, and the "free fishermen" started up into dark and swarthy pirates; and longer and blacker grew their leader's jetty beard, while his deep stern voice rang out on the waters thus, —

> *"Oh, the rover's life is free as air:*
> *We sail the world around;*
> *For winds or storms we never care—*
> *So pass the bottle round.*
> *For who would wish to change, boys,*
> *The life that suits the free?*
> *We're outlaws on the land, boys,*

But we're lords upon the sea.
Our ship she lightly skims her way,
Full freighted, o'er the wave;
With gallant souls and hearts so gay,
All dangers we can brave.
Then who would wish to change, boys,
The life that suits the free?
We're outlaws on the land, boys,
But we're lords upon the sea.
When cannons boom across the wave,
We hoist the black flag high;
No quarter asks the rover brave, —
We conquer or we die.
For who would wish to change, boys,
The life that suits the free?
We're outlaws on the land, boys,
But we're lords upon the sea.
For wealth is ours from every soil;
Proud England's gold we gain —
The galliot strikes, how rich the spoil,
The silver ore of Spain.
Then who would wish to change, boys
The life that suits the free?
We're outlaws on the land, boys,
But we're lords upon the sea.
Drink, brothers, drink! the wine if old,
Madeira's vintage rare-Huzza! drink deep,
each rover bold, We never think of care.
For who would wish, to change, boys,
The life that suits the free?
We're outlaws on the land, boys,
But we're lords upon the sea."

As the concluding chorus burst full and loud on Solgard's ear, he attempted to awaken his dormant senses, but in vain; the forms around assumed fantastic shapes, — a thousand lights danced merrily before his eyes, — the sounds became more and more distant, until even these faint impressions were lost in total unconsciousness.

CHAPTER VI.

**"Barnaby, Barnaby, thou hast been drinking;
I can tell by thy nose, and thine eyes winking."
North Country Song.**

At this period of our colonial history, the duties of guarding the lives and property of the inhabitants of the town were entrusted, by the wise provision of municipal authority, to citizens alternately chosen to perform the functions of this important office. But in the primitive state of society which then existed, offences were rare, and evil-doers but seldom met with; so that these worthy men were wont to take their rounds in undisturbed quietude, and with no other inconvenience than the loss of their accustomed repose.

Much, therefore, was the surprise of William Palmer and Jeremiah Lloyd, while passing the court-house some little before daybreak, on observing the body of a man, seemingly dead, stretched at full length upon the pavement in front thereof. On maturer examination they were much scandalized, however, by discovering, in the supposed defunct, the person of Captain Solgard, of his majesty's ship *Greyhound* (well known, from his official station, to most of the inhabitants of the town), in a state of exceeding inebriety.

In ordinary cases the mode of proceeding was obvious, — to wit, the conveying of the delinquent, under such circumstances, to the watch-house. But in the present instance Jeremiah Lloyd was not clear as to the jurisdiction which they, as officers of the town, might rightfully exercise in the case of an individual holding an especial commission in his majesty's service. In sooth it was a knotty point; and yet something should be done, and that speedily, lest the affair should be noised abroad to the detriment of the captain, and the fair fame of the city. To obtain the counsel and advice of the mayor seemed both desirable and expedient, and yet the hour —

Here the victim of Bacchus made an ineffectual effort to rise, but only succeeded so far as to lean on his elbow, in which position he regarded the guardians of the night with a very unmeaning gaze, and attempted twice or thrice some fragment of a song. The watchmen now saluted him politely, inquiring, in a tone the least calculated to give offence, how he came there, and whither he would wish to be conducted; to which he answered, "We're outlaws on the land, boys, but we're lords upon the sea!"

The two citizens then quietly raised the captain; who offered no resistance to their proceedings, but accompanied them without any remark, supported mainly on each side by his conductors, with a gait marvelously unsteady, and pertinaciously answering every question as they proceeded with the refrain of, "We're outlaws on the land, boys, but we're lords upon the sea!"

At William Palmer's house they came to a stand; and after a brief consultation, no satisfaction being likely to be had for the present from the gallant captain, he was inducted, with as little noise as possible, into a small room in the third story, there laid upon a cot; and the door being fastened to prevent any sudden outbreak, he was left to sleep off the fumes of intoxication.

The mayor had just finished his third cup of chocolate, and was in the act of plunging his fork into a fresh slice of well-buttered toast, when a domestic opened the door to inform his worship that friends Lloyd and Palmer desired of him some private converse.

"Bid them in," said his worship: "and more chocolate and toast forthwith, Deborah! Another difference touching the tannery, I warrant me. Good-morrow, Jeremiah! How fares it with thee, William? Sit ye down and partake— nay, 'twill damage thee naught; the morning is somewhat raw, and — another cup, Deborah!"

So saying, the hospitable magistrate placed his two visitors at the table, and reseating himself, supplied them with ample portions of the abundance before him; then wiping his mouth with a napkin of spotless purity, he leaned back on his cushioned chair, intimating that he was at leisure to attend to any communication.

Jeremiah Lloyd looked at William Palmer, and receiving a significant nod, broke silence.

"We would consult thee, friend Hasell, in a weighty and not lightly to be disposed of matter.

The case standeth thus: — as we were leisurely passing the court-house, well-nigh upon four of the morning, we were aware of a man lying on the pavement, and, as we soon discovered, utterly overcome by strong drink — "

"And now that thou hast taken him," interrupted the mayor, "doth he refuse to pay the fine?"

"Not so," answered Jeremiah; "but as to arresting this person, and holding him in durance, we wot not well upon what authority we may proceed; for, as commanding a king's vessel, the laws of the city may, peradventure, touch him not."

The worthy magistrate had listened with an aspect of profound equanimity to the preceding part of the discourse; but when it was revealed that Captain Solgard, an officer of such high rank, and in whom the town trusted not a little for protection from piratical invasion, had been actually taken up by two city-watchmen, not to mince matters, dead drunk, Thomas Hasell looked the very picture of amazement, gazing earnestly and somewhat incredulously on the speaker, and his under jaw falling still lower as he gazed; being sorely grieved thereat, and scandalized beyond measure.

When William Palmer told him, however, that the young man had not been taken to the watchbouse, but quietly lodged in his own domicile, to the intent that after a sound sleep he might arise in a fitting state of sobriety, the mayor took exceeding comfort, advising the two men of the watch to confer privately with the delinquent, so that the town might not get wind of the matter; and hinted that, if the affair was hushed up, the captain would doubtless not object to contributing somewhat towards the repairs of the Guildhall.

The associates bade adieu to the mayor and departed, well pleased with their own politic and discreet conduct, and fully resolved to exact a heavy penalty from the delinquent, though as to the precise amount they differed — William Palmer being for *fifteen*, while Jeremiah Lloyd was for *twenty* shillings.

It had been some time broad daylight when Captain Solgard slowly and almost unconsciously unclosed his eyes, and, stretching his limbs with a heavy yawn, looked around him. He was very much puzzled to imagine where he was — endeavored to recollect himself — found his brain filled with indistinct ideas of pirates, wine, and witches, his eyes heavy and feverish, his mouth parched and dry, and his epaulets and dirk missing.

The room in which he lay was in nowise calculated to give him any distinct perceptions of his precise situation: it was small, low, and scantily furnished; in one corner, a wooden chest and two three-legged stools; the chimney-piece inlaid with Dutch tiles, quaintly representing the Acts of the Apostles; the walls of the chamber in wooden panels, unpainted, and considerably darkened through age; and, close by the bedside, a pitcher of stoneware filled with cool water — to which Solgard, without any hesitation, applied his lips, and took a draught, "deep as the rolling *Zuyder Zee*," with that exquisite sense of enjoyment that wine bibbers alone can appreciate.

Much invigorated, he approached the window, through which the morning sun cast a bright cheerful light, and looking forth beheld underneath the well-known waters of Dock Creek. Directly opposite lay a schooner discharging cargo into Smith's warehouse; towards the river he saw the masts of the larger vessels that lined the mouth of the creek; and turning his eyes in an opposite direction, viewed the clamorous wherrymen, plying their oars under Third Street bridge, over which the industrious citizens were passing and repassing, with interchange of grave and cordial greeting.

He was therefore in a house situated on the southern side of Dock Creek; but as, to the best of his recollection, he had fallen asleep in a tenement about half a mile below the Swedes' Church, he was almost tempted to ascribe this mysterious transfer of his person to the direct agency of witchcraft.

But an explanation of such circumstances as referred to his actual location was near at hand, for the door of the chamber was slowly opened and friends Lloyd and Palmer looked in upon the captain with an inquiring aspect, that still further excited his curiosity.

In answer to his questions, Jeremiah Lloyd informed him somewhat in detail of the peculiar situation in which he had been found by them the night previous; how that, to avoid scandal, they had carefully led him to the residence of William Palmer, in the third story of which house they were at the present; hoped that he felt no unpleasant effects from the late occurrence; hinted that some small contribution towards the repair of the Guildhall would be taken in good part; and intimated that, as none but the mayor (a very discreet and safe man) and the parties present were acquainted with the matter, the whole affair might, if the captain thought proper, be kept dark.

As the captain thought it exceedingly proper, he willingly acceded to this arrangement, and forthwith offered such a liberal contribution towards the completion of the aforesaid repairs as proved highly satisfactory to the municipal authorities; being duly entered on the minutes of the Council, as a "Donation of Captain Solgard towards the Guildhall."

The captain bent his steps towards his ship in no very good-humor: baffled in his endeavors to procure information concerning the witch; chafed at the traitorous treatment he had met with at the hands of his false friends the "free fishermen," who had not only tested the strength of his head, and enjoyed his subsequent discomfiture, but, as he concluded, had deprived him of his dirk and epaulets, in testimony of his total defeat; and inwardly vexed at the scandalous guise in which he had fallen under the notice of the city authorities.

Musing on these things, he proceeded; when, on turning the corner of the Crooked Billet, he almost started at the sound of a voice issuing from the doorway of the "Mariners' Retreat," a low-roofed, squat, one-storied pothouse, that bore the reputation of a disorderly house, being especially resorted to, and affording refreshment and accommodation to a most riotous set of jolly tars. The voice he could not mistake, and on looking up he beheld the black beard, the rough manly features, and the athletic form of his last night's host. Their eyes met, but no sign of recognition from the stranger; he looked upon Solgard with a glance of perfect indifference, and yet a lurking smile might almost be detected playing around the corners of his mouth. He paid, however, no further attention to his late guest, but continued his conversation with the landlord without interruption; so that the captain, who at first had intended to address him, was almost tempted to consider the whole as a wild dream; and feeling the absurdity of questioning a man whose easy deportment and unmoved aspect strongly indicated, what he possibly might be, an utter stranger and altogether unconscious of the transaction in which his very image seemed to have borne a prominent part, he resolved to inquire of the landlord touching this mysterious being, and passed on to his vessel.

On board the *Greyhound* he received the report of his lieutenant; which went on to state, among other things, that several boats' crews had returned without any intelligence of the pirates, but that Midshipman Grubb with his party had succeeded in obtaining a crew which he was in hopes would lead to very important discoveries; adding, that some entertained the belief that Captain Teach was actually lurking about the city, although his vessel had been lost sight of since the arrival of the *Greyhound*.

Solgard recommended vigilance and activity; hoped that ere long they would be enabled to meet with these buccaneers; and, exhorting the crew to steadiness and sobriety, turned in to rectify his disordered apparel and remove every vestige of the past debauch.

CHAPTER VII.

Piscator. **Now, sir, has not my hostess made haste? and does not the fish look lovely?**
Venator. **Both, upon my word, sir; and therefore let's say grace, and fall to eating of it.**
Piscator. **Well, sir, how do you like it?**
Venator. **Trust me, 'tis as good meat as I ever tasted.**

Complete Angler.

A few miles above the city, on the banks of the Manaiunk, in more modern times known as the River Schuylkill, stood a lodge, erected by a number of *bon vivants* of the day, who had associated themselves under the title of the "Fishing Club of Fort St. David;" an institution which has since acquired more celebrity under the appellation of the "Colony," and still more recently, "The State in Schuylkill."

Why the Welsh saint was adopted as the titular patron of the establishment does not clearly appear; but certain it is, that quite as much jollity and good cheer were enjoyed as though St. George himself had presided over the revels; for thither, at stated periods, were the members of the club wont to resort to indulge in a substantial repast, in the which, as the reward of the morning exertions, a noble mess of catfish was never wanting, nor the usual accompaniments of wine and song; and albeit excluded from participation in the periodical feastings of this bachelor-like society, yet had not the fairer portion of creation reasonable cause of complaint, for at all other times full liberty of ingress was allowed, and often had the pavilion of St. David rung with the mirth of the fair creatures that sported around its walls, and fall often had the merry dance shaken the old fort to its foundation.

BLACKBEARD

According to previous arrangement, a party had assembled at the house of Madam Markham, consisting of sundry belles, accompanied by their esquires, including the fair Barbara, under the escort of Captain Solgard, and the Chevalier Oxenstiern, at whose invitation, as a member of the club, the excursion was set on foot, and on whom, as being in possession of the localities and other necessary information, the general superintendence and especial guidance of the party devolved.

During the delay incidental to the preparations of the female portion of the party, which, as veritable chroniclers, we are compelled to record, the eye of the chevalier sought in vain the form of his old friend Major Scheveling, who, from his piscatory propensities, as well as the eager satisfaction with which he had received the announcement of the contemplated attack on the finny tribe, was of course expected, on this important occasion, fully equipped, and ready for the sport. On inquiry, however, into the cause of the major's non-appearance, he learned from the fair Barbara that her uncle had received important documents from abroad, which required his immediate investigation, — and that, she doubted not, much to his disappointment, as he had been occupied to a late hour the preceding evening in arranging and preparing various fish-hooks, flies, and the necessary appurtenances.

It was yet early when the company, striking across a footpath that led to the rear of Christ Church, crossed into High Street, and, proceeding onward with light steps and lighter hearts, took a little circuit northward to avoid the Duck Pond, that lay on the verge of the town towards "Fourth Street," and entered the woods, that from this point extended to the banks of the Manaiunk. The sun glanced brightly between the green leaves; the air, pure and mellow, seemed to be charged with fragrance from many a wild and unknown flower; birds caroled gayly around, as if they feared not the happy group; and now and then the graceful deer would bound across their path, snuffing the tainted gale, and startled at their bright array.

Fain would we record the conversation that took place before the Manaiunk came in view, — how Solgard regaled the ear of the gentle Barbara by marvelous tales of his famous exploits in shooting deer — to the which she credulously did attend, — how Oxenstiern indulged in predictions touching the future extent of the city, in which his vaticination took such unbounded range, that the gentlemen quietly shrugged up their shoulders (which fact clearly shows that this polite mode of expressing doubt is not peculiar to the French nation; as hath been unadvisedly asserted), and the ladies considered him very amusing,— how some of the esquires drew the attention of the fair ones towards the livid state of the atmosphere, and the balmy condition of the air, — how others, disappearing rather unaccountably for a time, lurked in advance and greeted the party with the genuine Indian war-whoop; but suffice it to say, that they reached the river-side in such a merry mood, that Miss Rachel Curtis, who had been educated by a very superstitious maiden aunt, albeit as merry as any on the route, whispered to Barbara that she hoped nothing unlucky might occur ere they ere turned home.

Several batteaux were in readiness for the accommodation of the party; but ere they embarked, Solgard, who had from an eminence on the bank been looking down the river for some time with an appearance of impatience and anxiety, drew the attention of all by a sudden exclamation of, "Thank God! there they come." On looking in the direction in which he gazed, the barge of the *Greyhound* was seen coming up rapidly, manned with a crew of lusty sailors, bending in perfect regularity to the long man-of-war stroke, that sent her dancing over the waters, their oars glancing at once in the bright sun, and the form of the tiny midshipman in the stern, swaying, seaman-like, to the onward motion of the boat.

The gallant officer then intimated, that believing the barge, from its size and accommodations, might possibly conduce to the comfort and convenience of the ladies more directly than the small boats prepared to convey them to the fort, he had ventured to have it sent around without consulting the committee of arrangements, for which offence he hoped the resulting benefits might claim absolution.

This polite attention on the part of the captain was duly appreciated; and the arrival of the barge requiring some alteration in the arrangements, the batteaux were entirely dispensed with; and a beautiful light clinker-built boat, yclept

"Izaak Walton," appurtenant to the aforesaid "Fishing Company," being, by good-fortune, in the immediate vicinity, was pressed for the service. Madam Markham, having observed, or, what is equally efficient in most cases, having fancied that Solgard, during the walk, had paid much more attention to Barbara than duly comported with his sworn allegiance to her own bright eyes, took occasion to address him in the most fascinating tone imaginable; and furtively stole a glance or two, so tenderly expressive that the happy man, hardly restraining his emotions of delight, handed her as it were a matter of course into the barge; in performing which courtesy he failed not to press somewhat warmly the little hand he held; and while others of the party entered, seemed not to notice (much to the satisfaction of Madam Christine) that the gentle Barbara, with the rest of the party, was accommodated in the "Izaak Walton," of which Oxenstiern took the helm.

The barge pushed off; at the word of command the English tars let fall their oars, and urged her on steadily with long and measured sweep. The "Izaak Walton" followed, manned by younger members of the club, nearly all powerful and athletic men, not unpracticed in remigial art, and of one mind as to the necessity of beating the barge. With the wild and romantic scene before her Barbara was delighted, — the winding river at times gliding with the calm and glassy beauty of a lake, and anon roughened into murmuring ripples over a rocky bed, — the spreading chestnut and towering sycamore, rearing their majestic trunks on every side, — the margin of the flood covered with a profusion of wild-flowers of rich and varied dies, and heavy masses of dark-colored rocks shooting their bold angles far into the stream. The Izaak Walton, as it were by stealth, gradually neared the barge, and then by a simultaneous and powerful effort, shot ahead; the crew of the barge, meanwhile, by a movement extremely natural, increased their speed with an evident disinclination to be outstripped by their competitors. The contest continued for some time without any decided advantage being gained by either side; but when the Izaak Walton finally gained upon the barge, it became a perfect race.

"Give way, boys!" shouted Solgard. "Hold your own!" cried the chevalier; and for some time they kept on a rapid course, neither apparently gaining one inch, although the most miraculous efforts were made for that purpose. The long and powerful sweep of the barge was met by the more rapid strokes of the Izaak Walton; and the ardent and enthusiastic energy of the amateur oarsmen fully countervailed the practiced movement and indurated muscle of the jolly tars. During the heat of the contest an incident occurred, which added still further to the interest of the scene, more particularly in the estimation of the ladies, as invested with somewhat of a mysterious and totally unlooked-for character. On turning a bend of the river a canoe was seen close under the shade of an oak, whose branches completely overhung the water, containing but one solitary form, apparently that of an Indian, reclining in a state of listless repose. As they approached he raised his head, and after gazing for a short space on the passing boats, suddenly rose, seized his paddle, and made after them.

"Note you that solitary red man?" said Solgard; "observe, fair Christine, how even he, in his light canoe, would rival the white man; he carries light weight, 'tis true, yet that may hardly gain him vantage in such a race."

"He moves by magic, then," replied Madam Markham, with a smile; "for his canoe barely touches the water. See! it moves still faster," added she, gazing earnestly; "he will soon pass us like the wind."

And in truth, although both the barge and Izaak Walton still pressed onward with unabated speed, the Sagamore, as Solgard now called him, came up literally like the wind, handling his paddle with a grace and dexterity that were marvelous to behold. In a space of time incredibly brief he shot by, and passing athwart the bows of the rival boats, kept on with undiminished rapidity until a bend in the river concealed him from their view. As he passed, however, it was remarked that instead of being an aboriginal chieftain, he was a well formed and remarkably handsome young man, whose features rather indicated European origin, although bronzed to a degree that might readily, at a distance, be mistaken for the tawny complexion of a savage.

BLACKBEARD

As the party approached what was termed, rather paradoxically, the Fishing-ground, the crew of the Izaak Walton, despite their hearty goodwill, were unable to keep up those really vigorous efforts which had characterized the beginning of the race. Solgard's watchful eye immediately noticed the falling off, and he took advantage of the circumstance; the barge soon traversed the short distance that had hitherto separated her from her opponent, and the Izaak Walton seemed doomed to inevitable defeat, when the superior local knowledge of the chevalier stood him in happy stead; whirling off suddenly, he ran into a peculiar eddy that prevailed for a considerable distance on the right bank of the river; thus, favored by the direction of the current, he gained ground rapidly, while the barge, struggling against all the force of the main current, lost far more than she had previously gained. This critical advantage gave the victory to Oxenstiern; — the Izaak Walton came in about three boats' lengths ahead of the *Greyhound*'s barge.

The amateur boatmen were exceedingly delighted with their success, affecting, however, that moderation which victors so good-naturedly put on; and the captain, although sorely chagrined at the result, smiled in the most perfect good humor, as he congratulated the chevalier on the success of his maneuver; "although the real victor," added he, "was that mahogany-colored personage, who so completely distanced both of us." Solgard's sailors, however, disdaining such hypocritical complacency, pulled long faces, grumbled grievously among each other, and took no pains whatever to modify their rueful and vinegar aspects; the authority of the little mid (as Solgard and the rest of the party had now left the boats) alone checking the vent of sundry horrible forecastle profanities.

The fort itself, which Barbara now beheld for the first time, was a long wooden hall, say some seventy feet in length, by a breadth of twenty feet, in such manner framed with hinges that the walls thereof were naught but folding-doors, so that in summer, being thrown open on all sides, it was equally pervious in every part; and again being well closed, and properly fastened against inclement weather, it served well for indoor recreation.

Again, being set truly against the bank, one might step from the upper part to the very floor, and thence passing on to the other extremity, must descend to the river's edge by a flight of twenty steps. Against the walls hung fishing rods of all sizes, buffalo-robes and moccasins, war-clubs, bows of all shapes and sizes, and great store of arrows; together with panther-hides, enormous antlers, stuffed snake-skins, and similar spoils of the forest. A few shelves at the extremity of the hall contained matters principally appertaining to the piscatory art; to wit, — single hooks and double, snappers and spring-hooks, floats of divers kinds, lines of twisted hair and silk and Indian grass, books filled with great store of flies, such as the dun-fly, the stone-fly, the ruddy, the moorish, the greenish, and the drake-fly; and some few appropriate books, namely, "The Complete Angler,"

"The Contemplative Fisherman", "The Secrets of Angling," a delectable poem in three books, a mutilated copy of "Country Contentments,"and a very ancient volume, being a small folio in black letter, containing three parts— one on hawking, another on hunting, and a third entitled "The Treatyse of Fysshynge wyth an Angle;" which last Barbara opened, and fell upon a very entertaining passage: the style is somewhat quaint, and the mode of spelling different from modern usage; the following portion is on this score extracted for the edification of our fair readers, premising that the aforesaid treatises were compiled by dame Julyans Berners, a noble and learned lady, and also prioress of a nunnery near St. Alban's.

"The angler," says she, "at the least, hath his wholesome walk, and merry at his ease, a sweet air of the sweet savour of the mead, that maketh him hungry: he heareth the melodious harmony of fowls; he seeth the young swans, herons, ducks, cotes, and many other fowls, with their broods; which may seemeth better than all the noise of foundries, the blast of horns, and the cry of fowls, that hunters, falconers, and fowlers can make. And if the angler take fish, surely then is there no man merrier than he is in his spirit."

"So much for theory," said Oxenstiern, gayly, looking over Barbara's shoulder as he spoke; "now for practice."

BLACKBEARD

Duly equipped, the party separated into groups, each selecting such spots as seemed most likely to ensure success; some casting in their lines under the shade of a great tree, — others taking position on jutting points of the rocks, — the ladies in such noisy good-humor that the woods rang with their merriment, until the gentlemen were constrained to state the fisherman's adage, "Those who make most noise catch fewest fish."

Whether it be that ladies lack patience, or from a habit of paying attention to more than one thing at a time, or to compensate for their undoubted superiority in other respects, certain it is, that from the earliest ages to the present day, they have a notable want of success in angling. This is a fact well known to experienced anglers, some of whom, with much simplicity, suppose it to proceed from constitutional inability to maintain silence. Be that as it may, the present case proved no exception; for although the "sterner sex" were kept busy, every now and then pulling in a fish, none of the ladies obtained more encouragement than a few adventitious nibbles, which the fair anglers could not refrain from noticing, perhaps too audibly, at the moment of occurrence.

Barbara, in despair, threw down her rod, and playfully clambered among the rocks; amply compensated for her exertion, by attaining a projecting point that commanded a view of the most picturesque description. Being at some distance from the party, she turned, and was about to retrace her steps, when a distant and indistinct sound of music in the opposite direction struck her ear. She stopped short — listened — hesitated for a moment, and then, still keeping in view of her friends, approached the point from which it proceeded. The sound of a flute, under ordinary circumstances, would excite but little attention; but in such a wild, sequestered situation, music invested itself with a peculiar charm: the performance, too, was certainly good; the air entirely new to Barbara, wild and plaintive; and the player, although near at hand, yet entirely hidden from view. Curious to discover this melancholy Orpheus, she stepped cautiously along a ledge of rock that here lined the river, when a loose mass of granite gave way beneath her feet, and she slipped down towards the water. With great presence of mind, she gave a shriek sufficiently loud to call the attention of her friends to her critical situation. The mass, which still supported her, hung partly over the water's edge, and hardly sustained her weight: a single step, or any exertion on her part, might detach it from its insecure foundation; and, clinging to the edge of the rock overhead, she bitterly repented her thoughtless temerity.

The instant her voice reached the party, responsive shrieks from her female friends increased the confusion into which the gentlemen were at first thrown, on discovering her perilous condition. Some of the gallants rushed up the rocks, choosing the most direct route, regardless of all intervening obstacles, while Solgard and Oxenstiern, as by common impulse, leaped into the nearest boat, and, each seizing an oar, pulled manfully to the rescue. Barbara felt her strength rapidly diminishing, and it must forever remain matter of conjecture whether she could have retained her hold until the coming up of her friends; for suddenly she felt herself gently lifted into a canoe, which had rapidly shot out of a deep nook above, and by the same Indian-like individual who had skimmed past the rival boats in the morning.

The scene was witnessed by the two cavaliers in the approaching boat, and much to their satisfaction; for they feared lest Barbara, during the interval of time that must necessarily elapse, would become entirely exhausted. When they came up, they found Barbara reclining in the canoe, pale and still trembling with agitation, yet endeavoring to express her grateful feelings to the stranger who had so opportunely come to her assistance. Grasping his hand, the chevalier briefly and sincerely thanked him for his timely aid; and was well pleased to learn from the trembling girl that, although much alarmed, she had sustained no personal injury; while Solgard archly observed, that this was not the first race in which they had been beaten by their unknown friend. At this the stranger smiled, and replied in a manner that indicated a perfect acquaintance with the polished courtesy of social life; addressing Barbara also with a delicate and unobtrusive attention to her comfort, that hardly corresponded with his rude and almost savage-like attire.

BLACKBEARD

As the boats moved down together to the landing, the stranger was made acquainted with the names of the party, and in return, much to their disappointment, merely announced himself as a hunter, as if he considered his name of no importance whatever; further intimating that he but rarely visited the city, preferring, he confessed, the purer air of the forest. No further explanation being offered, the conversation became more general, and the boats reached the landing.

"Bless me, Barbara," cried Miss Rachel Curtis, "how could you be so imprudent! and such dangerous rocks, too! For my part, I can't imagine what under the sun could tempt you to go so far."

The color began to return to Barbara's pale cheeks; for although her motive was but an innocent curiosity, she was not inclined to reveal it in the presence of the hunter, whose music she doubted not that she had heard, and whose eyes at the moment met her own in an inquiring glance that seemed to watch her reply, and of course added somewhat to her confusion. She gayly replied, however, "Such a lovely landscape, my dear Rachel, were worth some danger; but, in good sooth, I thought not the feat so perilous." To the congratulations of the gallants who had sped to her relief by the terra firma route, and their felicitations on her narrow escape, she replied with a good-humor and vivacity that indicated the recovery of her natural spirits, and rendered her beautiful countenance so charming, that Madam Christine might well be pardoned an involuntary pang of jealousy, as she observed Solgard's eyes fixed upon the fair girl with an expression of interest and admiration. Owing to this, perhaps, she noted not that the young hunter, as his eye rested on the fair dames around, regarded her own graceful figure and elastic step with marked admiration, — certes, a form of such voluptuous mold, so bright an eye, and a complexion, not fair, but so darkly rich, were meet to win a stranger's eye.

And Oxenstiern had not been idle: the curling smoke, rising among the tall trees, spoke of culinary deeds; a fragrant and alluring odor came on the passing breeze; and in due season smoked the promise of a feast, ordered in fair array, on St. David's ample board.

"To the hall, fair dames! to the banquet, gentles all! Nay, thou escapest not so, Sir Hunter,"

added the chevalier, as he observed the stranger now bidding a graceful adieu to the ladies, with the intention of taking his departure. "Credit me," continued Oxenstiern, "thou shalt have fishermen's fare; and thou art a very hermit if those bright eyes tempt thee not."

To these potent arguments the stranger properly gave way, influenced, doubtless, by the all-powerful fascination of female beauty; and, ere long, be found himself seated at the table, and by no means indisposed to do justice to the more solid arguments before him.

The conversation, as usual on such occasions, commenced with laudatory remarks on the viands generally, and on the exquisite flavor of the catfish particularly, and ultimately turned on the current news of the day, during which the long threatened incursion of the pirates came in due course under consideration; and many details were given of the extreme boldness of these outlaws.

It was even asserted roundly by one of the party, that he had it on the authority of an eyewitness, that Blackbeard himself was actually seen in the city within a few days past. This assertion startled the ladies, who had accustomed themselves to consider the presence of his majesty's ship of war as ample security against the reappearance of this desperado; and the other gentlemen present, although, from the known character or the man, inwardly inclined to give credence to the story, affected, however, to believe that some supposed resemblance had given origin to the rumor.

"Pray, sir," said Captain Solgard, addressing himself to the individual who had first spoken, "is there aught especially remarkable in the voice and figure of this Captain Teach?"

"His voice," replied the person thus appealed to, "is peculiarly deep, clear, and thrilling in its effect; few can listen to its mildest tones without experiencing unwonted sensations; And in battle, men say, 'tis as the roar of a lion. As to his person, — he is low in stature, with a neck more like that of a bull than a human being, and a form so strikingly athletic as to warrant the many tales touching his extraordinary personal strength. He may be known also by his carrying arms at all times, and by constantly wearing a little three-cornered hat."

To this account both Solgard and the young hunter listened with much attention: the latter excited probably by the interest which, in the young, is always excited by aught akin to the marvelous; and the former comparing this description with his confused recollections of the "free fisherman," and his subsequent dubious recognition of the same individual at the "Mariners' Retreat;" from a view of which circumstances, he entertained but little doubt that he had been actually in company with, feasted, and outwitted by Blackbeard himself.

Before sunset the company were on their return to the city; and ere the hunter left them, he avowed his determination to "avail himself of the pressing invitations so kindly tendered by his friends; and on bidding them farewell, was amply repaid for the service he had been so fortunate as to render in the morning, by the grateful look with which the fair Barbara accompanied her parting wishes for his future welfare.

On reaching home, Barbara found the major so entirely engrossed by the voluminous body of documents which had, by their arrival, prevented his participation in the pleasures of the day, as to pay but a cursory attention to her statement of the interesting occurrences that so materially contributed to vary the anticipated routine of the day. Aroused for a moment from the absorbing tenor of his researches, as his niece informed him of her unexpected rescue from threatened danger, he chided her venturous rashness with a father's tenderness, and again relapsed into his contemplative reverie, as Barbara in few words described the reserve of the young hunter, and spoke more at large of the different ladies who were present, and numberless scenes of sylvan beauty.

CHAPTER VIII.

**"Some have delivered the polity of spirits, and left an
account that they stand in awe of charms, spells, cats, and
conjurations—that they are afraid of letters and
characters, which signify much in the subtle vocabulary of
Satan."**
Brown's Vulgar Errors.

Seated in a comfortable little apartment, into which
sufficient light was admitted through the lozenge shaped and
leaden-sashed panes of glass that occupied the upper half of a
door opening into the garden, and which apartment, under the
denomination of library and study, in fact constituted a species
of sanctum sanctorum, Major Scheveling had been throughout
the day busily engaged in writing; which, being a process not
very familiar to the old gentleman, may account for the limited
result of his operations, — the sum total of the unremitted labors
of the day producing but a single, though long and compactly
written, epistle. The old man was regularly ensconced in a very
high-backed elbow-chair, lined with crimson velvet, and right
comfortably stuffed; and before him stood an antique writing
desk of dark mahogany, on which lay the letter, at length
brought to a conclusion: this he folded with deliberation, and
directed it to the address of the extensive and wealthy
commercial house of "Widow Van Skeyp and Co.," at
Amsterdam.

Then sealing the same, and affixing the impress of the
family signet, he sallied forth just as the sun was about setting,
and mounting his quiet little Shetland pony, without saying a
word to any of his household, he rode rapidly into town, nor
once drew rein until be alighted at the London Coffee-house;
where, giving his steed in charge to one of the many idle boys

who habitually infested the purlieus, he inquired of a very respectable old merchant, who was gravely looking forth on the river from the northeast window, with both hands in his breeches pockets, how soon the first vessel for Amsterdam might be expected to leave the port.

"The ship *Santa Claus*, so please St. Nicolas, will go down, as the tide serves, to-morrow morning at daybreak," uttered a voice behind the major, the thick and somewhat asthmatic tones of which were certainly familiar to his ear. On turning round to the speaker, a dense cloud of smoke hovering over a little table intercepted his view for a moment; but as it cleared away, he beheld his old acquaintance Captain Oster, luxuriating, as in times past, in his short Dutch pipe, and contemplating a huge tankard that had erst been filled with mighty ale, immersed, as it were, in a melancholy yet not unhappy reverie.

The outward man of the worthy Heindrich was in nowise altered: the same scarlet waistcoat, the same indefinable breeches, the same flaxen wig, and the same woolen hose formed part of his habiliments; his eyes also bore their usual somnolent glassy expression, and his nasal organ, save an increment in rubicundity of hue, was still unchanged"

The recognition was mutual; and the major, well pleased with having an opportunity of transmitting his letter by a well-known hand, confided the same to Captain Oster; and, wishing the good ship a speedy and prosperous voyage, he again mounted his little nag, and returning without accident to Erigson House, found the Chevalier Oxenstiern ready to take a game of chess; and by checkmating him thrice in succession, put an agreeable climax to the fortunate occurrences of the day.

Early the next morning all was bustle and activity on board the *Santa Claus*; the tall form of Jeptha Dobbs, who still acted as mate, was seen gliding in many directions with accustomed celerity, although without the least appearance of haste, as, owing to the unusual elongation of the lower extremities, his lazy swinging gait was fully equal to the hurried step of his shorter legged contemporaries. So favorable were both wind and tide, that the ship made rapid way down the river, and having avoided all the perils incident to the difficult navigation of the Delaware, beheld the land growing more distant on each side of the bay; and at length, as the capes in turn sank below the horizon, boldly stretched out into the broad Atlantic, a fine breeze bearing her onward towards the well-known dikes of Holland and little dreaming of the approaching danger that awaited her on the mighty deep.

Towards sunset of the second day a sail was descried to windward: at first sight she might be easily taken for a light cloud hovering on the horizon; but subsequent observations not only established the existence of a vessel in that quarter, but went far to induce a belief, not very agreeable in those ticklish times, that she was bearing down upon the *Santa Claus*. The distance, however, was still too great to warrant any definite conjecture as to her intentions; and although inwardly revolving the possibility of being chased and brought-to by a buccaneer, Captain Oster thought fit to conceal for the present all such apprehensions; and by way of veiling his discomfort, addressed his mate with an appearance of hilarity, not usually resident in his physiognomy.

"Some coaster, I suppose, Mr. Dobbs; it will be an excellent joke to see him 'bout ship when he comes within sight of our guns."

Mr. Dobbs gave a dance at the wooden emblems which the captain facetiously termed guns, and shrugging up his shoulders, intimated that for his own part he would dispense with the anticipated amusement, and would prefer losing sight of the strange sail to any entertainment likely to arise from witnessing her alarm at the armament of the *Santa Claus*. With these observations, so ill adapted to administer consolation or encouragement to the captain, Jeptha returned to his post of observation; peering earnestly at the object of attention, with his head thrust forward in a horizontal plane, his body and legs at their uttermost elongation, and his hands dangling crosswise behind his back. In this position he remained, until it became evident that the vessel, whose approach now rendered her much more distinct, was so little like a mere coaster, that she carried guns, bore directly down upon the *Santa Claus*, and sailed so rapidly that a meeting of the two ships must inevitably take place.

Jeptha now seriously proposed overhauling the arm-chest, but Captain Oster in turn shrugged up his shoulders, — being well aware that the majority of his crew, although sturdy trenchermen, would by no means be so efficient in case of an engagement; and lighting his pipe with a desperate calmness, privately invoked the powerful intervention of St. Nicolas, in case of any danger, at the same time indulging openly the hope that their apprehensions might prove groundless.

And in good sooth the speedy interference of St, Nicolas seemed likely to be required; for, as the strange vessel came within bail, she ran up an ominous black flag, which, added to her threatening range of guns, and sudden show of armed men upon her decks, left no possible doubt in regard to her real character. The *Santa Claus* was without any ceremony directed by the pirate to lie-to, and send a boat aboard with the captain and papers. This peremptory mandate was obeyed, and thereupon the *Santa Claus* was boarded by a boat's crew of ruffians, at whose head appeared a tall swarthy West Indian, whose hair, curly and black as jet, shadowed his features in wild profusion, descending from his temples in two glossy ringlets of singular lengthy and luxuriance, and having his ears pierced with massive circlets of gold, betraying both the barbaric taste and the singular foppery of the savage buccaneer.

The lieutenant, for such apparently was his rank, looked around with a careless and almost a laughing eye on the little Dutch sailors, whose countenances exhibited no slight degree of terror and anxiety; then calling loudly for the mate, he scanned the long figure and equally long visage which Mr. Dobbs presented in obedience to his summons, with a manifest inclination to risibility.

"By what name art thou commonly known, master mate?"

"Answer as often to Jeptha, as Mr. Dobbs," replied the mate, laconically.

"You then, Mr. Dobbs, or Jeptha, if it please you better," observed the lieutenant, "descend with me into the cabin, and we will discuss matters more at our ease — forward, sir."

Jeptha was rather puzzled to account for the facetious disposition, and to him utterly unexpected good-humor, of the buccaneer; but feeling naturally more disposed to encourage such jocundity than to do aught that would by any means arouse the savage temper so generally ascribed to these lawless tyrants of the deep; he obeyed the command of the lieutenant with alacrity; and entering the cabin, was followed by the West Indian, who immediately stationed one of his own boat's croAr as sentinel on the outside, and making fast the door, seemed disposed to secure Jeptha and himself from any interruption.

"Now, Mr. Dobbs, this good ship, the *Santa Claus* I think you call her, is doubtless not deficient in the ordinary supplies of a well-provisioned vessel — such as good store of brandies, gin, rum, and sour kraut; -but I would more particularly speak of a certain hamper of choice Madeira, sent on board by Jonathan Dickinson, for the especial comfort and refreshment of Captain Oster during his present voyage; for a sample of which I will be indebted to you, lest our throats become parched with this dry-lipped conversation."

Jeptha was well aware that the worthy Heinrich had actually received, the day before leaving port, from his friend Jonathan Dickinson, a parcel of wine, in the precise manner and form above stated, and that the said wine had been carefully deposited in a secret crypt in the cabin; and his surprise was great to find that this stranger was possessed with a knowledge of the transaction. He however craftily stated that Captain Oster had himself put away this wine in some private nook, which it might be difficult to discover, but that in lieu of the wine some genuine cognac might perhaps — "You do very well," interrupted the West Indian, "if no wine is to be had; but do me the favor, Mr. Dobbs, to take hold of that brass ring that is set into the larboard-side of the transom, and pull gently upon the same." Jeptha looked at the speaker in greater perplexity than ever, took courage from the arch expression of his dark eye, and seizing the ring according to the directions given, lifted a species of trap-door, nicely framed in the wood-work, and displayed a recess of tolerable dimensions, in the which lay packed the hamper already alluded to. As no further concealment was now available, the mate extracted a bottle of the ruby-colored liquid and set it before the lieutenant, who held it up to the light, handling it as gently as possible, anticipating, by an involuntary and audible smack of the lips, that exquisite and soul-entrancing flavor that the pure grape-like cordial was soon to impart It was so evident that Captain Oster would experience a total loss of these private stores, that Jeptha considered himself in duty bound to drink on the invitation of the lieutenant; and as he filled up and tossed off glass for glass, it was under the sincere conviction that the act was meritorious, inasmuch as he only partook of what was actually now in possession of the enemy. The wine had its usual effect, and the awe that had hitherto restrained the curiosity of the mate giving way to the energy of the vintage, he ventured to inquire how the lieutenant had become acquainted, not only with the shipment of the wine, but the secret repository of the same.

"Our captain," replied the lieutenant, slowly pouring out another glass, "received this information from a particular friend of his, to whom we will, Mr. Dobbs, drink a bumper, — fill up, sir — no heeltaps: now sir, to our best friend — the devil."

"The devil!" ejaculated Jeptha, and started as if his Satanic majesty were coming to do honor to the toast in proper person, as the sentry, knocking suddenly and loudly at the door, called to his officer.

But to explain the cause of this interruption we must return to the worthy Heinrich, who in much trepidation had made his way on board the piratical vessel, and was immediately brought before the commander. This truculent-looking personage eyed the captain, as he approached, with a cool and penetrating glance, and observed, in a calm and quiet manner, —

"You were on board the *Greyhound* the day before you sailed — heard you anything, or saw you aught yourself, that induced you to believe she was getting ready for sea?"

Heinrich was of a mind too lazy and inactive to reason with himself on the singularity of the circumstance implied in the question thus abruptly advanced; the knowledge, to wit, that the commander of this piratical vessel so far at sea possessed of his movements on the day before his departure from Philadelphia. He answered, therefore, without any hesitation, that no actual preparations had met his eye; but that, from accidentally having overheard a conversation between Captain Solgard and hts first lieutenant, he was led to believe that ere long an attempt would be made to capture the notorious Blackbeard, who had been reported as actually off the capes at the time.

As he delivered this in his usual sententious and unmoved manner, the commander eyed him with a calm and rather pleased countenance, curling his upper lip slightly as Captain Solgard's intentions were revealed, and was proceeding to ask some further queries touching the force and armament of the *Greyhound*, when the lookout on the foretop announced a sail on the starboard bow. This occasioned a sudden change in the previously calm and indifferent bearing of the buccaneer; he immediately called for a glass, and for a few moments looked steadily in the quarter indicated. When he withdrew his eyes from the glass, his countenance had become serious; he directed Captain Oster to return immediately on board of his own ship, and in case he should be overhauled by the line-of-battle ship then in sight, to give to the commander of the tame the compliments of Captain Teach, and his sincere regret that the great disproportion in size between their respective vessels would oblige him to avoid a meeting. Word was then passed for the lieutenant, who was at the time luxuriating in Captain Oster's prime Madeira, to repair to his station; and the startling effect of the summons on the excited nerves of Jeptha we have already commemorated.

Heinrich's exceeding amazement may readily be conceived, when it was thus revealed that this mild, cheerful-spoken, agreeable, and polite personage, who had neither robbed, insulted, maltreated, nor murdered him, was no less than the famous Captain Teach, usually termed Blackbeard; whose bloody deeds of cruelty, and well-known delight in feats of rapine and murder, had been spread far and wide, formed the text of many colonial addresses, and were vividly set forth in a ballad sung to the tune of the "Jew's Daughter." But Heinrich should have bethought him of the adage that runs thus, "The cat will play and after slay;" for Blackbeard was said to possess that feline propensity, which would lead him to deceive his unsuspecting victims, lulling their suspicions for a time by a well -feigned semblance of courtesy and good-will; and when the illusion was complete, and a change least thought of, the buccaneer would give loose to the most horrid cruelties; or, if at the time disposed to mercy, he would content himself with plundering his prisoners, and, sparing their lives, divert himself with the jocular proceeding of his men; who, in such cases, by way of a good jest, would cut off incidentally an ear or a nose as they dismissed each captive, thereby provoking a series of groans, shrieks, and yells that much amused their facetious commander.

By the time the line-of-battle ship came up to the *Santa Claus*, the buccaneer had stretched far away to windward and altogether disappeared; and Captain Oster, being a second time forced to leave his ship, repaired, with more alacrity than he had manifested on the preceding occasion, on board the man-of-war (which proved to be a heavy seventy-four), and delivered Blackbeard's valedictory message, word for word. This aroused the indignation of the captain, and after a brief interview Heinrich was dismissed, and the seventy-four bore away in full chase of the bold buccaneer.

The wrath of Captain Oster was not a little excited on witnessing the unexpected violation of his private stores; and he took occasion to curse the swarthy lieutenant in a series of the most powerful and approved oaths at that time extant in the Dutch language, until Jeptha expressed his suspicions that the said lieutenant had doubtless dealings with the evil one, with whom rumor was that Blackbeard himself was actually in league; upon which Heinrich considered it most prudent to stay his imprecations, lest some familiar spirit might accidentally be within hearing. He contented himself, therefore, with an occasional growl, as he replaced the covering over the eight remaining bottles. The contents of three bottles had been absorbed with almost incredible rapidity by the joint efforts of the lieutenant and the mate; the former pouring down the rare and enlivening juice of the grape with the energy of a man who knows that no time is to be lost, and Jeptha resolutely exerting his best abilities in endeavoring to save as much as possible.

But about one-third of the fourth bottle had been decanted at the time the interruption above mentioned had taken place; but while Captain Oster listened to the details which the sympathizing Jeptha gave of the mysterious and unjustifiable conduct of the West Indian, he took, without reflection, glass after glass, as a man in trouble will generally do; so that by the time the mate bad arrived at the conclusion of his tale, and finally in a low and solemn tone revealed the terrific name which his suspicious boon companion had proposed for a toast, the captain stood aghast, and the bottle was empty.

But the attention of both captain and mate was soon to be directed to another and perhaps almost equally perplexing subject: a sailor in perilous haste rushed down the cabin stairs, and, missing his foothold near the top, or, it may be, not advancing bit head and lower extremities with equal celerity, be turned topsy-turvy ere he reached the bottom, and bursting open the door with alarming impetus, rolled, as it were, in a heap into the presence of his officers.

Jeptha assisted the little man. to regain his feet, and the captain, after ascertaining that both neck and limbs were unscathed, gave him a kick on the breech, and desired to know the cause of his intra" pion. As soon as' the man could collect those scattered ideas which his projectile movement had materially disarranged, he informed the captain that the devil himself in the shape of a huge black cat, had just taken possession of the ship: that the men had chased it until they discovered that all their efforts were nugatory; when suddenly it turned upon and chased them, biting, scratching, and clapper clawing more like a demon than a cat, and eluding continually the blows of her terror-struck assailants.

The usually imperturbable Heinrich had already during the day been constrained to abide numerous assaults against jis equanimity: he had been overhauled by a pirate, molested with questions by a man who knew more than he asked for, and only released from this imperious questioner to be again overhauled by a British man-of-war; he had been lawlessly robbed also of a portion of choice wine; and had, as misfortunes never come alone, accidentally fractured an old and much-valued pipe. It was then r as naturally may be supposed, in a state of high wrought and unusual excitement, that Captain Oster received the startling intelligence that Old Nick had taken actual possession of the *Santa Claus* in the appropriate incarnation of an enormous black cat. With a resolute expression of countenance, and without addressing a single word indicative of his intentions either to the sailor or Mr. Dobbs, he placed a pair of large horseman's pistols in his belt, and left the cabin.

Jeptha immediately followed, and in silence; on reaching the deck a very singular spectacle presented itself. Behind the mainmast, and crowding towards the companion-way, the whole crew had mustered in a state of awe and excitement. Blood was streaming freely from the faces of some, others had their shirts rent in many places, and all bore indubitable evidence of the demoniac power and ferocity of their sable enemy. The cat itself had run up the main rigging, and stood on the very extremity of the royal-studding-sail boom to leeward, with back arched, tail erect, and more than double the ordinary thickness, eyes flashing a horrible green fire, and claws crimsoned with blood: the appearance of the huge, swart, and grim animal was decidedly preternatural.

"This is horrible, Mr. Dobbs!" observed Captain Oster, turning suddenly round to Jeptha, and speaking in a low and hurried voice; "I surely meant to have shot the creature as I came on deck, but, as you see, I could scarce carry so far with a pistol to any certainty; and moreover," added he, in a still lower tone, "it favoreth a likeness of the evil one."

To one less superstitious than Heinrich Oster, who perhaps was in this respect fully imbued with the inveterate prejudices and traditionary beliefs that custom and the lapse of ages hare but more fully sanctioned as portion of the sailor's creed, certain circumstances connected with, or, to say the least, coincident with, the mysterious appearance on board of the equally mysterious animal, might have appeared incapable of rational explanation, save by a reference to a direct agency or sinister influence exercised by the aforesaid sable personification of evil. As soon as the cat bad stationed itself as above stated, it was evident to all that the lee lurches of the ship increased in violence, her masts bending and straining heavily ere they rose with the return of the hull, and the water running freely through her lee scuppers as she laid over; the wind came in sudden and powerful blasts, and dark threatening clouds were rising to windward, although but an hour before not even a fleecy vapor was visible in the unclouded expanse of the heavens. It was easy for all hands to see that a storm was brewing, and Captain Oster, breaking silence, gave orders to take in sail. Not a single man stirred; every one stood as it were paralyzed by an undefinable sensation of awe and terror; and a very ancient mariner, whom Captain Oster asked individually if he, as well as the rest, had gone mad with fright, answered solemnly, shaking his head with a melancholy earnestness, — "I have sailed with you, Captain Oster, and with your father before you, man and boy, this three-and-forty years, and I should be the last man to hang back or disobey orders: but it's all to no use to turn to, as long as that black fiend aloft is weighing down the ship to one side, and maybe'll capsize us without any warning."

Jeptha had been absent for a short time, and now appeared, bearing in his left hand a long rusty rifle which he prized exceedingly, and concerning the rare merits of which he had a fund of marvelous stories, to which his shipmates would listen with all the necessary gravity of apparent belief, such as courtesy demanded to the statements of a superior, although among themselves doubts of their claim to gospel verity were freely suggested.

"By the big Salem squash!" exclaimed Jeptha, elevating his piece to his shoulder, and taking a steady aim at the demon-cat, whose appearance seemed to grow more frightful, as if conscious of his hostile intention, "I'll try the virtue of silver slugs; and I reckon if Ironsides" (a familiar cognomen of his favorite gun) "stands fast, we'll see Old Nick drop in less than no time."

The seamen shuddered at the ill-timed levity of the mate, and every one gazed in breathless and mute expectation as he fired.

"Down he goes!" shouted Jeptha; "Martha's Vinyard! but that was a good shot;" and he rushed to the bulwarks to behold the floating corpse. It was nowhere to be seen; and

Jeptha concluded that it must have sunk suddenly, while the ancient mariner astounded the mystified tars still further by a solemn asseveration that the moment Mr. Dobbs drew trigger the black cat turned into a ball of fire and then disappeared; others backed this declaration by regular statements of similar import, and all were aware of an unearthly sulphurous smell left behind by the foul fiend, saving Jeptha, who, in his skeptical" way, would have it to be nothing but gunpowder. Singular as it may appear, no sooner had this supposed evil spirit disappeared than the dark clouds seemed to retire as by some hidden agency; the wind, that erst whistled so fierce and high, lulled into a favorable though powerful breeze, and the good ship *Santa Claus*, that worked so heavily under the potent spell of the feline incubus, seemed to rejoice in her deliverance, so lightly and buoyantly did she dance along the wave.

As if to compensate for the danger and vexation that impeded the commencement of the voyage, the weather now became favorable, and Heinrich's good-humor returned as he calculated how short a time would present to his sight the beloved spires and belfries of Amsterdam. Nothing occurred to mar these fair prospects; and no material mistake having been made in the reckoning, the "Broad Fourteen Sand" was passed without heaving the lead; and that skillful pilot Oud Karspel, coming on board, told all the latest news from Amsterdam, congratulated Captain Oster on his short passage, and having drunk several rounds with him by way of more thorough felicitation, he took charge of the *"Santa Claus*; left the *"Duyneker Diep,"* entered the *"Slenk,"* and carefully threading the narrow *"Muscovische Ree,"* and still more dangerous *"Texel Stroom,"* came out gloriously into the broad expanse of the *Zuyder Zee.* The *Santa Claus* now slackened her speed, hugging the coast of West Friesland, and not only Heinrich, but every little Dutch sailor on board, gazed at the low shores, bounded by broad dikes, the innumerable canals that meandered in all directions, and the whitewashed villages and comfortable farmhouses that dotted the lovely landscape, with emotions of delight, that the coldest heart must prove on the sight of his native land.

MATHILDA DOUGLAS

As night came on, and the passage -directly up to the city was somewhat perilous (although the pilot on making the observation professed his willingness to proceed and encounter any risk), it was concluded to remain for the night where they were at the time, and the anchor was let down in about twenty-four fathoms, hard rocky bottom. A large bowl of punch made its appearance in the cabin, and a small tub filled with a grateful compound of similar ingredients indicated rejoicings on a larger scale in the forecastle. Before midnight, Captain Heinrich Oster and that veteran toper Oud Karspel lay in a loving embrace on the floor of the cabin, each having held out with emulating firmness to the last, and sinking simultaneously from their chairs. At the table, as the sole survivor of the onslaught, sat the unconquerable Jeptha Dobbs; the peculiar" feature in whose constitution consisted in getting half-seas over in a short time, and with an unusually small amount of imbibed fluids, and again becoming more sober in exact proportion to the continuance of any given debauch. In the present instance he was, as may be supposed from the above premises, and the condition of his companions, perfectly himself, he gazed every now and then upon the prostrate form before him with a mock solemnity of visage, filling and slowly quaffing at each such cursory view his own goblet from the yet undepleted punch-bowl. From the forecastle arose shouts of merry uproar; all hands joined in celebrating the successful termination of the voyage; and marvel not that when the mate had accomplished the remainder of the bowl, by a sponge-like process of absorption peculiar to himself, and came on deck at eight bells to relieve the watch, he discovered the whole ship's company, without a solitary exception, dead drunk, and, with the usual gregarious impulse of jolly tars, collected in one confused heap around an empty tub on the starboard-side of the caboose. As it was fruitless to attempt to arouse men who were entirely insensible to the most energetic kicks which he dealt liberally among them, the mate leaned over the bulwarks and fell into a sentimental reverie. His thoughts reverted to the time when, on the deck of this very ship, he had almost declared his love to the fair Barbara: he pictured to himself the heavenly blue eye, that, when the tempest approached in fierce and wild career, had by chance met his own in a timid and melancholy gaze that went to his very heart; and, the peril past, again beamed with the charming light ot innocent gayety: that lovely form, firm and elastic in its youthful movements; those ruddy pouting lips that — unconsciously had Jeptha suffered his relaxed frame to sink upon the deck, and in a deep and quiet slumber he dreamed of love and happiness.

On the next day the *Santa Claus*, with a fair wind, sailed up the Amstel, and the queenly city rose into view. Everything reminded the happy voyagers of home: the numerous spires, the distant and confused chime of the mighty bells, the familiar dikes and sluices, and the well-known bastions capped with windmills, the countless signals and streamers floating from the shipping that lined the magnificent harbor— all told of the power, the wealth, and extensive commerce of the peerless city.

CHAPTER IX.

"I am not justly to be taxed with any presumption for meddling with matters wherein I have no dealing."—
Raleigh.

Let the reader imagine that from some convenient position he commands a view of the interior of the hidden laboratory, cell, study,, or workshop, as it may be termed, of the Chevalier Oxenstiern, which has been described in an earlier chapter, and he will behold two individuals, — one of whom, although altered in his appearance by a long apron of dark-colored serge, and sleeves of the same, as well as by a cap of green silk, fitting close to the circumference of the head and terminating in a floating tassel, will be recognized as the chevalier himself; and the other conceals under similar habiliments the spare and diminutive figure, the withered yet vivacious countenance, and the spectacled nose of Sir William Keith.

Anyone who might have noted the studiously polite and yet reserved manner of Sir William Keith towards Oxenstiern as often as they met in public, and the scanty and rare conversation that passed between them, would have been tempted to ascribe that distant and cold intercourse to feelings of personal dislike or secret aversion; and might well be induced to suspect motives of a mysterious, not to say sinister, nature, from a confidential and secret meeting of the said personages in this hidden chamber.

Sir William was of that class of persons who take every opportunity to avow an entire disbelief in everything that was referred to supernatural agencies; he ridiculed the believers in witchcraft and necromancy, — professed an utter contempt for omens, charms, talismans, incantations, and amulets, — and affected to laugh to scorn the vain and futile pretensions, as he termed them, of all such as held in judicial astrology, and sought the philosopher's stone; he even chose to doubt whether the disembodied spirits of the dead were ever permitted to revisit the earth; and was generally considered a bold and daring skeptic. But this outward scoffing at everything that might be deemed the creation of distempered imagination, or superstitious weakness, concealed, as with a mask, the most ardent zeal for hidden knowledge, and the most profound devotion for the mysterious and lofty aspirations of occult philosophy, ever cherished by mortal man. Oxenstiern blamed not, for he hardly heeded, the crafty policy which bade Sir William greet him before men with cold and stranger-like reserve; and if indeed he craved honor from his fellow-men, he must have been fully content with the unfeigned awe and profound respect with which Sir William treated him, when, in this solitary recess, he expounded to his attentive scholar the sublime doctrines of an unseen world.

The furnace that we have already spoken of glowed with the ruddy heat of a powerful and steadily regulated flame, which Oxenstiern fed from time to time, while Sir William on his knees plied a pair of bellows as often as directed. Both watched a small crucible, containing a grayish-colored liquid, that lay imbedded in the upper stratum of the glowing coals; and it appeared, from the fixed and grave attention of both, that a highly important process was going on. As Oxenstiern, with his arms folded across his breast, stood gazing upon the furnace, a supernatural change seemed to have passed over his wonted gay and courtier-like features, — instead of the ruddy hue of manhood, a wan and fearful paleness had overspread his noble countenance, and a stern unyielding gravity rested on his rigid brow. His eye was lighted up with the fire of earnest and lofty thought; and his whole appearance was so strikingly impressive, that Sir William surveyed him with an awe bordering on veneration, and perhaps imagined that the spirit of the Hermit of Hohenheim, or the more renowned Cornelius Agrippa, was embodied in the form of his master.

The language in which the chevalier expounded to his pupil the mysteries and practice of this hid" den science was peculiar to the art, the meaning thereof being couched in-dark and cabalistic words; which, though by no means intelligible to such as were yet among the uninitiated, and entirely under" stood alone by the great masters themselves, yet served to increase the deep reverence that Sir William entertained for his instructor.

It was therefore with a hesitating and timid voice that Sir William broke silence in the following terms: —

"You were kind enough, good master, to promise somewhat touching the action, or *modus operandi*, of the tincture."

A pause of a few moments ensued; during which Oxenstiern bowed his head upon his hand, as if in search of a fleeting reverie, and then spoke in low, distinct, and sweetly modulated tones: — "After this manner is the arcanum of the tincture to be understood, — to wit, that it taketh all the unwieldiness of old age, and every disease, and whatever corrupts the health, and that hath an inclination contrary thereunto. Nor doth it otherwise than so. Perfect its operations in the body likewise, — so as to transmute the corrupt and disorderly complexions into sound and healthy, like that tincture that makes luna of mercury; it separates not the evil therefrom, but tingeth both the good and the evil, that they finally become together most excellent. So likewise doth this tincture tinge the hydropical and icteritial body into a sound state: not that the dropsy is taken away, the original driven out, or separated from the good, but is transmuted into good, even as is behooveful and is constituted in its high, yea, best degree; even as the corrupted mud may, by the subtle corruption of art, be brought into an elixir, able to drive forth every corruption; and that corruption is not separated, but the whole substance is transmuted into another quality and nature."

Oxenstiern suddenly ceased; while a feeble blue flame shot out of the crucible, becoming by degrees brighter and steadier, and then again losing it£ brilliancy, and, gently wavering, finally died away. With a cup in his hand, containing a portion of transparent liquid, the chevalier stood by; and just as the flame disappeared, he carefully poured it into the crucible, muttering, as he did so, "Verily was Venus brought beyond twenty-four degrees, so that the color of Sol could ascend no higher — and this by quartation."

"And now, Sir William," continued Oxenstiern, "watch thou the alkahest; and when that it rises to within three fingers of the top, do thou mingle with it the magistery of pearls, which is contained in that iron flask behind the alembic: and now will I seek the further process"

So saying, he unclasped a small volume, entitled "Paracelsus his Paramirum;"and turning over the leaves until he found that part wherein is expounded the true and only process for the marvelous arcanum of the tincture, he diligently set about the proper understanding of the same, seeking to extract the veritable meaning of that great master out of the dark expressions and cabalistic form of words whereby he thought fit to conceal from the vulgar the divine secrets of alchemy.

Sir William watched the alkahest until it rose to within three fingers, and, in obedience to his master's directions, sought for the iron flask which stood behind the alembic. Two flasks were there, of different sizes; and taking the smaller of the two, which happened to be the nearest, he unscrewed the top, and inverted it over the crucible.

Oxenstiern accidentally looked up, and observing too late that the wrong flask had been taken, exclaimed, in a quick and eager voice, "Hold! thou art wrong;" but Sir William had already inverted the flask. Falling flat upon the floor, Oxenstiern cried, "Down, for thy life P and the dark liquid that fell into the crucible boiled up and exploded with terrific violence. The crucible split into a thousand fragments, and flew in all directions, and a dense mephitic vapor filled the apartment. Oxenstiern rose slowly, but Sir William lay stunned and senseless. "No wonder," observed the chevalier, speaking slowly, as if to account to himself for the cause of this explosive phenomenon; "fool that he was, to take the sublimated kaneth"

Sir William had received no wound, but, as if struck by a severe concussion, lay with his eyes closed and lips apart, in a state of apparent unconsciousness. The chevalier opened a small mahogany case, from which he took a vial, and poured a small portion of the contents, drop by drop, into his pupil's mouth. The effect was instant, and almost magical; the eyes opened, the mouth simultaneously closed, and the corpse-like flaccid limbs became endowed with life and motion. Sir William rose/ and, unable to discover that he had sustained any injury, reproached himself bitterly with having caused, by an unpardonable error, the destruction of a compound which the labor of months had nearly brought to perfection.

It was past midnight when Sir William arose to depart; all was silent and dark in the mansion of the chevalier; and master and pupil, with noiseless and stealthy tread, traversed the obscure chambers, and descended the broad flight of steps that led into the hall, with confidence and security. A door at the termination of a passage, giving access from the northern side of the hall into the garden, was opened by the chevalier with the same caution which had hitherto marked his proceedings, and his friend followed him into the open air. The night was perfectly clear, and the stars shone with sparkling brilliancy, diffusing a mild and gentle light upon the surface of the earth, and revealing, with sufficient distinctness, the narrow winding path in which lay the shortest route through the woods to the city. Sir William loved not to walk alone by night, especially after having been for several hours in close communion with an individual whom some hesitated not to terra a necromancer, and felt much satisfaction when the chevalier intimated his intention of keeping company as far as the western foot of Society Hill. Every step that Sir William took lightened his hearty as it increased the distance between himself and the abode of his master; around the precincts of which, at that lone hour, perhaps lurked the wild spirits of the air, awaiting his stern behest He listened too with greedy ear as his preceptor pointing out the various planetary orbs, taught him the motion of each fiery sphere, and obscurely hinted at those viewless messengers that, in unwearied flight, traverse the boundless realms of ether.

"That they may be summoned into visible presence," continued Oxenstiern, "is not to be denied; but it requireth a purification and preparation of mind and body that but few can hope to accomplish; together with a performance of certain rites and invocations, even to witness which needs a stout and fearless heart — but here we part, Sir William; so, God speed you."

BLACKBEARD

Sir William was surprised to find himself so near home as the foot of Society Hill, so entirely had the discourse of the chevalier prevented the note of time; and gazing in the direction of the city, he observed a few twinkling lights; towards which, after bidding adieu to the chevalier, he took his solitary way.

Oxenstiern watched the retreating form of Sir William until it was lost behind the intervening clumps of trees, and then continued for some time wrapped in meditation; gazing at times, perhaps, to read the book of fate spread out in the starry cope of heaven; and, as if he gathered somewhat from the luster of a distant star that, far in the west, shed an intense yet wavering light, he fixed his eyes upon that alone, in profound and almost melancholy reverie. His meditations were interrupted in a manner rather unexpected; for a dark figure, issuing from the obscurity, came directly towards him. The thought that Sir William had retraced his steps to seek him, was at first in his mind; but another glance convinced him that this opinion was incorrect. The intruder was a man of about the height of the knight, but of a breadth of frame utterly disproportioned to his low stature. His gait was unsteady and reeling, like that of a drunken man; and Oxenstiern, concealing his person behind an immense chestnut that stood hard by, determined to watch unseen the movements of this singular-looking personage.

He came forward, rolling heavily, — stopped for a moment within a few feet of Oxenstiern, — and, muttering deep and horrible imprecations, struck into the path that led to the mansion of the chevalier; in which direction his huge form gradually disappeared.

"Tis Blackbeard himself," said Oxenstiern; "and ripe for any devil's deed." So saying, he issued forth from his concealment, and again intently fixed his gaze on the single star that burned so brightly in the west. Its clear blue luster gradually dimmed, and then remained faint and pale. Again it waxed bright, but with a redder and more threatening glow; and Oxenstiern started as the change took place. "Ha!" exclaimed he, in slow and earnest tones, "there is blood upon the path of the buccaneer!"

Adding, more quickly, as he abruptly set forward in pursuit of the pirate, "God grant I be timely in the rescue."

Between Oxenstiern's house and the town stood a low one-storied cottage, the ruinous and dilapidated appearance of which sufficiently indicated the poverty of its occupant. An old woman, almost bent double by age and infirmities, dwelt therein; and a pretty girl, who called her grandmother, and who might be, at this time, about seventeen or eighteen years of age,' resided with and nursed the ancient dame. Without any visible means of livelihood, they seemed never in absolute want; and although presenting an appearance of the most abject poverty, the grandmother had more than once declined the offer of charitable assistance from the chevalier, as well as others. A little kitchen-garden, from which the subsistence of the owners was chiefly derived, separated the cottage, or rather hovel, from the path already mentioned. Oxenstiern approached the cottage; and quickened his pace as he observed light faintly glimmering through the chinks and crevices of the ill-constructed dwelling. As he came more near, a supplicating voice, broken by sobs and exclamations of agony, fell upon his ear. Bounding from the path, he cleared the little garden with a few active leaps; and bursting open the frail door of the tenement, was, for a moment, horror-struck with the scene. On the floor lay the dead body of the old Woman, her face fearfully tinged with the dark hue of suffocation by violence, and her aged limbs contorted in the agony of her dying struggles; while Blackbeard, having perpetrated this cruel murder, turned upon the poor girl an eye glaring with inebriation and unbridled appetite, and seizing upon the innocent young creature, in spite of tears and entreaties, would have doubtless accomplished his brutal purpose, but for the timely interposition of Oxenstiern. Seizing the buccaneer at the instant, and before he could turn to face the intruder, he planted one hand firmly among his thick black curls, and grasping his belt with the other, he raised his ponderous frame aloft in the air, as if it were that of an infant, then dashed it to the floor with a stunning violence, that made the roof above him tremble. The poor girl was no sooner liberated from the grasp of the ruthless pirate, than casting herself on the body of her murdered relative, she wept in the silent anguish of bereavement and despair. When Blackboard partially recovered from the effect of the shock he had received, he beheld Oxenstiern fixing him with a glance so terribly vindictive, that his own stern eye, which had never yet quailed to mortal man, and which more than once bad awed the boldest mutineers, unconsciously fell before it Unable to account for the superhuman strength which the chevalier possessed, and had just employed so evidently to his discomfiture, his superstitious dread of magic, to which he was disposed to attribute such an amazing exhibition of force, would have repressed his rising indignation, had he been otherwise than maddened by the most ardent and stimulating potations. Plucking a pistol suddenly from his belt, he fired full at the chevalier, and attempted to rise: this attempt was frustrated by a foot planted upon his breast with the tread of a giant; and the smoke clearing away, discovered that his accustomed certainty of aim had deceived him, for Oxenstiern stood over him uninjured, without the slightest change on his stern, vindictive aspect.

"Thy life I take not," said Oxenstiern; "nor yet hath been fulfilled thy bloody destiny, — thou mayst not now die by my hand, but on the trackless ocean shall stern and speedy vengeance overtake thee."

As he spoke this, in a voice of prophetic energy, that, by its low but fearfully distinct tones, excited an unwonted emotion, passing with somewhat of a cold and unpleasant thrill over the nerves of the hardened buccaneer, he raised the foot which pressed him to the earth, and, with brief sternness, bade him depart. Blackbeard arose, bewildered and amazed; for although his savage spirit burned for revenge, a consciousness of his own insignificance, when arrayed against the power of the majestic being who had so fiercely spurned him to the dust, forced him to obey; and he departed, muttering imprecations so horrible and deep, that the young girl shuddered, and clung to Oxenstiern for protection.

The chevalier learned, to his astonishment, that Blackbeard had long been known by the old woman; and that his visits to the cottage were invariably made under cover of darkness, and without a companion. The artless Susan further informed him, that her grandmother had always maintained an ascendency over her visitor; though latterly he had become more violent, and at times absolutely threatening in his demand for some concealed treasure; for her own part, she trembled at the appearance of this dark savage-looking man; felt uneasy, she knew not why, even when he smiled upon her, and rejoiced at his departure. "He came tonight," continued she, "with a reeling step, his face flushed and swollen, and his bloodshot eye glaring with excited passions. My poor grandmother harshly bade him begone and get sober; which, instead of checking him, only served to inflame his wrath: cursing her with dreadful maledictions, he told her at her peril to deny him the treasure; and when she refused, with scornful and shrill defiance, he dragged her from the bed with a horrid demoniac laugh, and choked her, as she feebly screamed and struggled on the floor of the apartment. He then turned to me, and would soon have added another murder to his bloody list, when God sent you to prevent it"

Oxenstiern listened with various emotions to the statement of the gentle orphan: indignant feelings knit his brow at the recital of the atrocious villany of the pirate; and compassionate benevolence warmed his heart towards the young creature so wickedly and suddenly deprived of her natural protector. He answered, however, in a kind and cheerful voice—

"Despair not entirely, gentle maiden; thy grandmother peradventure doth even yet retain somewhat of vitality; and if so be, by the grace of God, I may kindle up anew the spirit of lire. A greater marvel than this hath been wrought by leechcraft, in the which noble science I am indifferently skilled, having studied seven years under the renowned Frascati of Padua."

To all this the maiden replied not, but wept the more bitterly, thinking that leechcraft could be of no avail to her murdered relative. And had she known that the famous physician of whom he spoke had been dead himself upwards of a century, any hopes that she might have entertained had certainly been crushed by such an unquestionable indication of insanity on the part of her protector. This she knew not; and yet she hoped not, but regarded his proceedings with a degree of feminine curiosity that at least had the effect of arresting her despairing lamentations.

Oxenstiern applied his fingers to the wrist of the corpse, and then his palm upon the breast; but mournfully shook his head, as if he failed in discovering the feeble pulsations of lingering life that be had hoped for: he then approached his ear to the chest, and listened long and anxiously, the simple girl gazing the while in mute amazement. As e raised his head, joy sparkled in his eyes; and bidding the damsel be of good cheer, he produced a small vial of bright scarlet liquid, from which he poured a few drops down the throat of the corpse, and motioning to the girl to be quiet, watched for the anticipated result. Powerful was the essence, and of rare virtue, for presently a convulsive movement took place in the chest, increasing in violence; but as yet the eves opened not, and the limbs were cold and perfectly motionless.

"She is aged," said Oxenstiern; "another drop will assuredly suffice f and he added another drop of the elixir. He was right, for heavy and laborious inspirations ensued, the eyes opened, though at first with the ghastly glare of wild delirium; and spasmodic twitches in the limbs, and a firm clenching of the fingers, indicated the sudden infusion of vital energy. Then followed more regular and natural breathing; the eyes became more steadily fixed on surrounding objects, with an expression of recognition and returning consciousness; and the convulsive agitation of the limbs subsided, until the body lay relaxed in the calm and easy position of repose. The chevalier then gently raised her from her prostrate attitude, and conveyed her to the bed; while the poor girl, wild with delight, caressed alternately her aged grandmother and her benevolent protector.

Hardly had the old woman made use of her voice to assure the chevalier that she felt quite, nay, unusually well, when she demanded an explanation of her present situation. To give this was the task of the happy Susan; and the courage and benevolence of Oxenstiern were extolled in terms that fully repaid him for his exertions. Gratitude frequently becomes annoying; and Oxenstiern was compelled to cut short the expression of grateful feeling, by bidding them fear no further molestation from Blackbeard, recommending repose and sleep to the resuscitated old dame, and promising an early visit, as he took his departure. He departed; but the grandmother and granddaughter kept up a tolerably incessant interchange of words, until Susan fell asleep from pure weariness, and the old woman, for want of an auditor, followed her example.

The baffled buccaneer, as we have seen, retired from the scene of his villany stung with mortification, and breathing naught but fury and vengeance. He was, from the peculiar nature of the incidents he had encountered, completely restored to the sober exercise of his faculties, and traversed the forest with a firm and rapid tread, pursuing his course with the unhesitating step of one to whom the ground was familiar, until he reached the tenement on the bank of the Delaware, already alluded to as the scene of revel to which Captain Solgard was so unexpectedly introduced by the pirate chief. The first faint light of dawn stole upon Blackbeard as he entered the hut, and rudely awakened his sleeping associates. To them he explained in brief his project of vengeance upon Oxenstiern; and as the execution of what he intended required their co-operation, he announced the necessity of deferring their putting out to sea, which should have taken place that very day, until the scheme which he now meditated, and of which he had given all hands the particulars, should be accomplished, Some of the objects to be attained by a successful prosecution of the scheme proposed were of a nature well calculated to secure the good-will and aid of these marine depredators, and their cheerful looks and joyous assent satisfied the captain that they would second all his attempts.

Towards evening of the same day Barbara Scheveling wandered alone in the woods that separated Erigson House from that of the Chevalier Oxenstiem, searching for plants and mosses to enrich a botanical collection lately presented to her by the chevalier — gathering in one place most beautiful and delicate specimens of the graceful fern, and meeting in others with masses of modest lichen — roaming without fear of aught, for innocence, especially youthful innocence, seldom apprehends an unseen evil,— when she was aware of two men approaching her in deep and earnest conversation. Timid as a startled fawn, Barbara trembled with alarm equal to her former confidence, both perhaps equally causeless, and thought instantly of flight; but perceiving at the same moment that the intruders were directly between her and trigson House, and that they approached without observing her, she, by a rapid revulsion of feeling, laughed at her foolish alarm, and resolved to continue her occupation until they passed by. Another glance, however, again altered her determination, and hastily concealing herself behind a cluster of bushes, that effectually screened her from observation; she stood with a beating heart, while they passed within a few feet of her person. In this situation she overheard part of a conversation that caused her inwardly to rejoice in her concealment.

One of the speakers, although she knew him not, was Captain Teach, and the other a man considerably taller than Blackbeard himself, but by no means of so truculent an aspect, — Blackbeard's lieutenant, in fact — the swarthy yet elegant West Indian who so cavalierly disposed of Heinrich Oster's choice wine on board the *Santa Claus.*

"Seize him!" grumbled the captain; "ay, bind him! but let no one dare kill him, — he must fall under this knife;" and he grasped firmly the long Spanish blade which he wore over his right hip, regarding the keen edge and sharpened point with a grim and malevolent look of determination.

"So be it," replied the West Indian, with as much nonchalance as if a party of pleasure, and • got the life of a human being, were under discussion; u kill the chevalier yourself, an you will; but are you well assured that the casket you spoke of still remaineth in the eastern chamber."

The speakers passed on, and their voices became indistinct in the distance; but Barbara had heard enough to quicken painfully the beating of her trembling heart, and blanch her roseate cheek with death-like paleness. A plot had been laid to murder Oxenstiern, her best and most esteemed friend, her kindest and truest benefactor; when it was to be put into execution, or how, she had no means of ascertaining, — darkness covers most deeds of crime, and perhaps this very night might consummate the horrid design. Intelligence must be conveyed to Oxenstiern, and that instantly. She would hasten home, and her father should dispatch a messenger to the chevalier forthwith. Breathless with haste, she entered Erigson

House, and, to her surprise and gratification, found the chevalier indulging himself in a game of chess with the major.

The quick eye of the chevalier immediately observed that she had no usual cause of agitation, as he silently awaited the explanation; while an excellent combination of maneuvers, which the major had diligently planned for the defeat of his antagonist, was put to flight by the unaccountable behavior of his fair niece, who, throwing her arms about his neck, rested her head upon his shoulder and wept. Her excitement being thus calmed by the effusion of tears, she whispered, "I am so happy, dear uncle!" at which her uncle only wondered the more.

"Truly, my dear niece," said the major, audibly responding to the whisper of the fair girl, who still clung to him with filial fondness, "hadst thou not informed me, I should have thought some sudden grief possessed thee: but thou resemblest in this thy poor mother; for I well remember, how she actually wept fo joy when my brother returned from Dunquerque after being reported among the killed."

Oxenstiern thought it best to allow Barbara time to calm her emotion, and accordingly diverted the questions which the major would inevitably have propounded as a sequence to his last observations, by taking up the discourse, and making a series of desultory and entertaining remarks touching the proneness with which women fall to shedding of tears, on any occasion of unusual excitement, be it joyful or otherwise; during which Barbara resumed her self-possession, and the chevalier, on observing it, came to a conclusion.

The major listened with kindling wrath, and Oxenstiern with the most perfect equanimity, as Barbara gave a detail of what she had seen and heard in the woods; describing the hardened indifference of the taller ruffian, and dwelling with more horror on the dreadful threats and malignant aspect of the other.

"Many thanks to you, fair Barbara," said Oxenstiern, as she concluded by conjuring him to provide speedily for his safety. "As to these villains, 1 have been, ere this, made acquainted with their plot, which is to attack my house to-night at twelve; and I have already made such arrangements as shall effectually defeat them."

"Requested a detachment of marines from Captain Solgard, I presume?" inquired the major.

"Not so," answered the chevalier; "but my precautions, I doubt not, will prove altogether effectual; and, with your favor, I would resume our game, in which, methinks, I had you somewhat at a vantage."

"You have been a soldier!" exclaimed the major.

"Tis many years," replied the chevalier.

"One might know it," resumed the veteran, "to behold you with such composure sitting at a game of chess, when you are aware that in about four hours some ruffians are to make a desperate attempt on your life. Why not remain with us tonight?"

"That were impossible, my kind sir, for my plan of defense requires my personal superintendence, and my house would be plundered else."

"Then must I reinforce your garrison," said the veteran; "there are Fritz and the gardener; and although my own arm has become somewhat stiff of late, I can still handle a Toledo, as the knaves may find to their cost."

"My dear sir," resumed the chevalier, "your aid were more than sufficient in this mailer j but you must absolutely remain to take charge of your niece, who has been sufficiently alarmed by these rogues already \ and I will give you an early call in the morning, and acquaint you with the result of my proceedings,"

Barbara disclaimed all apprehension in regard to the safety of Erigson House, and earnestly besought Oxenstiern to accept the proffered assistance of her uncle; but he was inflexible on this point, and only went so far as to promise, at the particular request of the major, that in case of any unfavorable emergency two guns should be fired, at a minute's interval, to signify his want of further assistance. With this the major was fain to be content; and finishing the game in which he had been engaged with his guest, he immediately sallied forth, and calling together his force, to wit, the gardener and Fritz, set about drilling them with military exactitude, having first furnished his little corps with arms offensive and defensive,

— leaving Oxenstiern to entertain Barbara, until such time as he might think fit to retire to his own domicile.

About an hour before midnight he accordingly Bet forth j shaking hands with Barbara, who endeavored to appear composed, while a tear stole down her cheek, and discovered the major sedulously attempting to impart regular discipline to his raw recruits, who, although able-bodied men, and willing enough to take an active part in any irregular skirmish, as the major himself alleged, had merely, by the greatest exertions on his part, been able to acquire a very small portion of the regular drill; in which, however, they had attained a tolerable degree of expertness, as he would take the liberty of exemplifying in the presence of his friend the chevalier. Fritz and the gardener accordingly stood forth, but, much to the mortification of the commanding officer, utterly failed in the few simple maneuvers to which their attention had been so devotedly directed: when Fritz was correct, the gardener was generally deficient; and whenever the gardener Failed not, the other half of the corps would invariably blunder. Oxenstiern assured the major, who was not a little confused, that under present circumstances, irregular troops would be likely to prove much more efficient than regular soldiers, and took his departure, while the major bade him be sure to recollect the signal.

Barbara sat by herself, starting at every little noise, and even annoyed by the cricket, that, emboldened by the quietude of the apartment, began to chirp from among the asparagus branches in the fireplace. The screech-owl, too, at intervals, poured forth his hideous note; and, under the existing circumstances, a less superstitious imagination might have deemed that mournful cry $n inauspicious omen. As the hour of midnight approached, the major ever and anon consulted the massive Dutch clock that stood sentinel on the first landing of the staircase. The clock struck, — the twelfth chime gradually died away — and hardly had the last echo ceased, when the report of a single gun echoed through the forest,

"Look to your priming, lads!" exclaimed the old officer, promptly unsheathing his sabre; "and when I give the word, follow me — double-quick step."

No second report, however, followed, — much to the disappointment of the major, who awaited the signal with all the ardour of his youthful days. For the space of an hour he controlled his impatience; the end of which period, leaving Fritz with instructions to guard the premises until his return, he made a sortie towards the field of battle, — himself, sword in hand, urging the advance, and the gardener closely following in the rear.

CHAPTER X.

"By this the drooping daylight began to fade,
And yield his room to sad succeeding night;
Who with her sable mantle 'gan to shade
The face of earth, and ways of living wight."
Spenser.

The evening was calm and beautiful; the fading rays of a glorious summer sunset had left the glassy surface of the "hidden river" covered with a dense shade, when the light of the rising moon disclosed a canoe, propelled by a solitary individual, wending its way between the forests which lined its banks.

From the apparent inattention to the course of his little vessel, it would seem that the thoughts of its occupant were wandering on other matters; for his paddle, after a vigorous stroke or two, would fall carelessly into the water, and a state of listless inactivity succeed these almost unconscious efforts.

"'Tis strange," at length exclaimed he, starting from his reverie; "it may he fancy, but those features, my memory seems to tell me, have been elsewhere seen." So saying, the hunter (for he it was, already mentioned in a former chapter) diligently plied his neglected paddle, and soon the light ripple before the canoe gave token of its rapid progress; and on approaching a deep cove, nearly concealed by the overhanging branches of the surrounding forest, by a dexterous sweep it was whirled deep into its shades.

A few minutes afterward the active form of the hunter might be seen gliding among the trees with the quick noiseless tread of an Indian, until, on reaching a more open spot of ground at the top of the bank, the loud bark of a noble staghound, subsiding to an affectionate whine of recognition, welcomed its owner to his habitation.

Wedged, as it were, in the masses of rocks that rose precipitously from the water's edge, stood a low log-cabin, with thatched roof, sufficiently rude and sylvan in its aspect.

The furniture of the interior did not belie its external appearance: consisting of a rough table and bench, — a seaman's chest in one corner, on which was spread a bear-skin, as a couch, — a shelf or two, containing sundry fishing-tackle, and a very scanty supply of culinary utensils; a rifle, with its attendant powder-horn and pouch, formed the only decoration of the wall.

The night was wearing on; and after pacing his hut for some time in a state of abstraction, followed by his faithful hound, that sought in vain to attract his notice, and seemed, by his inquiring looks, to wonder at his master's unwonted humor, the hunter threw himself upon his rude couch, with the determination of seeking repose: but, whether from the excitement produced by the events of the day, or from the effects of the good cheer at the fishing club, sleep came not at his bidding. Wearied at length with the restlessness of over-excitement, increased by the sultriness of the night, he sprang from his couch, and, lighting an Indian pipe, seated himself on a log in front of his hut.

Soothing is the influence of tobacco to a mind ill at ease; and as he watched the rising vapor of his calumet, curling itself into fantastic wreaths, the hunter felt a pleasing calm stealing upon him. The scene, moreover, which presented itself, together with the stillness of the night, was favorable to uninterrupted contemplation. Far as the eye could reach, the mighty forest, as yet untouched by the axe of civilization, stretched away in all the lonely grandeur of its native wildness, unbroken, save by the serpentine winding of the placid stream glittering like silver in the moonbeams,

A casual observer might have been led to suppose, from the immoveable posture of the hunter, and the fixedness of his gaze, that his imagination was entirely absorbed in the wild beauty of the prospect before him. But the ideal visions which flitted before his mind's eye were widely different.

Recollections of earlier days were crowding on his memory: the ancient gable-fronted mansion, with its pleasure-grounds reaching to a sluggish canal, on the margin of which stood the well-remembered Lusthaus, or small pavilion, the scene of many a youthful frolic, — the venerable figure of an ancient gentleman caressing the little flaxen-haired damsel on his knee, and enjoying the luxury of the ample stoop or porch of the aforesaid mansion. Then would the scene suddenly change to the roughness of the sea-boy's life, — the horrors of shipwreck — the bustle of cities— the Indian war-whoop — while ever and anon the form of the fair damsel he had so opportunely succored would flit among these ill-assorted fantasies.

What strange confused assemblage of recollections does the mind engender, when ransacking and groping into every corner of the memory in search of a familiar yet forgotten countenance, to which it has, as it were, the shadow of a clew— a vague outline constantly within reach, but which flies in the attempt to grasp it!

Thus it was with our hunter: and doubtless the grateful smile and exquisite proportions of the gentle Barbara imparted an interest to his researches which they might not otherwise have possessed; albeit he might be willing to persuade himself that the mental' puzzlement was the offspring of pure philosophical investigation.

The hunter started from his reverie — the gray dawn of morning was spreading itself around the horizon," and the refreshing breeze of the soft South wind roused him from his cramped position. He must have slept, for his pipe had fallen from his hand unobserved; and, on raising his eyes, the figure of a stranger, whose approach he had not noted, stood before him. The external appearance of the intruder was by no means calculated to allay the surprise created by his sudden presence; for, in addition to his low square-built figure, garnished with a portentous looking pair of pistols, ostentatiously displayed in his belt, a single glance would reveal the characteristic features of the notorious Blackbeard.

For one moment the eyes of the hunter were fixed upon the sea-robber with an expression of perplexed doubt as to his identity; in the next, the angry flash that deepened his sunburnt cheeks told plainly that the feelings awakened by this unexpected visitor were far from being of an amicable nature. » Firmly grasping the hunting-knife which he plucked from his belt, as he started to his feet, and rushed with rapid strides towards the pirate, he burst forth, in a voice nearly choked with rage, —

"Ruffian! we meet at last — in a fair field— on equal terms — knife to knife — and no quarter P

"Avast P growled the rough voice of Blackbeard, at the same time presenting a pistol; "not so fast, messmate I one step nearer, and you are on the road to Davy Jones's locker I — no ripping up of old sores! I see you haven't forgot my capsizing you with a handspike for disobeying orders, when we first run up the black flag, eh! and then sending you adrift in the jolly without a pilot! and, but that on a former occasion your cutlass had done its duty on a cursed Spaniard who left this gash on my cheek, the carcass of Captain Teaches first officer would have swung as a pistolmark from the yard-arm! — But you were nothing but a crack-brained youngster then — your notions may be changed now; you are -a brave fellow, withal, and I want such a one. The Peaceful Mariner is the road to riches; I offer you a berth — be my lieutenant, and you will. Show your colors, friend or foe!"

During the whole of thjs persuasive and, for Blackbeard (whose arguments were generally of a practical nature), remarkably lengthy and argumentative harangue, the hunter stood in an attitude of stern defiance.

The sudden frenzy excited by the appearance of the freebooter, which associated itself with the recollection of former injuries and insult, had given place to a feeling of indignation at his proposal, mingled with that of long-nourished and ungratified revenge.

Casting on him then a glance of unqualified scorn and detestation, he answered, —

"I hold no terms with a cowardly assassin!"

The dark eyes of the buccaneer flashed fire, and his pistol also flashed in the pan, else would the hunter have dearly paid the forfeit of his rashness, in thus provoking the fury of his lawless adversary.

Hurling the faithless instrument of his vengeance into the river, the buccaneer drew another, and cocked it: but now he hesitated, ere he pulled the trigger; his countenance gradually resumed its calm and settled expression of sternness.

"You must be mine, Marx!" said he, in a low tone, intended to imitate the gentle language of a forgiving spirit. "In spite of all this, sleep on it, and meet me a week hence at Caller's Cove."

With this the rover rapidly descended the ledge of rocks that here grew up out of the water; and the hunter, watching his progress with a grim dissatisfied air, beheld him leap into a boat below, and could even hear him growl out, "Shove off I" which order was obeyed without delay by the old sea-dog who sat in the boat; and pulling briskly down the river, a curve in the stream ere long concealed their farther progress from the eyes of the disappointed hunter.

The day was fine for hunting, — the air cool, clear, and bracing; and the young man, equipping himself for the chase, whistled to his staghound, which bounded before and upon him in rapturous enthusiasm, giving short yelps of pleasure, and chasing hither and thither in the exuberance of his happiness. The hunter plunged deep into the forest, seeking he cared not what, so it but proved sufficient matter of excitement: and, certes, ere long he did find ample food for the same; his dog roused a noble buck, and away they flew with lightning speed. The hunter watched their course, and darted across the forest to meet the antlered monarch on the turn. Ere he took his stand, he cast his eyes around as usual, to see if haply others than himself might be near. On either side of a small open space stood an enormous sycamore, as much alike as could be in size and verdure, giant brothers, Otus and Ephialtus like, to guard the sacred recesses of the sylvan realm. On the tree to the right, as the hunter looked up, he beheld a huge panther crouched in wary expectation, his superbly spotted skin partially gleaming in the sun, that hardly found its way through the branches of the tall tree. The animal appeared not to be aware of his approach, but employed itself in gazing in another direction, and now and then looking over, with what seemed to the puzzled hunter, an expression of intelligence, into the tree opposite.

What was the surprise of the hunter to discover, on turning his gaze in the same direction, another enormous panther on the other tree, It was precisely at the same height from the ground, lay crouched in a similar manner, and paid no more attention to the motions of the hunter than the other had done.

Here was a curious predicament to be placed in: the opportunity would have been irresistible, had but one of these spotted Dromios been thus presented; and even before the double foe the hunter was full loath to retreat without pulling trigger,

"If Fleance were but here," said he to himself, "it would go hard but we should manage both of them,"

Even as he thus soliloquized, as if his wishes had been heard by some propitious deity, a bark, a familiar bark too, was heard by intervals at a distance, telling full well that Fleance was hard upon the buck.

The panthers heard it toe, for they stirred simultaneously, and looked in the direction whence proceeded the sounds; and then, as these indicated, by becoming more distinctly audible, that the chase was rapidly nearing them, they drew up their catlike figures for a spring, and eagerly awaited their prey.

On came the buck at speed, panting and crashing through the bushes, bounding beautifully over the brush, — laying back his huge antlers, until they overhung his broad flanks, streaked here and there with blood, where the sharp thorns, in passing, had torn the sleek velvet of his skin, — and thinking little, as he left Fleance behind, that he was madly rushing into the very fangs of a far more cruel and relentless foe.

On came the hound also, steady to the track; and the -stag is now within twenty yards of the panthers— he is still nearer — and, with a fierce unerring leap, and wild startling yell, the panther on the left drops like a thunderbolt upon the hapless buck. Happy was it for Fleance that thus the warning came. Stopping short, as the other panther sprang upon him, he started aside, and the disappointed monster came hurtling to the earth. Recovering himself, he growled horribly, and rushed upon the hound; but he had to deal with no feeble foe, — Fleance was a dog of exceeding strength and fierceness.

"To him, Fleance! shake him, sir!" cried the hunter; and, watching his opportunity, he released his hound from his furious adversary, by lodging a ball in the brain of the panther, which immediately fell over to one side; upon which Fleance gave him a rough shake or so, by way of a piling endearment, and then approached his master wagging his tail with pleasure, and licking his hand fondly with a tongue smeared with gore.

The hunter instantly set about reloading; and well for him that he did, for no sooner did the report of his rifle ring through the woods, that the panther, which was until then busily engaged in sucking the heart-blood of the dear, turned and beheld the fate of his companion. He sprang towards the author of his comrade's death, and well then did the gallant staghound serve his master. With bristling back, eyes flashing, teeth displayed, and tail erect, he met the onset, and, as faithful hounds have done before and since, he saved the life of his beloved master. The contest was sharp, short, fierce, and bloody. Fleance was down, and the panther had seized him by the throat — the rifle was not yet loaded — the ramrod broke half-way down— down went the rifle to the earth— out flashed a keen Flemish knife — and deep did that dog's master bury it in the very heart of the fell monster that was tearing and gnawing at his throat.

The panther loosed his hold, but Fleance rose not. The hunter gazed around at the panthers and the buck, — "A sorry purchase with thy life, good Fleance!" cried he; and as he spoke he instinctively put his rifle in order.

Whence arises this singular attachment of dogs to the human race/ Something more, surely, than mere gratitude for services rendered — something more than a mere instinctive preference for the hand that feeds and caresses him, animates the noble creature 1

There is unquestionably an even more than hitman refinement of feeling — a disinterested and pure sentiment of affection, that ever swells within the breast of a brave and faithful hound. Let him but once deem a human being entitled to his devotion, and naught after can ever sever the enduring link. Unlike most friends, he adheres to his master in every circumstance of good and evil report; change, disease, loss, trouble, and disaster may come, and he changes not. The noble staghound, in princely hall, proudly and fondly licks the royal hand that feeds him j and his sentiments are not more pure, nor his attachment more elevated and ennobling, than the emotions of the bobtailed little cur, that, when his master is carted off to Tyburn, to partake of Turpin's fate, runs in between the hangman's feet, and whines piteously for a last look and a kind word from his degraded and guilty, yet still beloved " lord "

A dog is very much like some women; who, if they once take a fancy to a sweetheart, hold on to him, let the world find what fault it may, and determinate! y set down every censure and reproof which may be passed upon his conduct to the censorious and scandal-loving spirit of that age: his good qualities they magnify, — or invent, if none such there be; his awkwardness is graceful; his chattering a happy flow of words; his stupidity reserve; his want of modesty a frank and honest freedom. A dog, most unquestionably, is to his master's "follies ever blind," and bears no grudge for a whipping; he licks the hand that fits the halter to his throat; and let the ladies pardon us, if we recollect that the confiding heart of woman yearns, ever yearns towards her destroyer.

What doth the courtly Marquis of Chaste! tell us in his "Book of Pleasant Pastime," touching "Dogges?"— "A perfect hounde," saith he,-"is one among a thousand — a perle of quadrupeds; be flincheth not; he nestlyth no grutch; he disdayeth to consort with dogges of less degree; he barketh not, save in tyme and place; he loves the chase, both for itself and that hys master loves it; the fyrste in the feelde, and the last in the kennyl; quick as Argus, true as Steele, staunch as oake; clear-voiced, deep-mouthed, long-lymbed, broad-chested, thynne-flanked, sound-fanged, sharp-eyed, and rather tall than long; docile, kind, gentle, playful, unpresuming wyth hys master; taking no note of strangers; fierce and savage, and he suspects a foe."

CHAPTER XI.

"By dimpled brook, and fountain brim, The wood-nymphs, decked with daisies trim. Their merry wakes and pastimes keep— What hath night to do with sleep!"
Milton.

Although the comrades of Blackbeard bad so readily undertaken to aid him in the accomplishment of his revenge, further consideration and more mature Reflection resulted in a manifest and increasing reluctance among many of them for the undertaking. Few were unacquainted with the name of Oxenstiern; and those mysterious traits in his character, which had baffled the investigation of the educated and better informed, were magnified by the vulgar in exact proportion to their want of knowledge. When the buccaneer, therefore, on the night intended for the attack, summoned his forces for the enterprise, an old and weather-beaten pirate stepped forward in the name of his comrades, and bluntly divulged the scruples they entertained in regard to attacking an individual who was known to be cheekby-jowl with Beelzebub himself, and could call up legions of evil spirits to aid him on any emergency. To this his leader listened with a grim smile, that portended no good to the speaker; but being well convinced, that under such a belief their fears would only embarrass the prosecution of his scheme, be forbore attempting to argue the absurdity of their notions, but selecting two of the younger men of the crew, who professed to disbelieve the current reports about Oxenstiern as old women's tales, mud accompanied by his trusty lieutenant, in whose congeniality of disposition he placed a well-grounded reliance,— -all four fully armed, — he set forth.

It was near the appointed hour, when they entered the forest that surrounded the dwelling of their intended victim; the night was dark, and the wind moaned heavily through the tops of the gigantic trees that formed the avenue along which they pursued their route, Blackbeard and his lieutenant interchanging a few words in low whispers; and the two seamen, in spite of their boldness at the outset, gradually became infected with the fears which they had so lately derided, and kept close to their leader.

They had now arrived to within about one hundred yards of the house, when Blackbeard, motioning to his companions to stop and maintain silence, listened anxiously to ascertain if any sound from the building would indicate the watchfulness of the inmates. At the moment, a strain of wild and plaintive music stole upon his ear; at first so indistinct that he was disposed to question its reality; but anon it swelled to a louder and richer tone, floating upon the air as from a harp of some ethereal spirit, and then again subdued to a dream-like and dying melody.

The buccaneer looked at the West Indian, — he curled his lip in scornful derision: but the two seamen treat bid, for such melody came from no mortal hand; and they begged their chief to desist from attacking one who was protected by Satan himself. Blackbeard, although not unmoved by these wild and unearthly strains, cursed their cowardice in the bitterness of his heart, and bade them begone. This command they willingly obeyed; for, although they would have defied any mortal odds, the prospect of encountering the foul fiend completely unnerved them; and Blackbeard now found himself reduced to the assistance of the fearless West Indian. The courage of this last remaining ally was, however, to be put to a severer test. Directly in front of their path, a dark figure rose from the earth, increasing in stature until it had attained gigantic proportions; and the shapeless mass was distinctly seen by a blue flame issuing from the sightless orbits of a skull, which served as a head to the creature itself, and seemed to grin in horrible mockery as it approached.

At this ghastly phantom Blackbeard's resolution for a few moments faltered; and the lieutenant, reckless and undaunted under the most appalling circumstances of battle and shipwreck, suddenly began to manifest, by a lengthened and quivering manner of drawing in his breath, and by an involuntary and excessive trembling at the knee-joints, symptoms of great terror.

When the apparition had approached to within about thirty feet of the spot where the two pirates had taken a stand on its first appearance, it stopped short, and, protruding a lank fleshless arm, seemed to beckon to them in derision, and invite them to come on. At the same moment, from among the trees on every side came peals of fiendish laughter; and indistinct shapes and grinning faces, that bore some resemblance to the countenance of a man, arose out of the darkness, and, mouthing and sneering at Blackbeard, disappeared to give way to other and still more fantastic hobgoblins. «r

The appalling nature of the scene so overpowered the West Indian, that, fearing the legions of spirits would on a sudden seize and carry them off bodily, he began to retreat, facing the specter as he did so; and continued this retrograde motion until he had gained sufficient distance to turn about and increase the rapidity of his flight, leaving his commander, as he feared, in the clutches of the evil one.

Blackbeard, however, was not of a nature to be repelled by these appearances, terrifying as they undoubtedly were; for, considering them as phantoms, be concluded that they could offer no substantial resistance: his indignation too at the flight of his bravest men, and his vindictive and unsatisfied thirst for the blood of Oxenstiern, urged him to proceed at every hazard. He rushed forward, then, and fired on the grisly figure that checked his progress. It made no movement, but seemed to resolve into vapor, losing its bodily form, and becoming more dim, until it entirely disappeared.

The disappearance of the shadowy apparition, and the report of the pistol, were succeeded by loud and contemptuous peals of merriment, not only far off in the depths or the forest, but before, behind, and so close to the ear of the buccaneer, that the darkness seemed crowded by the swarming fiends.

Encouraged, however, by the disappearance of the obstruction which seemed ready to prevent his passage, the pirate speedily arrived at the entrance of the dwelling itself, where all, in spite of the uproar without, seemed enveloped in the unconsciousness of repose. To effect his entrance was the next object of the buccaneer; and he gnashed his teeth with rage, — for both axe and bar had been part of the equipment of the two seamen, and had been carried off by them in their retreat In this dilemma, Blackbeard formed the plan of rushing with the whole weight of his ponderous frame against the door, and bursting it open by main force. He withdrew, therefore, to a short distance, sufficient to give his bodily weight the greatest possible momentum, when the massive door slowly rolled back on its hinges, affording unimpeded entrance to the bold man, who dashed through without the least hesitation. The hall was almost dark, save where a small lamp, that burned in a niche over the first landing on the broad staircase, shed its feeble rays throughout the midnight gloom, revealing only more distinctly the darkness it sufficed not to illumine.

The eyes of Blackbeard sparkled as he beheld Oxenstiern himself on the landing already referred to; and yet he almost doubted his identity. His visage was pale as death, and his eyes brighter than Blackbeard could well gaze upon; on his head he wore a light yellow turban, and a rich cymar of the same color descended to his feet, secured at the waist by a belt of crimson velvet, in the clasp of which flashed a gem of inestimable value. His attitude was that of calm undisturbed meditation — his arms folded across his breast, and his eyes resting on the earth. Blackbeard grasped his knife firmly, and sprang up the steps. Oxenstiern moved not, nor even looked up at his approach, and the pirate was on the point of reaping his revenue; he trod upon the last step, and at the instant he tell, as if (truck by the hand of a giant, while a sudden sharp flash of light passed simultaneously athwart his eyes: Oxenstiern and the lamp disappeared, and he was left in utter darkness. He must have continued for some hours in a state of absolute unconsciousness; for, on looking about him, he discovered, to his no small surprise, that he was lying on the table in the large room of the rendezvous (as his companions were wont to term the old cabin on the Delaware, in which they were used to assemble for all purposes of consultation and reveling), with his crew all around him — some smoking, some talking, and others watching for his resuscitation. He was informed, that about an hour before day the lieutenant headed the whole crew, and marched them to the woods that begirt the haunted dwelling of the chevalier; at which point they came to a dead halt; and the lieutenant, advancing a little farther alone, fortunately discovered the body of his late commander, as he thought, on the verge of the forest; and they had brought it down accordingly, to give it decorous sepulture, when symptoms of life were manifested by occasional twitches; on which account the ceremony bad been deferred until further examination which -resulted in a happy recovery.

We roust now leave these rovers of the deep, and return to our old friend the major, whom we left sallying forth with the gardener, about one in the morning, towards the residence, of his neighbor, determined to put an end to the doubt and anxiety that he then entertained touching the safety of the beleaguered chevalier. "

Much to his surprise, the first object he fell in with was the chevalier himself" bearing on his shout der the huge inanimate frame of Blackbeard'; with which, after politely saluting the major, lie proceeded to the edge of the forest, where he cast it down as it had been a sack of wool, and then requested the major to accompany him to the house.

To the house they proceeded accordingly, where the following conversation took place: —

"I heard but one shot, chevalier; who fired that?"

"That arch villain Blackbeard; but he might as well have fired at the stars, as the object he aimed at"

"How many came to the attack?"

"Four ruffians in all; but two of than were put to flight by a serenade that I had prepared for them; and another, a bold West Indian by-the~by, mistook a very harmless specter that stood in his path for some dread spirit of the infernal regions, and fled incontinently."

"Then Blackbeard alone attacked you; did you cut him down?"

"Not exactly; I merely stunned him, so that in a few hours he will recover, and this by means of an invisible fluid that I create at pleasure/'

"Nay, my dear chevalier, you but make merry with me."

"To prove that I do by no means," responded Oxenstiern, "I will give you earnest thereof:" upon which he gave the major a small Jar coated with some bright metallic leaf, and desired him to place his hand upon the ball at the summit "As you touch it," continued he, "I will cause the fluid to pass" through your body, and yourself shall deckle whether I jest or not"

The major did as he was requested to do, and received a sharp and sudden blow: he started, and looked behind him, but no one was near; and Oxenstiern stood before him with an arch smile of triumph. "Art thou convinced?" added he; "or wilt thou abide a more positive demonstration."

"God forbid!" hastily replied the major; "my elbows even yet tingle with the blow: whence it came I know not, for I saw none near enough to strike."

"And no one did strike, my dear sir; nor did any human being smite the furious buccaneer, who would fain have slain me as I stood here unarmed; but the same subtle fluid that but now touched you so lightly fell upon him like a thunderbolt, and left him helpless, senseless, and motionless as death itself."

A thundering knock at the door was now heard, and it was opened for the admission of Fritz; who first looked around him with an inquiring glance, and then proceeded to inform the major that Miss Barbara had waited so long for his return that she became very uneasy, and Anally dispatched him to ascertain the cause of delay. Upon this Major Scheveling concluded to return home immediately, as well to relieve the anxiety of his niece as to take some repose; to the deprivation of which during the foregoing part of the night, he became by this time so sensible, as to remind him that youth no longer - enabled him to dispense with the necessary luxury of a comfortable couch, nor curiosity arrest the yearning for his accustomed sleep.

Barbara, whose feelings had been wrought up to a very uncomfortable and restless degree of excitement by the events of the evening, and the anticipation of some fearful catastrophe, soon after the departure of the major towards the dwelling of Oxenstiern imagined that she really entertained a deep presentiment of sudden danger, threatening the life of her uncle; and, without delay ordered Fritz to fly to the assistance of the old gentleman. To this Fritz objected, urging the impropriety of leaving his young mistress unprotected on such a critical occasion, whereupon the gentle Barbara, becoming more decidedly fixed in her intentions the more opposition she met with, reiterated her positive commands, and Fritz, having exhausted his stock of argument, at length obeyed.

The situation of Barbara was now far from enviable, — solitude, night, uncertainty, fatigue, and painful vigilance conspired against an imagination always ardent and susceptible; danger and distress appeared like dark shadows obscuring the picture that fearful fancy drew. The darkness without seemed to yield indistinct sounds of ominous import, prognosticating evil near at hand. With eager and intense watchfulness she listened, at times imagining that voices were on the breeze, and again that she perceived the tread of coming footsteps. Then all would become silent, save the south wind coming up with a melancholy pleasing murmur through the forest; and when that died away, succeeded a long, unbroken, and dreary stillness, so perfect that Barbara perceived her own repressed breathing.

Presently she heard, close under the window, where grew a natural arbor of grape-vine in unchecked luxuriance, a low but not unmusical voice humming the air of a song, which she recognized to be the very same as that played on the flute by the young hunter during the fishing excursion to Fort St. David, and which bore a peculiar impress of wildness and originality not easily to be mistaken for any other. This preparatory prelude finished, the invisible serenader sang, in a voice not remarkably loud, but singularly sweet *and clear, the following roundelay:* —

> *Can woman's heart be cold to love,*
> *Of a warm and silent night,*
> *When the heavens are glittering above*
> *With pare and starry light!*
> *When the night-wind slowly passes by,*
> *And seems itself to breathe a sigh?*

BLACKBEARD

It was not in the light of day,
Nor beneath a sultry sun —
But night o'ershadowed Helle's bay,
When Hero's heart was won;
And the star that guided love aright
Was the lamp that burned -on Sestos' height.

In Seville, where the orange-trees
Fling perfume on the air,
'Tis not until the vesper-breeze
Has breathed its freshness there,
And the sea has quenched the sun's last ray,
That maidens hear love's roundelay.

Thy gentle heart has naught to fear,
The stars are out to guide thee, —
The night so still, so calm, so clear, —
And I will be beside thee!
Then bie, my love, with me away,
Before the dawning of the day.

Barbara had never before been serenaded; but she had heard Oxenstiern tell how the Spanish cavalier was wont to chant his passionate ditty, with his guitar, by night beneath the balcony of his dark-eyed mistress; and she listened, probably, with less surprise than pleasure to the voice that so unexpectedly broke in upon the fearful silence around her. The song at once dispelled the feeling of loneliness that weighed so heavily upon her; and the agreeable sensations excited by the varied modulations of the strain produced a more cheerful train of anticipations. Hardly, too, had five minutes elapsed since she listened to the concluding verse of the song, when she heard, to her unspeakable satisfaction, the boisterous laugh of her hearty old uncle ringing loudly in the forest; the which, as affording unequivocal evidence of his being unharmed and near at hand, wag well calculated to remove all her anxiety, as well on his account as on that of the chevalier, for whose well-being the good spirits of his friend the major seemed sufficiently to vouch.

As the old gentleman entered the apartment in which his niece awaited his approach, he was immediately greeted with a shower of kisses from the happy girl, who hung upon his neck with all the fond ardor of a daughter; and when she looked up and beheld Oxenstiern gazing on the scene with a pleased yet half-envious eve, her innocent countenance became instantly suffused with blushes; which might either be interpreted as arising from surprise at the unexpected appearance of the chevalier, or, it may be, treacherously betraying to the maiden herself more tender emotions, of the existence of which she had been hitherto unconscious.

What impression this involuntary agitation on the part of Barbara produced in the mind of Oxenstiern was by no means clearly manifested: whether the sudden change in his demeanor was to be traced to such a cause, or arose from other sources, still it is certain that the kind and familiar manner in which he usually addressed her was now replaced by a respectful, yet somewhat cold and distant, demeanor. Instead of the pleased and encouraging attention which he usually paid to every word that fell from the lips of his young friend, he seemed almost disposed to neglect, if not absolutely to shun, her conversation. The replies he gave to the few questions which the curiosity of Barbara induced her to put touching the adventures of 'the night, were couched in few words, — evidencing no inclination on the part of the speaker to enter into any more copious detail; after which, directing his conversation exclusively to the major, Oxenstiern appeared to be unconscious of the presence of his niece.

All this to Barbara was of a nature the most perplexing that can well be imagined; and her uncle aroused her from the deep reverie into which she had insensibly fallen, by a suggestion that, as the night was now far spent, she would do well to seek some repose; adding, that his friend the chevalier and himself would fain be left to themselves, in order to discuss matters of some importance.

With this the veteran proceeded to uncork a dusty bottle; and as he was recommending to Oxenstiern the lighting of a pipe, Barbara withdrew, — but only to meditate more deeply on the singular conduct of the chevalier; to account for which her fancy invented a thousand causes, and in regard to which her conclusions were as uncertain and unsatisfactory as her first impressions.

Morning came; and Barbara, after superintending the duties of the household, seated herself at the breakfast-table, persuaded that something would now occur to elucidate the mystery that so strongly haunted her imagination. First appeared her uncle, yawning involuntarily, rubbing his eyes, and shaking his head, which plainly enough indicated the nature of his inward cogitations — the pernicious tendency, to wit, of all nocturnal vigils; against which he also mentally took a solemn oath, come they under whatsoever form or pretense. Under the influence of such thoughts, the major sat. down to his morning peal with more than ordinary gravity, and less than his usual appetite. The chevalier too sat down; but his conduct only served the more to perplex and embarrass Barbara: not a trace of the coldness and abstraction which had so suddenly on the previous night taken possession of the chevalier now remained, and Barbara was tempted to consider the whole as a dream; for his speech to her was accompanied by the bland smile that sat so well upon his noble features, and the tone of his voice was, as usual, kind and affectionate. He appeared not to notice the agitation which Barbara manifested when he entered; and in a short time matters appeared to be on their usual footing, — nothing indicating that anything unusual had occurred, save an occasional heightening of color in the cheeks of the maiden, as if the voice of Oxenstiern had suddenly acquired the power of calling up new and unusual emotions.

"By my faith," said Oxenstiern, locking across the table through a" window which commanded a view of the avenue leading to Erigson House, " yonder comes a gallant cortege, — plumes and caps, dames and squires, in goodly number; nay, if my eyes deceive me not, the fair Markham herself in the midst, a very Calypso among her nymphs7 and the gay Captain Solgard, obedient to her enchantments, riding by her side, the happiest of mortal men. Prithee, fair hostess, purvey somewhat substantial for these errant knights and damsels: a cold ham, an it were to be had, with an Amstel pie or so, were to the purpose; for, what with a brisk canter and the fresh morning air, toast and coffee would never stay them."

Barbara hastily ran to the window; and when she ascertained, by the nearer approach of the party, that the chevalier was right in his conjectures as to some of the individuals who belonged to it; she left the room, with some little of that momentary embarrassment which housekeepers generally experience, when their *ménage* is invaded at an unseasonble hour.

As to the major, he leisurely finished his cup of coffee, commended, ad interim, the suggestions of the chevalier touching the preparation "of some solid nutriment for (he approaching party, and then, with all the coolness and self-possession of an old soldier, proceeded to reconnoiter the cavalcade.

Considerably in advance rode William Hasell, a son of the mayor, a youth of some seventeen years of age, managing with much address the powerful and fiery steed which he bestrode, and which ill-brooked the occasional touch of the spurs, with which superfluities the boy had armed his heels, having, in his fourth attempt to run away with his rider, got thus far beyond the party.

Madam Markham bore herself proudly and gracefully, about the center of the party, on a spirited little jennet, — her cheeks flushed with exercise, her dark eyes sparkling with enjoyment,— in a dark green riding-dress, that displayed to advantage the voluptuous -contour of her person, and now and then endeavoring to replace the rich profusion of curls which the wanton wind had disarranged in charming disorder.

On one side of the fair Christine, Captain Solgard displayed his elegant and graceful horsemanship; and she ever and anon inclined her head to the opposite side, as listening to the remarks of Doctor Eastlake, who was mounted on a steed the plump sides of which the more set forth his own professional lankness.

Among the ladies in the rear, the restless and unceasing movements of Bob Asterley, as he was generally denominated, were manifestly prominent; his black pony, whose cropped mane and tail gave evidence of the nicety which in other things distinguished his master, might be seen at one time on the right, then on the left, and anon curvetting in the midst of the other horses, much to the discomposure of his more sedate brethren; whereupon Bob, being duly reprimanded by some one or another of the damsels for this indiscreet management of his steed, would show a set of handsome white teeth> push his hat back from his forehead, so that his laughing blue eyes might gaze full upon the lady who addressed him, make some jocund observation, then profess much contrition for his offence, and forthwith watch for another convenient opportunity of renewing his criminal proceedings "

Robert Asterley was in stature somewhat deficient, — measuring exactly five feet five inches in boots; well made, and naturally compact of limb, but by habits of luxurious indolence his person had attained that degree of pinguitude which consorts well with florid health, but any considerable addition to which were matter of no slight inconvenience to the possessor. Being the sole remaining representative of a wealthy family, his circumstances at no time peremptorily argued the necessity of any laborious occupation; and in devoting a few years to the study of medicine, he but obeyed that national feeling which induces every man, however independent, to acquire the capacity of rendering himself useful to his fellow-creatures. We have alluded to his habits as being luxurious y in fact they may be so considered, for he rarely forsook his couch before nine of the morning, sat down to the daintiest table in Philadelphia, smoked much, and of the primest Havana cigars, and every day had the trouble of choosing between pale sherry, pert, and madeira. His countenance presented a singular composition of features; he had the tall forehead of a popular preacher, the small inquisitive nose of a bon vivant, and the stern shaggy eyebrows of a justice of the peace " In addition to these circumstances, his hands and feet were remarkably small; his light chestnut hair, straight like that of an Indian, was sedulously brushed in such wise as to conceal an incipient baldness on the crown; his expletives eschewed all manner of profanity; his greatest delight was to romp with the ladies, — who, in return, handled him on such occasions with sufficient roughness to manifest clearly how much they disliked such excessively rude conduct, with a declaration, however, which operated as a salvo to the wounded feelings of the little man, that he was a merry little man in spite of his impudence, and that his saucy laugh displayed a splendid set of teeth.

Doctor Eastlake, whom we have already spoken of as riding near Madam Markham, was of good repute as a physician, in appearance saturnine and sallow, in disposition reserved and eccentric; supposed by strangers, who formed an estimate of his character from the nature of his caustic remarks, to be sour, miserly, misanthropic, and wretchedly miserable; while those who knew him better were fully aware of his practical good-nature, liberality, secret beneficence, quiet philanthropy, and philosophic contentment. To a general acquaintance with the fundamental principles of language, he was constantly adding a specific knowledge of someone or other of its conventional divisions. In this manner he had added to a familiar acquaintance with the classic tongues of Italy and Greece, the copious Teutonic, the flowery Tuscan, the godlike language of Iberia, the gay dialect of France, and the modern Romaic, besides being versed in Hebrew, Chaldee, and Syriac; having also some skill in the Russian tongue, and being used diurnally to hold converse with an ancient Netherlander fish " woman in the grave and weighty Low Dutch.

The party now drew up on the verdant lawn in front of the mansion, and Major Scheveling, his niece the beautiful and blushing Barbara, and the Chevalier Oxenstiern, issued from the hall-door to assist them to alight, and to bid them welcome. As soon as Madam Markham had reached the earth with the ready aid of the devoted Captain Solgard, she ran up to and embraced Barbara with the most sisterly affection, and saluting the major with a degree of deferential respect that absolutely fascinated the old gentleman, she recognized the chevalier with a pleased yet somewhat quiet smile.

Bob Asterley the while was creating no little confusion,— offering to assist one of the fair dames to alight from her saddle, and, at the moment when she was prepared to leap into his arms, rushing off at a tangent to offer like assistance to another lady under similar circumstances; vowing himself to be the most unlucky man alive, in not being able to devote himself to both at once; and flying from one to the other in whimsical incertitude, alternately, until his friend Doctor Eastlake relieved him, and no less the ladies themselves, from this dilemma, by assisting one of the two himself, and leaving to Bob the sole care of the other; observing, at the same time, to the damsel whom he had thus put under obligation to his politeness, as if to relieve her from any such burden, that he had known many a pleasant ride marred by the presence of ladies.

The prudent suggestion of the chevalier in regard to making due purveyance for the wants of the morning visitors had not been neglected by Barbara; and, much to the contentment, doubtless, of the travelers, their eyes were saluted, on entering the breakfast-room, by a fair table, spread with an ample snow-white table-cloth, and duly garnished with sundry solid, substantial, and savory dishes.

CHAPTER XII.

**"The bashful blood her sunny cheeks did spread,
That her become as polished ivory,
Which cunning craftsman's band hath overlaid
With fair vermilion, or pure lastery."**
Spencer.

All the fashion and beauty of Guanives had been invited to a ball to be given by the Senor Garcilaso de Vega at his country house, about three miles from town. This port, which had long been familiarly known to privateersmen and contrabandists as the most secure and unmolested haven on the northwestern part of the coast of Hispaniola, was famous for the beauty of the senoritas, and the lawless character of the male population, The Sen or Garcilaso was unquestionably the most influential as well as the wealthiest caballero in Guanives; and it in no degree detracted from the estimation in which he was held in this community, that, in his youth, he had sailed under the black flag of the notorious Marino.

It was in celebration of the birthday of his daughter and only child, that the old hidalgo had made preparation for a most sumptuous fete. Everything that wealth could procure, and the imagination could devise, of splendor and magnificence, was lavished in the adornment of the palace, which he termed his country-house, the portrait of his ancestor the great Lopez de Vega was carefully transported from town, and assumed a conspicuous station at the upper end of the ball mom, seeming to overlook and smile upon the fairy scene. There was a singular mystery always attached to this picture, concerning which tradition ran as follows: — When the great Lopez was yet a youth, his charity was invoked by an aged mendicant, whose hoary locks and venerable appearance most strongly excited his compassion. He learned from the lips of the old man himself that he was in the most absolute indigence, without a friend to cherish or a home to shelter him. Moved by his story, Lopez led him to his own lodging, and, impelled by an irresistible emotion of kindness towards the aged sufferer, nourished and provided for him in all affection until his death, which shortly after took place. Three days previous to his dissolution, the old man requested his benefactor to procure for him the requisite materials for painting a portrait; his last hour, he observed, was nigh, and he wished to leave behind him some slight memorial of his gratitude. His request was complied with, although Lopez was disposed to consider it but the fantasy of an unsound and distempered imagination. Lopez sat for his portrait: for two days the aged painter suffered no food to pass his lips, nor closed his eyelids in slumber; steadily he sat before the canvass, with silent untiring perseverance; and on the evening of the third day a perfect likeness of the immortal De Vega was accomplished. The glorious rays of the setting sun fell full upon the picture, and Lopez almost started as the semblance of himself seemed to return his gaze with a benignant smile.

"Thou mayst know," exclaimed the painter, "from the radiant smile that illumes yonder countenance, that thy career is yet unclouded and happy: the time may come when it shall be otherwise; and then, when thou art in peril, shall the dark and frowning aspect of that very picture warn thee of impending danger Let thy descendants also preserve the gift; to them it shall ever be as a beacon in the path of life — forever shall its aspect change as danger threatens, or death is at hand." Having spoken thus, be stretched himself upon his couch, closed his eyes, and died. And still, as gay and happy days were the portion of De Vega, did the dark eyes of the portrait gaze with a calm, unwavering luster: but the day on which Lopez died it bore a sad and melancholy aspect; and ever as a De Vega died would this mysteriously prophetic countenance forebode the sinister event. Such was the portrait that the lineal descendant of the great Lopez now transferred to the ball-room already spoken of, there, as it were, to overlook and protect the last and most beautiful of his noble race.

Evening came on, and the sun had hardly set ere the magnificent mansion was lighted by brilliant chandeliers and innumerable lamps in rich profusion, and such variety of hue and form as might well have been deemed the costly garniture of some fairy palace.

Fair dames and gallant cavaliers moved through, the rich saloons, flooded in mellow radiance and breathing fragrance from a thousand flowers; strains of exquisite music at times stole upon the ear, subdued and at a distance, soothing the melancholy meditation of the musing lover, and haply melting the tender heart of some dark-eyed beauty, as the mellow strains mingled with the pleading voice of passion. Mark, too, with what a queenly step advances the peerless Estifania! In years, in the innocence and fearfulness of a young heart, still a girl; in stature, form, and grace, a most lovely and perfect woman. Her attire was rich with most costly gems; but as her snowy bosom rose beneath t her kerchief, few would mark the rare necklace of pearls, and the bandeau of precious diamonds that circled her divine brow sparkled with less fascinating effect than the brilliant rays that beamed from her large dark eyes. Conscious of beauty, she received with an indifference almost scornful the homage paid to her matchless charms. Yet there was one before whose gaze her cheek had burned with conscious blushes, at whose approach her heart would beat quickly and with pleased emotion, and in the warm pressure of whose hand her own would tremble, but not with fear. And this one her father hated; not that he was a nameless man, of obscure or ignoble race, for Alonzo de Melendez took his name from an ancient and noble house, — a man of approved valor and still in the prime of life, handsome, soldier-like, and haughty; and in this last particular had he accidentally offended the proud Garcilaso; who, letting slip no opportunity of satisfying his vindictive spirit, had the inexpressible gratification of refusing him his daughter. But as daughters are generally disposed to consider right what fathers would seriously persuade them to be wrong, the more the Senor Garcilaso disparaged the haughty De Melendez, the more earnestly did the divine Estifania ponder on the excellent qualities of the cavalier; so that as her father grew more bitter in his hostility, so much the more deeply did the daughter fall in love.

The ball went on, and frolicsome maskers passed to and fro. There might you see a cavalier biting his lips at the caustic jest that issued from a dull looking wizard; and there again a whisper from the same unknown mummer calls forth a deep blush on the brow of that fair damsel. And to lively strains of music glide graceful and active figures in the mazes of the lively fandango and the light bolero, with the merry snapping of the castanets; and the portrait of the poet smiles on the throng beneath.

Estifania was wearied; the rich and glorious festival, the bright throng of guests, the devotion of many a gallant heart, the vows of adoration, and the envy of many a dark-eyed beauty, gave her but little pleasure: her heart bounded when at times some tall graceful figure approached *en masque* to salute her; but hitherto she had met with naught but disappointment: she had listened, but in vain, for the deep clear voice of De Melendez. Unconsciously she wandered from the dancers, until she issued into the open air upon a terrace, from which she commanded a view of an extensive garden, where thousands of lamps twinkled like fire-flies in each cool grotto and shaded bower; a figure slowly approached her, removed its mask, and revealed the noble countenance of her lover.

On the same day in which the whole town of Guanives had been put into commotion in expectation of the fete to be given that evening by the Senor Garcilaso, an armed vessel had been descried hovering off the harbor during the day. By the aid of good glasses, it was discovered that she carried at least twenty-two guns; and although no flag or signal of any kind was visible, some of the oldest and most experienced seamen pronounced her to be an English privateer. Towards dusk she stood out to sea, leaving many who had watched her during the day in a state of complete uncertainty in regard to her maneuvers. Among those who had gazed upon the strange sail with no little interest was Alonzo de Melendez, who was well aware that cruisers of suspicious character infested the neighboring waters; and whose tender interest for the beautiful Estifania led him to meditate seriously upon the danger to be encountered by the fair object of his passion, in case of an unexpected piratical descent upon this almost unprotected part of the island.

In such meditations he pursued his lonely walk along the beach, until he had turned a point, which entirely hid the town and harbor from his view. Here seating himself upon the fragment of a rock, he gazed out upon the ocean, that insensibly through the dim twilight blended itself with the clouded horizon. Could his eyes deceive him?

Was it a trick of his imagination, or did he actually behold a tail making for the secluded and unfrequented nook in which he was seated?

He gated earnestly; nearer approached the dim ambiance that at first, as it were, floated among the clouds, now clearly to be distinguished as a ship under easy sail. Alonzo now secreted himself carefully among the rocks, and continued to watch the progress of the vessel. A shadowy apprehension of evil arose before him, as he recollected the unexplained movements of the privateer off the harbor during the day; and the probability suggested itself, that the vessel now before him, and the privateer, were one and the same.

About an eighth of a mile from shore she came to anchor in smooth water, and a boat well filled put off for the beach. As the boat touched, two men leaped ashore, both heavily armed, and differing exceedingly in appearance; the one tall, light, and athletic, and the other, to whom the one already mentioned paid the deference due to a superior, although in a rough and unpolished manner, was none other, as might be conjectured, from his unusually short stature and Herculean breadth of frame, together with the eyes, that glowed like live coals from their deep sockets, than the notorious Captain Teach, more generally known under the name of Blackboard.

"And his richest jewels — "growled the pirate.

"Are to be worn to-night," answered the lieutenant," by his daughter, a beautiful little senorita, by-the-by, as Miguel tells me; and 1 think if once snug aboard, she would hardly object to receiving the attentions of the. lieutenant of the — "

"Nonsense," again muttered he of the beard; "the girl may come aboard an you will; but no private love-making among free-traders; share and share alike. And that dog Miguel I he comes not yet, hell seize him!"

Miguel, however, did come; and just as Blackbeard was uttering this friendly wish, a dark-browed, mean-looking Spaniard issued from a passage in the cliffs, and stood before them.

Alonzo no sooner beheld them in secret conference, than, quietly withdrawing himself from his hiding-place, he retraced his steps to Guanines, in order to take such measures as would frustrate their design, which appeared to him to be sufficiently obvious; the plunder, to wit, of the rich Senor Garcilaso, and, if convenient, the abduction of the lovely Estifania, With all the alacrity and energy of a lover, therefore, De Melendez armed a body of his friends; and with a force as strong as he could possibly muster, repaired instantaneously to the gardens of the Senor de Vega, where his men-at-arms were placed so ambush, it was after having taken these precautionary measures that he sought his mistress— a quest which resulted, as we have already seen, in an interview upon the terrace.

As Estifania again entered the ball-room, from the conference with her lover, the scene before her strongly arrested her attention — the gay and happy guests whom she had left in the enjoyment of the voluptuous movements of the dance, excited by the liveliest strains of exhilarating music, were now congregated into groups, whispering one to another, and gazing, as by common impulse, on the portrait of her ancestor. There stood her father also, regarding the picture with a sad and anxious eye, as he wist not what manner of evil were at hand.

Estifania looked up at the portrait, and suddenly shrank back in terror; ever from her youth had she beheld that mysterious countenance bent upon her with a benevolent smile of kind and almost paternal feeling; but now a stern and vindictive compression of the lips, a fearful frown, and a piercing and fiery glance, directed as to some distant object, strangely altered the mysterious image.

Gradually the eyes of the picture dilated with a fearful expression of wrath, and now rested upon the door opposite, as if the object of its indignation were at the entrance of the saloon.

With a yell of ferocious triumph, Blackbeard and his ruffians sprang into the apartment. Quick as light Don Garcilaso drew his dirk, and planted himself before his daughter, when the flashing cutlass of the merciless lieutenant in full sweep cut down Estifania's bold defender. Amid the confusion the lieutenant hesitated not a moment, but seizing the struggling beauty in his arms, was bearing her off, when his progress was impeded by a most unlooked for obstacle, namely, the gallant De Melendez, who, raging like a lioness protecting her young, now, with his party, rushed fiercely to the rescue. Tearing with one hand his mistress from the hot grasp of the sea-robber, with the other tie planted a pistol to his head, and killed him on the spot Desperately brave and determined as were the pirates, yet, fiercely assailed by more than double their number, and aware that every delay was adding strength to the ranks of their opponents, they gave way reluctantly, and retreated in tolerably good order to their vessel; on gaining which, they made no delay, but, weighing anchor, immediately stood out to sea, with the loss of three men killed, and eleven others, among whom was Blackbeard himself, seriously wounded.

The Senor Garcilaso recovered slowly; and as if anxious to repair the injustice done to the gallant De Melendez, he not only gave his consent to his marriage with his child, but urged the immediate celebration of the nuptials, with such eagerness that the blushing girl put herself under the protection of her lover, and obtained from his delicacy that delay which her father could not well appreciate, and which, sooth to say, the ardent lover but ill-brooked himself, although his young mistress rewarded his forbearance by her sweetest smiles, and but faintly struggled to disengage herself, as he almost devoured her pouting lips in passionate lingering kisses.

CHAPTER XIII.

Are ye fair as opening roses? Tender maidens, on, beware!
When its bloom the heart discloses,
Lore will find a dwelling there.
Prudence then in vain opposes —
Youth is never wise as love!
PRINCE HOULB, ESQUIRE.

During the repast which had been hastily provided for the equestrian party who had honored Major Scheveling with a morning visit, Bob Asterley had been devotedly attentive to his fair hostess, endeavoring to assist her in all her arrangements, and laughing most heartily at the confusion which his well-meant efforts more than once created. Under plea of offering assistance, he would every now and then seize her by the elbow, much to her embarrassment: then the natural benevolence of his heart would invariably break forth, as she ascended or descended the broad staircase; on which occasions his arm was kindly passed round her waist, to guard against the possibility of her receiving any injury from a fall: in the heat of conversation, too, his hand would unconsciously grasp that of Barbara, — who was laughing heartily at these and other extravagances, when her eye accidentally met that of the Lie man. What lurked in those merry blue orbs is uncertain, but Barbara withdrew her hand silently and slowly; and as she turned to converse with Madam Markham, Bob might have observed her short upper lip curled with something else than merriment, but he observed it not; for he never observed, if he could by any means avoid such observation, anything that would be likely to displease him.

As Doctor Eastlake was riding back to town, he observed the little nag of Bob Asterley close beside him; and giving a preparatory hem, he addressed the rider, —

"You noticed, I suppose, that strong guttural accent of Major Scheveling?"

"Yes; I took particular notice of that," answered the little man, after Eastlake had twice repeated his observation, speaking more loudly and distinctly at each repetition. "But, by-the-by, what a heavenly creature is that niece of his! such a lovely mouth."

"Yes, very lovely! and the broad sound," continued Eastlake, "of the vowels, which must have struck you during the conversation."

"Very true! But do you think her shape as fine as that exquisite figure of Madam Markham? How delightful, Eastlake, to marry such a woman."

"You frequently speculate," observed Eastlake, "upon the soul-seducing, transporting prospects offered by the anticipations of married life, but I would wager my polyglot Bible against that nag of yours (heavy odds, by-the-by, in your favor) that you never call any woman wife. In the first place, your ordinary manner of addressing womankind is so much like courting them that it would cost you more time and trouble than you would be disposed to take to convince any of them that you actually intended aught serious. In the second place, you smoke, at a rough calculation — "

"Why!" ejaculated the little man, in a whisper, "what goddess of the woods have we here? Approach softly, and alarm her not, lest she take umbrage."

And, chuckling at his pun, Asterley held in his horse to a walk, while his friend followed his example; and they slowly approached the cottage of the old woman whom, after having been apparently put to death by the ferocious Blackbeard, Oxenstiern had, so much to the surprise and delight of her granddaughter, resuscitated The pretty Susan bad attracted the attention of the all-admiring Asterley, as she lightly tripped along to the well for water; and hearing the tramp of horses, she turned her sunny countenance to the strangers, and smiled so sweetly in answer to Asterley's "Good morning, miss!" that the heart of the comatose little man bounded with rapture.

"Fine pure water, Eastlake!" said he; alight and take some."

"Thank you," replied the doctor, "I have no thirst."

The maiden, blushing and smiling to be addressed, and yet so politely, by a strange gentleman, beard little Bob, in honeyed accents, request a little water to assuage his exceeding thirst; and setting down her pitcher, which was large and heavy, ran into the hut and procured a gourd, from which Asterley, who had now alighted, took a long, although it did not appear to be a very copious, draught.

"You must be very lonely, all by yourself here," said the little man, inquiringly.

"Oh no, sir! there's grandmother too; and she has been troubled with the rheumatics ever since last Sunday week," replied Susan, casting her eyes modestly to the ground.

"Descend, most -erudite Asclepiad," quoth Asterley, "and prescribe somewhat."

Eastlake alighted, and entered the cottage, where he found the aged dame crouched in a low-seated, rush-bottomed, high-backed chair, knitting sedulously, and humming the while snatches from ancient ditties. With the credulous garrulity of fourscore years and upward, she gave the doctor a circumstantial account of her present ailment: from that she insensibly glided into remarks touching other diseases incidental to old age, — speaking of such as she had labored under in a martyr-like tone, 'which insinuated no small commendation of her own fortitude, and alluding to others which she had never experienced, as if seeking from such review ground for reasonable self-congratulation. To all this the doctor listened with due gravity; while, on the outside, Bob Asterley, in a bland insinuating voice, was questioning Susan of her age and name — whether she had been much to school — how many brothers and sisters she had — whether or no she could knit —was she fond of flower " — he had in his garden in town beautiful tulips and carnations, almost as brilliant as her own complexion, which he would be proud to show to her — how could her grandmother permit her to go without shoes or stockings, and her feet so delicate and small — was she partial to straw bonnets — perhaps she could be induced to wear one of his selection — he would certainly bring one from town, together with a bottle of opodeldoc for her grandmother — in this warm weather the evenings were by far the most suitable times for walking — perhaps she rambled now and then in the woods by moonlight — he often did — he should not be much surprised if by chance he should meet her that very evening in the path that led through the forest to Erigson House — it would be so amusing, wouldn't it — who curled her hair so beautifully — what a pity this neck (suiting the action to the word) should get so sunburnt I

Susan was innocence and nature itself; and, delighted as she was with the flattering attention of the little gentleman, her countenance failed not to betray the pleasing nature of her emotions; smiles and blushes, in delicious rivalry, took possession of her lovely countenance, on which Asterley gazed with an ardent and voluptuous glance, that, innocent and unsuspicious as she was, filled her with peculiarly thrilling and indescribable sensations.

Doctor Eastlake gave the old woman some directions, and issued from the cottage; when, judging apparently from the animated manner of Asterley and the downcast confusion of the maiden, that the little man had been entertaining her with something more interesting than a homily, he gravely shook his head in disapprobation of such immoral conduct, and, mounting his steed, admonished Asterley that time was precious, and it were well to be moving.

Bob delayed no longer than to whisper something in the ear of Susan, that tinged her cheek with scarlet, and hastily stealing a kiss, which her confusion rendered her incapable of denying, bestrode his little nag, and followed the doctor at a full gallop.

That very evening, as the moon rose over the woods, Bob Asterley begged a set of boon companions to excuse him for a brief space, as some very important business, which brooked no delay, claimed his instant attention; and after offering and receiving many regrets on his forced departure from such agreeable society, he set forth at a brisk pace up Front

Street as far as High, then turning up to Second, he faced to the south, and by dint of steady walking, after crossing Dock-water, passed a little to the north-west of Society Hill, and found himself on the verge of those woods already mentioned as being interposed between Society Hill and Erigson House.

He entered the forest with a slower and more cautious step; approached the cottage, now so interesting as the home of the charming Susan; and bending his head in every direction, seemed as if desirous to leave no nook unexplored in search of some expected object. "Heigh ho!" uttered he at last, in a whisper, "if Eastlake but knew of this, he would moralize until he brought tears into his own eyes."

After this ejaculation, Bob leaned against the trunk of an immense sycamore, and surveyed the moon in mute admiration, as lovers ore wont to do, his eyes fixed on the orb of purest light, and his vagrant fancy reveling in imaginative dreams and ethereal visions, — a voice breaks in upon the silence around — a female voice, too, of most sweet and silvery tone— 'tis the tender and impassioned exclamation of a young girl, speaking low, and addressing one who has obtained her first and only disinterested love.

"Rather singular," again soliloquized Asterley, in a whisper, "that two sets of lovers should, on the same night, choose the same spot for a love-scene " By-the-by, as my little Susan is so very tardy in making her appearance, I may as well take a survey of these turtle-doves."

With this observation Bob cautiously crept around a low thicket that in some degree intercepted the voice he had heard, and by quietly drawing aside a few small tranches, brought into view two individuals seated upon a bank, thickly covered with moss, in a position that indicated a great deal of mutual good feeling. With his back against a tree, the cavalier supported in his arms a lovely young creature, on whose existence his own seemed to depend, — so perfect was the contentment that, to the utter abandonment of all other ideas, took possession of him, as his eyes met those melting lustrous orbs that gazed on his countenance with such tender and undisguised affection; his deep manly voice contrasted well with the light girlish tones that issued from her beautiful mouth, which, sooth to say, he sought ever and anon, despite her well-feigned struggles, as if he would fain devour her rosy lips.

Judge of the almost incredulous horror of Asterley, as the fair girl, turning up her bright countenance until it was accidentally exposed to the full radiance of the moon, revealed the features of the innocent " naive Susan.

Bob succeeded in restraining his wrathful emotions, but not without an effort, — it having cost him a lock or so of hair, which, in the agony of the moment, his hands had grasped with unconscious energy, and abstracted from his pericranium.

"Alas!" said Bob to himself, "what faith can be put in woman! By all that's lovely," continued he, "I forswear the sex! A man may be trusted, but as to a woman — Zounds! Eastlake was right, when he advised me, as 1 valued my peace of mind, and looked with pleasure to an approving conscience, to avoid womankind."

The lovers were about to separate: kisses, that seemed to Bob almost endless, and made his brain whirl with jealous envy, were interchanged. As Bob gazed, he could not help thinking that the figure of Susan's lover was not unfamiliar to his eye; and with his curiosity thus excited, he watched their lingering and reluctant farewell witty a grim sardonic smile. Susan bounded away with light and active grace, as fearing to tempt her resolution by any slower departure. Her lover watched her elegant form, sliding by the clear moonlight, until it disappeared under the roof of the cottage; then turning round so that his face was clearly visible to Asterley in the pale moonlight, he consulted, with much sang froid, his watch as to the hour of the night; gave a low peculiar laugh, that rang upon the ear of Asterley with a demoniac and hollow sound; and taking out of his pocket a small morocco wallet containing cigars, he lighted one by the aid of a flint and steel which were produced from the same receptacle, and resuming his seat on the moss-covered bank, watched, with epicurean contentment, the rings and waves of ash-colored vapor curling from his lips and obscuring the bright face of the moon.

"Good God!" cried Asterley, rushing in with much vehemence, "'tis Eastlake I Yes, sir," added he, clenching his fist and setting his teeth together firmly, "I have witnessed your perfidious conduct! and, by all — "

"Take a cigar!" interposed the doctor, looking up with the utmost nonchalance at the intruder; "I have always esteemed it a sovereign sedative: then, if you will be kind enough to make me acquainted with the circumstances that have given rise to this unusual effervescence, I shall be exceedingly happy if my experience or skill should enable me to suggest any thing that may tend to its alleviation. Try this — the dark browns are generally the best."

The undisturbed coolness of the doctor produced almost instantaneously a sympathetic effect on his little friend. During the utterance of the verbose formula with which Eastlake had interrupted his angry address, his feelings quickly subsided from that elevation to which they had been so lately excited by the pungent sense of injury, and soothed involuntarily by the hope of something like a reasonable, if not a satisfactory, explanation. Bob mechanically obeyed the impulse of habit, by accepting, as the doctor concluded his unctuous response, the proffered cigar.

For a while both puffed away in silence: Eastlake well aware that the delay of every moment served in a degree to re-establish that tacitly understood ascendency which, almost imperceptibly, he yet actually exercised over his volatile companion; and unwilling, by any unseasonable remarks, to disturb that feeling of bonhomie which he was conscious would, under the soothing influence of a good cigar, gradually take possession of Asterley. Bob was also silent; for he could not altogether make up his mind in what manner to commence the conversation, — somewhat ashamed of the exceeding wrath which he had at first manifested, and somewhat confused at having so suddenly relented,— uncertain whether to assume the tone of injured confidence, or to imitate the philosophical nonchalance of the doctor, — becoming the more undecided the longer he continued silent, and feeling unfortunately more embarrassed as he became more convinced that he ought not to appear so. At length he observed, very calmly, —

"Solgard informed me, doctor, that you were invited to Delbitt's this evening."

"Very true; but, under the rose, I had a more interesting engagement elsewhere."

Bob started as if an adder had by chance crawled upon him; but composing his features, he requested a light, and presumed that the lady was some new acquaintance.

"By no means," answered the doctor; "it must be now at least two weeks since I fortuned to meet her, as I took a morning ride in this neighborhood/"

"Her name?" observed Bob.

"Is Susan,'" continued Eastlake. "By-the-by, Bob, you might have observed a young girl at the cottage where you quenched your thirst this morning — true! you did make some observations at the very time touching her personal appearance — 'tis the very same, I assure you."

"But, doctor," exclaimed Asterley, with a sudden emotion of disinterestedness, "you, of course, intend no harm to the poor girl! It were, a circumstance but little creditable, you know, to the honor and humanity of our sex, that the simplicity and unsuspecting confidence of this poor young creature should prove the very means of her dishonor."

"Nay, Bob, I can assure you it is naught but a mere platonic liaison. In sooth, could you accidentally witness an interview, our mutual reserve would not fail to strike you with admiration, and convince vou of the guarded nature of our attachment."

An extraordinary cloud of smoke was the sequel to these assertions; so that for a short time Asterley sought in vain to note the expression of the speaker's countenance. When the vapor cleared away, nothing further was to be discerned on the lank sallow features of Eastlake than a settled expression of the most inflexible gravity.

The little man triumphantly advanced the forefinger of his right hand until it had been brought almost into juxtaposition with the nose of Eastlake, and whispered, but in a voice remarkably clear and distinct, "This evening I did accidentally witness your interview;" then elevating his voice somewhat, he added, letting down his finger, and resuming his usual mild and unctuous manner of speaking, "I feel particularly happy that I can conscientiously bear testimony to what you have so justly denominated mutual reserve; and although I could hardly speak as to what ideas might have been formed in the imagination of the young lady, I would be loath to hazard a doubt as to the purity of your platonic attachment!"

As Asterley concluded, the doctor stretched himself at full length on the mossy bank, and indulged for some moments in a low but cordial chuckle; to which contagious demonstration of risibility the sympathetic Bob soon responded in a ringing burst of merry laughter; upon which the doctor frankly confessed all that Bob had discovered, and in a merry mood the friends passed to town together.

CHAPTER XIV.

As lamps burn steadiest when un glaring light,
So modesty in beauty shines most bright:
Charms unambitious powers resistless boast;
And she who means no mischief, does the most. — Ignot.

Captain Solgard was in the act of raising the heavy black knocker which served to apprize Madam Markham of the arrival of guests at her hospitable portal, when his thundering double rap was arrested by the unexpected opening of the door.

Out came Oxenstiern. To Captain Solgard's complimentary salute his reply was brief, and unmarked by the accustomed polish of his manner. To the captain's inquiry touching the state of his health, he made no reply, save an indistinct "Thank you, sir," which rather escaped mechanically than by any active utterance, — gazing on the astounded captain with just such a look as a man might naturally wear whose thoughts were wholly devoted to that abstruse and perplexing search after the lost tribes of Israel.

This reverie, or brown study, of the chevalier, however, quickly passed away; and the rapid or almost instantaneous assumption of his ordinary graceful and insinuating manner might have well caused the officer to doubt the reality of the previous impressions produced on his senses.

The chevalier requested most courteously that Captain Solgard would honor him with his presence at a small entertainment which he purposed giving to a few friends on that very evening; and, professing great pleasure on his ready acceptance of the invitation, passed onward.

At Philip Tyebout's fishing-tackle store, which stood in those days at the upper corner where Pewter Platter Alley now issues into Front Street, our friend the young hunter, with whom we have already made acquaintance at the festival of Fort St David, formerly treated of, stood reclining somewhat over the counter, and much puzzled to decide between the respective merits of several fishing lines that lay spread out before him in most attractive rivalry.

A sudden and familiar tap on the shoulder forced him to look around, and recognize an acquaintance in Oxenstiern, who, entering still farther into the store, assumed an easy position on the counter, and commenced a discussion on various subjects connected with the chase, and also indulged his young friend with a dissertation, not only instructive but highly entertaining, on the mysteries and pleasant ways of fly-fishing; giving him at the same time the advantage of his experience in the selection of a good line, and promising him, as he gave him goodbye, that he should behold something well worth seeing at his house that evening.

At Erigson House the chevalier was directed to seek for his old friend the major, and the gentle Barbara, at the farthest and most shaded part of the garden. There he accordingly found them, enjoying the fragrant perfume of sweet flowers, and listening to the rich and powerful warbling of a mockingbird, perched high upon the branch of an elm, and making the whole forest ring with the echoes of his eccentric and ever varying music.

To the major and his niece, the chevalier addressed the same invitation which had been extended previously to Solgard and the young hunter; and with equal readiness was it accepted. Barbara's curiosity failed not to become excited when Oxenstiern declined staying to dinner, under plea of his presN3 being indispensably requisite at home, in order to perfect tome arrangements which he purposed introducing as part of the evening's entertainment During the day her imagination was busy in fancying a thousand things, no little to the detriment of household matters; and as evening drew nigh, her heart, she knew not why, beat high with undefined anticipations.

In the evening Oxenstiern received his guests, as they assembled at his house, with his usual urbanity and refinement Not a few fair dames honored his invitation by their presence;

among whom we will only note at present that fascinating coquette the lovely Markham, and the gentle and beautiful Barbara. There, also, appeared the gay Solgard; the romantic and interestingly mysterious hunter; the grave, sarcastic, and profound Doctor Eastlake; the decrepit beau, and restless plotter, Sir William Keith; the volatile and amorous Bob Asterley; the unassuming, insinuating, and inquisitive young Franklin; and that very worthy and erudite personage yclept "Master Nicolas Salomon."

After the ordinary refreshments had been duly discussed, and the conversation had -become interesting, instructive, amusing, and exciting, according to the nature of the various subjects under consideration, and the peculiarities of disposition and sentiment of each particular individual, the whole company was politely requested by Oxenstiern to enter another apartment, through a door which was now thrown open for their passage. The room which they entered was of unusually large dimensions, and presented a truly singular appearance. Its form was such, that the door by which they entered was the central part of that portion of the wall which bore a semicircular form, while the chord of this arc was the rectilinear extent of the wall opposite to the entrance. When the door was closed

behind them, the visitors remarked a circumstance which, to say the least, was sufficiently singular, — the non-existence, namely, of any aperture for the admission of light from without to supply this deficiency, a dim and almost amber-colored light pervaded the chamber, although none could divine from what quarter it proceeded. It illuminated the countenance of every guest, giving what might be termed a radiant paleness to the face, so that each one marveled exceedingly at the supernatural appearance of the others.

By slow degrees the light began to lose its golden luster, and waxed less and less; then becoming a mere twilight, that still grew duskier, until at length succeeded darkness so deep that it might be almost felt, which continued for about the space of eight minutes.

"Of a truth," uttered a melancholy voice, which was recognized as that of the worthy Master Nicolas, "the light hath utterly departed. Verily, I will hold firmly the garment of someone, for 1 have many doubts touching this matter."

"Prithee, good Master Salomen, handle not my sleeve so roughly, an it please you," uttered the clear silvery voice of Madam Markham, who, being in the immediate vicinity of the pedagogue, had thus fallen within his grasp.

"Of all dark places," exclaimed the major, "that I have yet fortuned in, this exceeds all save one, and that is the lower dungeon of Potsdam."

"I have put my hand on somebody's head," quoth Doctor Eastlake; "and, from the altitude of the same, I take it to be the pate of Bob Asterley."

"You are perfectly correct in your conjecture," replied the individual thus unceremoniously subjected to the imposition of hands. "But, bless my soul I what does the chevalier mean by shutting us up in this dark room? — I beg your pardon, madam, I really did not intend — gracious heavens! who trod on my toe?"

"Pardon me, sir," said Sir William Keith; "I really was not aware that your foot was so near. It shows, however, that we cannot be too cautious how we make any movement in the dark; this accident, in fact, arose, I feel morally convinced, from the mere circumstance of my shifting from the left leg to the right."

"I perceive," observed the young hunter, who had been hitherto perfectly silent, "something like daybreak in yonder direction."

It was of course utterly impossible to ascertain in what direction the speaker pointed; but, by dint of investigating all points of the compass, every individual of the party did perceive in one particular direction a very faint dawn of light, which discovery had a strong effect upon the spirits of the company, affording much relief to those who, with the erudite Master Nicolas, had been afflicted with doubt as regarded both the cause and the probable duration of the obscurity.

As the light increased, all became aware that it proceeded from a large square opening in the wall opposite the doorway, the boundaries of which aperture were but ill-defined, presenting a vapory and indistinct outline. Beyond the opening nothing could be seen but a gray mist of a cloud-like appearance. In the midst of this the figure of Oxenstiern appeared, singularly attired in a vest and turban of orange-colored silk, at first bearing the semblance of an indistinct and shadowy form, then growing into a more perfect and stronger likeness, and finally standing forth in all the clear and vivid outlines of breathing life. A low murmur of admiration and recognition arose at this unlooked-for spectacle; but, with a calm and rather severe aspect, Oxenstiern pressed his finger to his lips in token of silence, and continued gazing fixedly upon the wondering spectators, until, in the same mysterious manner in which he had made his appearance, he gradually faded away, melting, as it were, insensibly into the gray fleecy atmosphere around him.

Presently the mass of vapor that filled up the body of the picture rolled away, and" a scene of singular beauty presented itself. A rich and verdant landscape unfolded its beauties to the eye, blending many a lovely and picturesque feature of a fertile and peaceful country. A broad canal, reflecting from its glassy surface the over-arching branches of the tall trees that lined its borders, passed through extensive meadows of luxuriant vegetation. An antique mansion stood near, with a garden that stretched down to the very edge of the water, adorned with luxuriant verdure and flowers of gorgeous hue. On the porch of the house, which looked directly over this fair garden, sat a man somewhat beyond the prime of life, bearing a most striking similitude to Major Scheveling, yet of a more youthful appearance, and in frame considerably fuller and more athletic. He gazed in abstracted musing on an arbor at a little distance, where a beautiful little child sat playing amid the flowers which her companion, a boy some years older, had gathered for her amusement, and sportively strewed over her in youthful enjoyment.

All gazed on this scene with admiration; but none with such highly wrought feelings as old Major Scheveling, his niece Barbara, and the young hunter. The old man's eyes filled with tears, for he well remembered that pleasant summer day when he sat in that very porch, inhaling the fragrance of his beloved garden, and planning in his mind the marriage of those beautiful children, so innocently disporting themselves in the arbor before him. The youngest now stood beside him, a lovely girl almost matured to womanhood; bat that dark-eyed boy, that wild and wayward son, whither had he wandered?

As Barbara recognized the " form 'and features of her beloved uncle, she scarce refrained from an exclamation of surprise. She too remembered the well-known garden, and the cool shaded arbor, in which many a time she had sat by the hour perusing some favorite book, soothed by the birds warbling around her, and the rustling murmur of the pleasant breeze: but she wist not what little children those were who sported among the flowers; and she turned from the fairy vision and watched her uncle, who with fixed attention stood wrapped in the scene before him, unable to control his mournful emotions.

One other person in, the group beheld the landscape as if it were not unfamiliar to iris eye. The hunter made a step or two in advance on the first appearance of the vision, and looked alternately at the major and his more youthful semblance in the magic picture; he then stepped back, and, folding his arms, looked calmly on the scene, although his eyes now and then were turned, as if doubtingly, upon Barbara, and when she accidentally encountered his inquiring gaze, she marveled much at the deep blush that immediately suffused his swarthy features.

The worthy Master Nicolas took off his spectacles, wiped them carefully, and with curious eagerness again placed them in their natural position, and surveyed the picture. Once he opened his mouth, as about to utter some pithy and erudite observation, but a feeling of awe, for which he could ill account, restrained him.

The figures in the picture are in motion— the little girl runs playfully to the canal — a beautiful water-lily attracts her attention — the boy endeavors to reach it — it hangs far over the water — he hastily breaks off a twig, by which he can bring it within reach — the child is eager to possess it, and stretches forth her little hand to touch it-she slips, and plunges into the water.

"Save her! oh, save her!" cried Barbara, and the hunter" sprang forward as if to obey her supplication: but the sound of her voice seemed to dissolve the elements of the picture; it slowly faded away, but all might see, through the gathering dimness, the old man in the porch, wringing his hands in anguish, and the boy boldly plunging into the canal to the rescue of his little playmate; and presently naught remained but a thin vapor.

Then came on a great darkness; and when the light appeared, naught could be seen but the room with its bare - walls, and the door, by which they entered, opened and there stood Oxenstiern, nowise changed from his usual garb and demeanor. He courteously prayed his guests to leave the chamber, and partake of some refreshments, hoping that what he had presented had conduced to their entertainment, and remarking that the spectacle would have endured for a longer space if entirely uninterrupted.

"Was that yourself, chevalier?" exclaimed Bob Asterley, "or some familiar spirit, conjured by the potency of the black art to assume your identity?"

Oxenstiern smiled upon the little man and bowed, but made no answer, as if to intimate that he was unwilling to enter into any explanation; while Doctor Eastlake told Bob that he must seek another opportunity to learn the secrets of natural magic.

"If I would not dare ask such a question," continued the doctor, addressing himself in a low whisper to Miss Phoebe Danvers, who listened with profound attention; "but my friend Bob is such a daring fellow!"

"He is, indeed," responded the lady, with emphasis, as certain passages between tbe little man and herself suddenly occurred to her recollection.

"Pray, Master Salomen," exclaimed the lively widow Markham, "where be those verses that you have promised me for so long a time?"

"And that exposition on the text of Rabbi Fronts, that I have been anxiously looking for the last three months?" continued Doctor Eastlake.

"I dare to say you have entirely forgotten that pretty missal, good Master Nicolas, that I was to have a sight of," observed Barbara, with an arch smile on her rosy lips.

BLACKBEARD

The worthy pedagogue turned his honest countenance with much gravity to each one who addressed him, and then looking down for a brief space, as pondering on the subject, spake with suitable deliberation, —

"Touching the madrigal, gentle lady, whereof you make mention, I do remember me of certain verses, which I have but hastily put together, the which as yet require further digestion and revision. And in the matter of that exposition, good sir, I should have completed the same ere this; but there is one small passage in the original concerning the which I have still my doubts. As to the illuminated missal, methinks, Miss Barbara, that I have it even now with me."

Master Salomen began to institute a search forthwith into the capacious abyss formed by his right hand coat-pocket; and from amid a vast multitude of anomalous articles, finally produced the book in question, — a manuscript on vellum, covered richly with blue velvet, and curiously fastened with silver clasps. It was opened, and attracted admiration, — each letter separately formed with pious care, and the broad margin streaked with gold, and heavily charged with illuminations of most gorgeous and vivid coloring.

There was a brilliant representation of the lovely wife of Uriah, innocently disporting herself in the clear cool wave of a lake at the bottom of a garden, and King David, on a terrace overhead, casting an unhallowed gaze over her unconscious charms. In another page the vainglorious Philistine advances to meet the son of Jesse. The holy zeal of the painter has induced him to contrast as strongly as possible the relative stature of each hero; so that Goliah looks down contemptuously on the trees that grow near, while little David hardly reaches to the knee of the giant; and the tents and men-at-arms of the hostile camps overhang the scene, in utter defiance of the laws of perspective.

Birds, too, of richest plumage and graceful form, hover over many a page; and golden-winged cherubim with radiant hair seem to forbid any sacrilegious imagination.

A sudden concussion threw Master Salomen from his equilibrium; and in his effort to recover himself the book fell from his hands. On looking round to ascertain the cause of this" unexpected shock, he discovered the offender in the person of his quondam pupil, little Bob Asterley.

"Ah! Robert," said he, shaking his head in admonition, "when thou wert but a lad, thy headlong vivacity not unfrequently required correction, and I fear me exceedingly that years have not, in any perceptible measure, amplified thy discretion."

"You must really pardon me, my very good sir," answered the culprit, "for I was endeavoring, you know, to escape from the wrath of Miss Phoebe Danvers; although I must confess that I am entirely unconscious of having given her any just cause for indignation."

Miss Phoebe shook her finger at him in a threatening manner, while her sparkling eyes and heightened color led to the suspicion that Bob had been guilty of some impropriety that had justly aroused r maidenly ire.

Doctor Eastlake, as was his wont in such cases, turned upon his little friend his usual glance of grave reproof, but in vain. Certain circumstances, of which, as we have related in a preceding chapter, Bob had accidentally become cognizant, went, in the opinion of the little man, to detract much from the moral weight of his friend's character; and he returned the glance in a manner at once so triumphant and so familiar, that the doctor became aware, in a moment, that the prestige of superior purity and decorum, which had hitherto given so much weight to his counsels, had entirely disappeared.

The doctor was aroused from these reflections by the voice of Madam Markham, inquiring whether he put faith in the generally received opinions concerning witches, hobgoblins, necromancy, apparitions, and so forth.

Master Salomen adjusted his spectacles, and awaited his answer; for he ever esteemed the doctor a man of much erudition, although unfortunately, too much addicted to lighter and less important subjects — such as a knowledge of the modern languages, and the trifling accomplishments of fencing, riding, and so forth, altogether unworthy the attention of such an excellent classical scholar.

The soi-disant skeptic Sir William Keith also approached as the beautiful coquette propounded this interesting question, while his protégé Franklin put on an expression of respectful gravity, although a sneer faintly lurked on his placid countenance.

"It has been too much the custom with philosophers in our modern age," commenced Eastlake, "to decry many things which seemed sanctioned alone by the impress of popular traditional belief; and in no instance, perhaps, is this more strikingly verified than in reference to the vulgar superstition,

as they term It, touching the apparitions of the dead. The enthusiastic pride, also, of many highly cultivated minds, and a zeal for the dignity of science, have led them to class all the phenomena of nature under certain physical laws. To their laborious investigations we owe much j and the daring flight of science is no longer bounded by the orb on which we dwell: but there still seemed to exist a dark and unknown world, immeasurably removed from human ken, into whose dreary confines, we learn, a few gifted sages have in times past entered with a fearful tread, Even to them this unhallowed knowledge was the price of many years of long and painful study; and the possessor of such dread mysteries was ever as one estranged from the familiar communion of his fellow-men. Of such the life has endured far beyond the given years of man: their spirits have departed, one by one, but no human eye beheld them in the hour of death. Few would dare to seek"— he looked earnestly at Oxenstiern, who smiled almost imperceptibly — "or commune with the spirits of the departed; but that they do at times appear to mortal man, we dare not disbelieve,"

Bob Asterley turned more than once a puzzled and hesitating glance at the speaker, as if he would satisfy himself that this laconic, skeptical, and philosophizing companion was actually guilty of this long, imaginative, and unscientific oration,

"I must acknowledge my surprise, Doctor Eastlake" observed Sir William Keith, "to perceive these antiquated notions countenanced by a man of your scientific attainments."

Eastlake immediately entered into an animated and ingenious defense of the popular belief on this as well as other subjects, — -much to the edification of his friend Bob, who had heard him equally eloquent in favor of the contrary opinion.

The chevalier was engaged in pointing oat to the hunter the beauties and prominent features in several paintings and sketches which lay in a portfolio on the table, and Barbara drew near, interested in the remarks which Oxenstiern indulged in from time to time, as successive scenes recalled to his memory circumstances under which he had personally beheld them.

"Many travelers affect to disbelieve/' observed the chevalier, with his finger resting on a view of Gibraltar, "in the existence of the subterraneous, or if you will, subaqueous communication between the Rock and the African main; but having on a certain occasion passed through, I can bear personal testimony to its actual existence."

"Under the ocean?" inquired Barbara; "how could vou venture into such a place?"

"Through sheer necessity," replied the chevalier; "and if my memory fails me not, the circumstances were sufficiently pressing: I had spent some time in Ceuta, and was becoming somewhat weary of the hospitality of the King of Fez, when I mounted my dromedary and rode to the summit of Abyla, in hopes of getting a glimpse of some vessel approaching Ceuta, on which I could take passage for a Christian land. I had alighted, and was looking over the edge of a large abyss on the mountain, supposed by the natives thereabouts to be the crater of an extinct volcano, when I was suddenly aware of a party of wandering Arabs coming upon me like the wind. The sons of Ishmael are no respecters of persons. I accordingly descended into the crater very cautiously, but with more speed than I should have thought proper to make use of on an occasion of less immediate emergency. In my haste I slipped, and how I reached the bottom uninjured, I know not; over bushes, brambles" and heaps of scoriae" I continued rolling for a most unreasonable length of time, — a pitch from the Peak of Teneriffe will give you an adequate idea of the distance. Well, I did come to the bottom at last, and had the satisfaction to hear three or four shots, as it were from the clouds, fired doubtless by my friends above. To return by the way in which I had got down was out of the question. A dark cavern of immense height and breadth seemed inviting me to enter: with a bag of dates, and a goat-skin filled with water slung around me, I proceeded; and, save being obliged once to lie down and suffer a troop of monkeys to pass over me on their route to Africa, I met nothing to molest me, until I came to Spanish daylight!"

"What a singular scene!" exclaimed Barbara, as her eyes rested on the following picture; "strange men and stranger looking boats plunging and sinking in all directions on a broad river — waves running mountain high, as if agitated by a violent storm — trees bending before the wind — and one little boat, apparently undisturbed amid the general commotion; the helmsman, attired after the English fashion, sitting in the stern, calmly smoking a pipe — even the smoke curling up undisturbed to the heavens, as in the midst of a perfect calm. Pray, chevalier, explain!"

"You have before you," said Oxenstiern, "one of the most esteemed productions of the justly celebrated Quang, — a Chinese painter, who flourished in the early part of the last century. The subject therein immortalized is the great typhoon of the vear 1621: it swept with unexampled fury over the broad waters of the Hoangho, capsizing and destroying junks without number; one boat, guided by a stranger, riding out the tempest in security, owing to the potent interposition, as the Chines^ believed, of the mighty Chin-Jos."

The features of the individual in the boat, although small, were minutely distinct, and the hunter recognized in them the very countenance of Oxenstiern.

He was about to call the attention of Barbara to this singular coincidence, when Captain Solgard approached the fair lady in question, with that agreeable assurance which so well became him, and taking her reluctant hand, led her forward to the harpsichord (on which, by-the-by, the chevalier, whose taste in music had been highly cultivated, was no mean proficient), craving one of his favorite songs.

The hunter was conscious that his feelings had been in some degree interested in, the fair creature who had but just left him, ever since the day of the festival at Fort St David; the grateful expression of her sweet countenance had, in fact, been more than once recalled to his recollection, and stole in upon his meditations perhaps more frequently than he was aware of. A certain feeling of uneasiness came over him as Solgard led her away f and Oxenstiern smiled, as he observed with what an air of abstractedness his young friend began to receive his remarks, and how every now and then his eye would furtively glance from the portfolio to the harpsichord.

"Prithee, Bob," said Eastlake, "do you notice the lover-like air of impressment with which our son of Neptune hovers around Miss Scheveling 1 I warrant me now, that I give him a hint to keep in the proper channel."

With this intimation, the doctor, as if accidentally, commenced by making some unimportant observations to the lovely widow; to which her lover, engaged as be then was, paid but little attention. His gestures then became more animated, and his conversation evidently of a more interesting nature. Solgard looked around rather more frequently. Madam Markham smiles and looks archly at the doctor — Solgard's countenance betrays a slight degree of impatience — the doctor inclines his head more near, and sinks his voice to a low and tender tone — the beautiful Christine blushes, but her sparkling eyes betoken anything but displeasure. What a trial to Solgard! That insidious, sallow-looking doctor was actually making love to Madam Markham! His own mistress too! at whose feet he had poured forth a thousand ardent vows of adoration, and in whose dark eyes he had read the sweet confession of a mutual flame! — "By heavens!" ejaculated the jealous lover, "I renounce her forever!"

The doctor casually encountered the angry scowl that unconsciously had taken possession of the gallant captain's brow: he smiled in secret triumph at the rapid success of his maneuver, and presently relapsed into the ordinary indifference of polite conversation^" when the officer's brow gradually cleared, although his jealous feelings failed not to manifest themselves by occasional glances in that direction.

It is more than probable that Solgard's angry feelings, having already partially subsided, might have totally disappeared, had it not been for the unguarded conduct of Bob Asterley on the occasion. He had watched, with much delight, the progress of his friend's attentions to the fair coquette; and when the doctor gave him a detail of his operations, the little man took no pains to suppress his gratification. The significant glances which he threw, during the doctor's recital, both on Solgard and Madam Markham, were noticed by the former with suspicion, and rekindled his jealous wrath, so that it wanted but a fair pretext to break out into a flame.

Solgard approached with somewhat of a grim smile,

—

"I perceive, doctor, that you have been making yourself agreeable to the fair lady in yonder corner.

"I flatter myself that I have not been altogether unsuccessful in that respect," responded the individual thus addressed, with a complacent smirk upon his countenance, that proved particularly disagreeable to the gallant officer.

Captain Solgard was a gentleman by birth and education, but he was now fairly under the dominion of the green-eyed monster, and resolved to find or make a quarrel.

He went on — "You must be aware, sir, that for some time past I have been paying serious attentions to Madam Markham, which she has not thought proper to discourage?"

"A matter of much notoriety," answered the doctor, dryly.

Bob Asterley was emphatically a lover of peace, disliking in especial the smell of gunpowder, and finding no music in the whistling of a bullet. It is true he got into many a quarrel by volunteering to prevent a fight, but his zeal suffered thereby no diminution: he persevered through good and through evil report; and though at times his well-meant efforts to conciliate served but the more rapidly to establish a misunderstanding, yet the benevolence of his motives was never for a moment brought into question.

Solgard for a moment paused, as if to calm himself, and Eastlake continued, —

"Your manner, even more than your language, Captain Solgard, leads me to infer that you are disposed to take in high dudgeon the mode in which have entertained Madam Markham this evening. Now, sir, I would have you know, that we of the Colonies make love when and where it listeth us. By my faith! an you frown so haughtily, you will tempt me to marry the fair widow."

"This trifling, sir, is unbecoming; and by the great —

"

"Gentlemen," interposed Asterley, who, in his character of pacificator, now hastened to interfere, "let me beg of you not to view this matter in so serious a light. I assure you, Captain Solgard, that my friend the doctor had nothing whatever in view but a mere joke — upon my word, it was an excellent device — and so he fairly aroused your jealousy!" Here Bob laughed as cordially as possible, trusting to the effect of sympathy.

If the lover had been angry before, this unfortunate observation of the little man redoubled his indignation. Doctor Eastlake then dared to consider his passion as a fit subject for burlesque, and courted his mistress to excite merriment at the expense of his jealous feelings! — Solgard became filled with wrath.

Bob looked up, and discovered his mistake: his mirth suddenly became mute. Doctor Eastlake had relaxed not a muscle of his grave and sallow countenance, and Solgard's face was crimsoned with angry emotion. As Bob turned his gaze from one to the other, and was ruminating some new idea of mediation, Solgard bowed, with what the doctor termed bitter politeness, and retired.

CHAPTER XV.

**"This gentleman must, for his honor's sake, have a bout
with you— be cannot, by the duello, avoid it."**
Shakespeare.

The bright chariot of Phoebus had already (to speak after the manner of the ingenious author of the Seven Champions of Christendom) been drawn by the fiery-footed steeds of day more than half the distance between the gates of Orient and the bright arch of Zenith, when Bob Asterley, enveloped in unusual gloom, and perplexed with many doubts, rapped mournfully at the portal of his medical comrade. The door was opened by a buxom wench, to whom the manners of Asterley were probably not unfamiliar, as she suffered, with but faint resistance, and not a word of remonstrance, the ravishment of sundry kisses from her rosy lips, as she led the little man into the study. Bob entered, and she ran to call the doctor.

Some time elapsed ere the professional man made his appearance; which he did in a pair of Turkish slippers, and a loose dressing-gown, or wrapper, of light-colored chintz. He yawned heavily as he shook hands with Asterley, complaining bitterly of having been kept up all night by certain professional duties; and gave directions to the maid, who answered to the appellation of Grace, to bring his toast and chocolate into the office.

"Upon my word, doctor," said Asterley, "this irregular mode of Living will injure your constitution. By-the-by, that was a foolish affair last evening"; though Solgard, I suppose, will get cool before long."

"A slight flesh-wound might satisfy him," observed Eastlake, musingly; "and will, I think, be decidedly preferable.

There is so little certainty in a pistol-ball, that my patients might be obliged to attend my own funeral, or his majesty lose the services of a gallant officer, without a sufficient degree of malice prepense to render the event agreeable to the survivor. — A little more cream, Grace, and another cup. I can recommend this chocolate, Bob."

"Why don't you put in cream first, doctor?"

"Because," replied Eastlake, "the flavor of the chocolate is less impaired by the addition of cream to the surface, than by its entire incorporation into the mass of the beverage itself. You will observe, also, that I cream twice to every cup; by which means the temperature of the liquid is not sensibly diminished, — always a desideratum to chocolate drinkers."

"Who is that beautiful creature opposite?" exclaimed Asterley, who, during the latter part of the doctor's observations, had been looking through the window into the street.

"Prithee, Bob, have some respect to the character of my office! That licentious gaze of yours will shock my female neighbors. Lo! the damsel already observes you, and discreetly retires from the porch! Ah! her grandmother has taken her place, and scans you with a curious eye: the old lady appears to apprehend no danger. I hope, by-the-by, that you have not attempted any liberties with Grace, for I have reason to know that she is a very modest girl."

"I doubt it not," quoth Bob; "but—" here a thundering rap at the door cut short his reply.

Grace ushered in a little curly-headed urchin.

"Mother wants you to come and see the baby, sir, as soon as possible."

"And what is your mother's name, my little man?"

"Peggy Dickson, sir."

"Where does she live?"

"In the little red house, sir, in Almond Street, next door to the baker's."

"Very well, my child; tell your mother I will be there directly."

Another rap at the door — enter a round-bellied, thick-necked Hollander.

The case was one of apoplectic tendency. He complained of difficult respiration; his face was highly flushed — veins swollen; and the details of the enormous breakfast he had but a short time previous devoured, almost startled the phlegmatic Eastlake.

A free use of the lancet operated much to the relief of the plethoric Dutchman. Bob held the basin, until he (that is to say, Bob) fainted, — the sight of blood being with him an antipathy for which we can ill account; upon which the Dutchman stared with stupid admiration, thanked the doctor, and departed.

As Bob recovered from his syncope, Eastlake advised him to amuse himself, until his return, with a cigar, and such books as lay upon the table, and issued forth to make such calls as required immediate attention.

The doctor's library, at a time when books on medical subjects were as scarce as they are now abundant, comprised divers antique folios, such as "Hippocratis Opera," "Hildani Observationes Chirurgicae," "Sennerti Medicina Practica," "Hoffmani Medicina Rationalis," and other musty tomes in the Latin tongue. It is, in fact, but in modern times that works on medical science have made their appearance in the vernacular. On the shelves reposed also volumes of a different cast: there stood the ponderous "Arcadia," esteemed at that time the flower of courtly invention; next came the dramatic works of "rare Ben Jonson" then Farquhar and Congréve, abounding in racy and sparkling wit; and on the end of the shelf, very dusty, "Newtoni Principia." There, too, were the poets of the Augustan era of Britain, — Waller and Cowley, Lovelace and Suckling, Dryden and Pope: several numbers, also, of a new piece entitled The Spectator, which at that time excited much attention, and was generally ascribed to Sir Richard Steele.

One of these numbers had attracted the attention of Asterley, and he was engaged in perusing it when Eastlake returned.

"The author of that piece," said Bob, as he laid down the paper, "is a sensible and well-informed man; he considers the custom of dueling as a heathenish and anti-Christian practice, on which point I fully coincide with him. By all that's lovely! no one shall catch me standing up in cold blood to be shot at! 'tis a tempting of Providence."

"'Tis singular," observed Eastlake, lighting a cigar, "to note how universally the practice has prevailed through all ages. It is recorded in Holy Writ that the patriarch Jacob wrestled with an angel; which species of duels is in much repute among Cornishmen at the present day: Samson, also, encountered a lion in single combat; from which circumstance the Greeks took the hint, and invented the fabulous feats of Hercules, Jason, Perseus, Bellerophon, and other worthies, who went about fighting duels with dragons, hydras, triple-headed and hundred-handed tyrants. The object, in these instances, was victory. Gradually, however, duels came to arise from more interested motives. As a legalized mode of proving innocence, or wiping away foul and calumnious aspersions, men in the darker ages found a convenient and conclusive resource in the issue of single combat" A sweeping blow of the mace at once killed and convicted the guilty; and the dagger of Mercy gave an impartial verdict Our courts of justice have superseded such trials; and some affect to consider this an improvement: in some few cases it may be so; but, generally speaking, whatever be the decision, the losing party complains of injustice; so that, on the whole, the ancient mode afforded more general satisfaction."

"Then you prefer," uttered Bob, inquiringly, "the test of single combat to the decision of an impartial and enlightened jury?"

"By no means," replied the doctor; "but juries are too often ignorant or interested, or both. A fact is presented to them by half a dozen ingenious lawyers, in as many different lights. Wearied by endless digression, blinded by curious sophistry, excited by brilliant declamation, and absolutely bewildered in the maze of legal jargon, they decide as hungry men, knowing that dinner depends on the verdict, satisfied that they can do no wrong, since both parties have been satisfactorily proved, by their eloquent advocates, to claim nothing but what is perfectly just and correct."

"Yet," continued Bob, "the issue of a duel in the present day has no judicial effect whatever; a man's guilt or unworthiness is in nowise established by the lodgment of a ball in the brain, or the passage, of a small-sword under the fifth rib."

"Your consideration," replied Eastlake, filling Bob's glass and his own as he spoke, "is in the main correct; and partly falls into the view under which I propose to consider the utility of dueling, as understood in the present day. — Do you like the flavor?"

The little man paused and replenished his glass — held up the golden liquid to the light, and demanded where the wine was to he met with.

"The wine may be had," replied the doctor, u of Jonathan Dickinson, near the drawbridge. Inquire for the pale sherry which he imported some years back in the brig Amity. — I imagined Solgard would have sent a challenge ere this."

A gentle rap at the door interrupted the conversation, whereupon entered a gentlemanly-looking man, in full uniform, and, in a manner ceremoniously polite, stated that he had been commissioned to deliver a note to Doctor Roger Eastlake; upon which the doctor acknowledged his identity, and received the missive. It ran thus, —

"In consequence of what took place last evening between Doctor Eastlake and Captain Solgard, an early interview is deemed necessary. Doctor Eastlake will please signify his choice of weapons, and designate time and place, as soon as may be convenient. Lieutenant Curt will agree upon preliminary arrangements."

The doctor perused this invitation with proper gravity; and, introducing Lieutenant Curt to his particular friend Mr. Robert Asterley, begged the indulgence of the gentlemen for a few moments, in order to indite an answer to Captain Solgard's billet.

The response was brief, — signifying an acceptance of the challenge — specifying the small sword as the weapon on the occasion — and leaving time and place to the discretion of the respective friends of the parties interested.

Lieutenant Curt met the smiling, welcome, and cordial invitation of little Bob to a glass of wine with uncompromising gravity of feature and laconic politeness. The wine, however, was not such as lieutenants in his majesty's service often meet with, and effected that which Asterley could not. An air of much satisfaction stole upon his rigid features as the delicious nutty flavor made itself sensible to his palate; and when he set down the glass on the table, an almost imperceptible smacking of the lips took place.

The lieutenant departed, and the friends lighted fresh cigars.

"Such wine as this," began Bob, interrupting his speech with an occasional application of the nectar to his lips, "could never injure a man of tolerable constitution; to me it has been for years a sovereign elixir: before dinner it whets the appetite; after dinner assists the digestive powers; relieves the gloom of a cloudy day, and harmonizes with sunshine; makes the happy gay, and comforts the mournful soul. I have had a headache all the morning, doctor; so prithee open another bottle!"

"A most logical argument," replied Eastlake. "Who is it that observes, much to the same purpose, —

"Si bene quid inemini, causn sunt quinque bibendi, Hospitis adventus, prssens sitis atque future, Aut vim bonitas, aut quelibet altera causa."

Which has been thus rendered by a disciple of the same school, —

"If memory serves me but a little, There are five reasons why we tipple, — Good wine — an old companion by — Because I am, or may be, dry — Or any other reason why."

"Bless my soul, doctor! I but this moment thought of it" (and his countenance deepened into unusual gravity); "have you made your will?"

"Very true, Bob! that should be attended to; several bequests I would fain make — in case I depart from this world to-morrow. I will write it myself — nay! a cramped hand might defeat the intention of the testator. Make you a good pen, Bob, and write as I dictate."

Behold Robert Asterley seated at the table, with a fair sheet of foolscap before him, dipping a fresh crow-quill into the inkstand, and executing airy flourishes at about half an inch above the paper, as one doubling his fists for a fight.

"Art thou prepared, most worthy scribe, for thy solemn office?"

"Ready, ay, ready!" responded Asterley.

"Set down, then, with thy speedy pen, as I give it thee."

Asterley wrote, and Eastlake dictated as follows:

"Be it remembered, that I, Roger Eastlake, in the city of Philadelphia, of the colony of Pennsylvania, physician, being of sound mind and body, do hereby ordain this to be my last will and testament.

"Imprimis — I give and bequeath my body to my friend Doctor Pemberton, for dissection; and would that he examine whether any morbid lesion exist in the hepatic duct or duodenum."

"Bless my soul, Eastlake!" ejaculated Bob, "I really believe you would like to witness your own post mortem examination; a lawyer would be tempted to view such a bequest in the light of a posthumous *felo de se*."

"As to my soul," resumed Eastlake, "having no further control over the same, I make no testamentary disposal thereof."

"Absolutely heathenish, Doctor Eastlake! upon my word, you are only fit to live among Indians!"

"To die among them, you would have said; but proceed! —

"I give and bequeath my professional assurance to the venerable Doctor Pemberton, — his more youthful brethren in the healing art being sufficiently provided with the same. Item. — My polyglot Bible to Master Nicolas Salomen. Item. — To Master Benjamin Franklin my copy of Newton's Principia, together with my case of mathematical instruments, and a rare work entitled "A True Guide to the Heavens, or Martyn's Astronomical Recreations." The remainder of my estate, real and personal, 1 hereby give and bequeath to my trusty and well-beloved friend Robert Asterley, whom I hereby appoint and confirm to be the sole executor of this my last will and testament"

"Well," observed Bob, flourishing his pen.

"Grace may now come in," resumed Eastlake, "and witness my signature."

Grace was called, — wiped the meal from her fingers, though her face might as well have participated in the act — smoothed her apron, and entered with her countenance reddened, partly through bashfulness, and partly by the fire in the kitchen.

She beheld in silent incomprehension, and with her lips unconsciously parting, the doctor sign and seal the document, and, grasping the pen as directed, inscribed her name as witness. Bob was unable to trace the faintest resemblance to any letter throughout her signature, and prudently surrounded it with the explanatory "Grace Bissel, her mark."

In the evening Bob again dropped into the office, and gave the doctor to understand that all necessary preliminaries had been arranged for the meeting, — the time, five o'clock the next morning — and the ground, a retired spot on the Jersey shore, a short distance below Kaighn's Point. No objection had been made to the proposed weapon; and Bob hinted that the captain flourished a cunning rapier.

The evening was rendered agreeable by cigars and wine; and Bob, being somewhat elevated, was giving the doctor much good advice, and indulging in a strain of moral reflection, when Eastlake, consulting his watch (a rare piece of mechanism in the colony in those days), informed Asterley that he must plead a pressing engagement in excuse for leaving him for a short time; and advised him, if he felt sleepy before his return, to turn in without any ceremony.

Bob did feel sleepy before his friend's return, and was awakened by the doctor tumbling over him, as he lay profound in the big elbow-chair.

All was as dark as Erebus — u Merciful Father V 9 ejaculated Bob; "what's that?"

The little man had altogether forgotten the circumstances of time and place under which sleep had insensibly taken possession of him, and was puzzled to account for a small fiery coal, glowing with remittent insulated ardor, in the midst of the darkness. A sulphurous flame suddenly shot up, and the doctor, applying the match to a little taper of green wax that stood hard by, enlightened the little man on the subject.

"What's the clock, doctor? I was almost asleep when you came in."

"Ten minutes lacking to three," replied Eastlake; "suppose we go to bed?"

Bob yawned, rubbed his eyes, and came to the conclusion that an hour of sleep was not worth undressing for; adding, somewhat dolorously, "We must be on the ground at five."

During the next hour, the doctor occupied himself in performing his ablutions, trimming his beard, effecting a change of apparel, and, towards daylight, discussing sundry slices of cold beef, in which solid viand Bob declined to participate, taking in lieu thereof a supplementary glass of wine or so — the doctor obstinately adhering to cold water.

Asterley and the doctor, accompanied by a medical friend, found their boat in waiting at the mouth of Dock-water; and stepping in without delay, the oarsmen went to work in silence, plying their lusty sinews with vigorous and well-timed strokes.

The sun rose in all the glorious effulgence so oft described by imaginative writers, as the little wherry came abreast of the island, and afforded Bob an opportunity of apostrophizing "bright Phoebus," as he termed it, with a running commentary on the indispensable importance of its light and heat to the human race; upon which the medical gentleman present ventured to deplore the partial illumination of the citizens of Nova Zembla, and the melancholy deprivation of children born in salt mines, who labored under an elusive species of contentment, although absolutely ignorant of the existence of this bright luminary, or at least imagined the light of the sun, which they heard spoken of, to proceed from a huge candle. Eastlake, contrary to his usual manner, took no part in the conversation, but reclined in contemplation of the beautiful scene around him, with a fixed and serious gaze.

The air was fresh on the water, and a strong tide running up forced them to head considerably down the river. The wherry, however, danced over the waves like a cork until they reached the Jersey shore, where a strong pull beached her well on the sand.

They had brought her to a little below the Point; and the party, breaking through the bushes that lined the beach, entered a tolerably heavy growth of pines, through which they kept on,

rousing the deer as they passed, until they came in sight of a stream of water since called Newton's Creek, which, becoming died, as it were, by tree roots of the trees that shade its margin, empties its mahogany-colored waves into the Delaware.

A short turn to the left, and a walk of about half a mile along the banks of the creek, brought them to the place of meeting; where Captain Solgard with his second, and Mr. Trocar, the surgeon of the *Greyhound*, awaited their approach.

Salutations were interchanged, rapiers measured, and superfluous garments laid aside.

Each stationed himself— the seconds withdrew.

Solgard's countenance expressed haughtiness and vindictive satisfaction. Eastlake's manner was perfectly cool and collected, indicating firm and serious determination.

"They salute, and recover — their swords clash as they cross each other *"en quarte"*— the doctor evidently disposed to stand on the defensive — Solgard eager to attack — both are skillful and practiced swordsmen, but no time is consumed in useless maneuvers, or cunning display of science — Sol

fard presses forward with bold and rapid thrusts — Eastlake parries coolly — Mr. Trocar interchanges glances with Lieutenant Curt, answering the lieutenant's doubtful shake of the head by an equally expressive shrug of the shoulders — Bob views with interest the composed demeanor of his friend in vain Solgard attempts to deceive his wary antagonist with the feint, the clash, the entanglement, the demi circle — prompt and active, with a firm foot and steady eye, Eastlake foils his impetuous attack— exasperated beyond measure at what he deems contemptuous forbearance, Solgard loses all prudence, and thrusts with furious and unguarded desperation — a sudden and powerful *"disengagé"* whirls his sword high in the air, and Eastlake's rapier presses against Solgard's "bosom.

"You have pressed me hard, Captain Solgard, " said the doctor, lowering his point as he spoke: then observing for the first time the blood tricking from a superficial wound in his sword-arm, which he had received without being aware of, during the violence of Solgard's final and desperate onset, he continued, — "Should you now be disposed, sir, to receive any explanation or apology on the subject of the misunderstanding which has led to the F resent meeting, do me the justice to believe that am inclined to offer it freely and sincerely. By my faith!" added he, smiling, "I have lost enough Wood already, considering my languid circulation."

Disarmed, and at the mercy of the antagonist whose life he had so lately sought, Solgard could not be insensible to his generous conduct. Under such circumstances, the gentlemanly deference which Eastlake paid to his wounded feelings at once soothed his pride and warmed his heart.

Extending his hand, he exclaimed, "You are a noble fellow, Eastlake!"

During the complimentary conversation that ensued, Eastlake's wound was attended to, and Asterley, delighted with the pacific issue of the reencounter, insisted upon the immediate adjournment of the whole party to his house, where, as he remarked, the matter would undergo a more satisfactory discussion over a bottle of wine.

It was still early when they landed at the city, and proceeded along Penn Street to the beautiful mansion which had been built by Asterley's grandfather, — a specimen of the solid and comfortable architecture of some of the wealthiest of the early settlers. A small court between the street and the house was shaded by two enormous button woodtrees, which stood there at the landing of Penn, and tad been spared when their brethren of the forest bowed before the axe. The main building was two-storied, and put together as usual, with alternate red and black bricks. A' single apartment on each side, which might be called wings, standing about twelve feet back from the facade of the main building, completed the front view of the edifice. A hedge of boxwood, neatly trimmed, lined the interior of the paling that enclosed the court, from the level of which three steps of dark gray stone mounted. into the old-fashioned porch that adorned the entrance.

The household of Robert Asterley, Esq., consisted oi an ancient negress, whom he had inherited with the rest of his grandfather's estate; and who, having been the family cook from time immemorial, now discharged the additional functions of housekeeper and *femme de chambre*. Also a nephew of this old lady, a stout strapping slave, who acted, in a measure, as his master's factotum; a sable Figaro, who shaved his master every morning, sat up for him every night, brushed his coat, powdered his hair, polished his buckles, and selected his waistcoat for the day. He also assisted Aunt Hebe in the culinary operations, had the sole charge of the garden, and occasionally interfered with the groom in the stable. He might be easily known at a distance by his white apron, in which he traversed the city at all hours and seasons, delivering messages, executing commissions, and idling away his leisure hours, which, sooth to say, were but few. ' This snow-white tablier formed an integral

Krtion of his equipment, whether he stood behind his master's chair at dinner, or followed, at a respectful distance, in his wake to Christ Church on the Sabbath. With equal pertinacity did this apron appear, whether the wearer was lent for a funeral or a wedding, on either which occasion Nero (for by this unchristian designation was he christened) officiated with peculiar propriety and decorum. His countenance was not adequately jocund to express the native benevolence of his disposition, — an iron gravity maintained itself invariably over his sable visage, respectful, deferential, and immoveable: the immutable Nero handed around cakes and wine at a funeral without a tear, and never showed his teeth "when beards wagged all."

Silently, and with a gliding and almost imperceptible motion, Nero ushered the guests of his master into the parlor, took charge of beavers, swords, and canes, and disappeared with noiseless celerity.

Aunt Hebe perceived him as he entered her domains,

—

"Good gracious me, Nero! who has Master Robert brought to breakfast? I reckon a power of

Gentlemen — and I never to know nothing about it! How many is there?"

"Five," replied Nero.

The old lady grumbled awfully, and took occasion to eulogize Robert's grandfather; who always, she remarked, gave her notice beforehand when any one was to breakfast, or dine, or take supper with him, except once; and that was no fault of his, when the Sagamore of the Delawares, and five or six of his warriors, came in from the woods back of the house just as dinner was getting ready. She continued such observations from time to time, and stirred about all the time with amazing briskness, enlarging and hastening her preparations with an alacrity astonishing in one who had nearly completed a century.

The morning was pleasant, — a bright warm sun, and the air fresh and fragrant. "Gentlemen,"

exclaimed Bob, "let us pass into the garden awhile."

They passed into the garden, which was extensive, and handsomely planted; flowering plants and shrubs, native and exotic; endless varieties of roses, tulips, lilies, hyacinths, violets, pinks, and honeysuckles; clumps of fragrant wild-locust and tail sycamores; natural arbors of broad-leaved clustering grape; — everything indicated the taste of the proprietor. But as a craving appetite receives little nutriment from aromatic odors (*malgre* the assertion of De Berg to the contrary), the natural beauties around were, under these circumstances, viewed with less satisfaction than the white apron of Nero, who approached, and summoned the gentlemen to breakfast.

Aunt Hebe, aided by the omnifarious Nero, had provided a solid, nutritious repast. It were useless to describe the demolition that ensued; suffice it to say, that, after the first impetuous onslaught had subsided into something like regular and deliberate operations, all due commendation was bestowed on the skill of the cook, as demonstrated in the excellence of the varied preparations, practical proof of which amply stood forth in the exhausted condition of the dishes.

After breakfast, and during that state of contented indolence that naturally accompanies the digestion of a hearty meal, Asterley suggested that a certain fish, which had been on table, and much approved of by all, would swim better on a little *haut barsac*, the quality of a lot of which in his cellar he wished to submit to their judgment.

This suggestion of the little man, however, was voted by his guests, unanimously, to be both unseasonable and unreasonable, and consequently inadmissible.

"Wine before dinner!" exclaimed Lieutenant Curt, with an affectation of much horror, expressed by a graceful elevation of the palms heavenward; "as bad as a cigar before breakfast."

"Cigars, Nero," whispered Bob; "a box of Ladesmas." Nero vanished.

It is mournful to reflect that we have so far departed from the manners and customs of our progenitors, that we actually follow the fashion of the present day, in drinking wine at eleven of the ante-meridian, and smoking before we are fairly up in the morning.

The tasteful and luxurious style in which the breakfast-room was fitted up induced Solgard to request that the gentlemen present might be indulged in a general survey of Asterley's *ménage*; and his intimation to that effect was cheerfully and promptly acquiesced in.

They first looked into the parlors, in which no expense had been spared to render the furniture rich and tasteful. Around the walls were suspended portraits of Bob's grandfather and grandmother, together with a maiden aunt, whose estate fell into his hands in consequence of her having taken a fancy to his blue eyes when he was a baby; also Bob's father, a remarkably handsome youth, in the costume of a British officer; finally, that of Bob himself, acknowledged by all present to be an excellent likeness; whereupon Eastlake gratuitously volunteered the information, that it was taken several years ago, when Asterley was quite a young man.

The library next in order came under examination, and was found to be well stored with books. The English classical writers, from the days of Chaucer down to Queen Anne's Augustan era, including Spenser, Drayton, Chatterton, James of Scotland, Donne, Parnell, and many others; a very extensive collection of all genera and species of novels and romances; a vast profusion of dramatic productions, — Shakespeare, Beaumont and Fletcher, and Ben Jonson, inclusive; Bibles of all sizes, from the venerable vellum-covered blackletter down to modern Roman character.

Our readers must not incautiously be persuaded, from the recapitulation of the various books in the library, that the owner thereof was exclusively a literary man, a mere "helluo librorum." It is true that the title of almost every work, and the date of its publication, were matters in which he possessed no inconsiderable depth. But we would wish it to be understood that Bob was eminently a practical man; and the uncut leaves of many of the volumes, as well as the compact arrangement and dusty covers of the whole, would tend to lend confirmation to this suggestion.

The library was further adorned with busts, both in bronze and marble — beautiful casts from celebrated models of Grecian sculpture, — and several choice paintings of the Flemish school, the subjects of which were principally bacchanalian; a pair of foils and masks on one side of the bookcase, and a guitar on the other, denoted still further the accomplishments of the proprietor. Three or four elbow-chairs of carved mahogany, with concave seats of black leather, stood as it were in attendance upon an octagonal table, covered with green cloth and supplied with writing materials, in the center of the apartment.

A staircase, springing from the noble hall in the middle of the building, led the way to the upper apartments; in three of which Asterley assured the company that the furniture and moveables had remained undisturbed since the time of his grandmother.

The fourth room, being the bedchamber of Asterley himself, had undergone various alterations. An air of epicurean luxury reigned throughout; the place of chairs was supplied by sofas, covered with blue damask — the toilet-table and appurtenances of lackered wood from China bowls and goblets from India — richly-framed plain and convex mirrors — a dressing-case of carved ivory — morning gowns in endless variety, and slippers of every hue.

MATHILDA DOUGLAS

The paintings and engravings that were suspended around the chamber were unfortunately of a character which would forbid our venturing upon too minute a description; none of the party, however, being emphatically moral men, we are compelled to admit that they refrained not from praising the beauty of the pictures, and the exquisite taste of the engraver.

Such, alas! is the depraved condition of morals in the present day, that our shop-windows and scrap-books display, for the edification of the rising generation, scenes and sketches of far more licentious and prurient tendency than any of those for which we would convict Asterley of indecorum; and could the Friends of those days now revisit the scenes of their colonial existence, they would doubtless groan in spirit, and grievously lament the unblushing wickedness of the age.

Asterley would have next submitted the kitchen and its purlieus to the " admiration of his friends, despite the irate countenance of Aunt Hebe, who planted herself, Cerberus-like, in the doorway to dispute the passage, had not Eastlake suddenly pleaded an indispensable engagement of immediate urgency; upon which Solgard and the others followed his example. And Bob no sooner beheld them fairly on their route along Penn Street, than he doffed his coat and waistcoat, kicked off his shoes, untied his cravat, unbuckled his knee-straps and turned in for a nap "

CHAPTER XVI.

**"If, when the darling maid is gone,
Thou dost not seek to be alone,
Rapt in a pleasing trance of tender wo,
And muse and fold thy languid arms,
Feeding thy fancy with her charms,
Thou dost not love— for love is nourished so."
Miss Aiken.**

"Heigh-ho! I am actually in love then with my own cousin Barbara!" Thus spoke the young hunter, soliloquizing, with his hand on his rifle, and his back to a tree, in a part of the forest from which Erigson House was partially visible, and whither he had, as he imagined, accidentally wandered. "Strange!" continued he, "that I, Marx Scheveling, should leave, twelve years ago, my old father in Amsterdam, and meet with him now in this part of the New World; and my little cousin too — good God! what a beautiful creature! Now, should my father discover me, he would immediately revive his original idea of a match between my cousin and myself; and of course the first interposition of her uncle's authority on my behalf would induce the dear girl to hunt up some reasonable, or some unreasonable, cause of dislike to my worthy self. It may be the best plan, therefore, to blind the old gentleman for a time, and save the lovely Barbara from domestic persecution; and if she be now heart-free, I may haply win her sweet love; and then will she listen, with dutiful acquiescence, her uncle's offer of his runaway son Marx."

"An excellent plan, and feasible, methinks, Master Marx!" uttered a voice close to his elbow, which Marx instantly recognized as that of Oxenstiern.

The chevalier stood beside him, equipped with rifle, powder-horn, and moccasins, his fine features flushed with exertion: he loved dearly to bring down a noble buck.

Marx was utterly astounded to find his Indian like vigilance so completely outwitted: the chevalier had closed upon him utterly unperceived. Ah! Dan Cupid! not only should sculptors bandage thine eyes, but thine ears also! Marx began to suspect now that he had seen nothing for the last fifteen minutes, and heard as little, until the voice of Oxenstiern disturbed his reverie; which thoughts now coming upon him, with the recollection that his soliloquy had been overheard, as implied in the chevalier's observation, made the young hunter blush exceedingly, so that his swarthy visage became suffused with a crimson glow.

"Think not," resumed the chevalier,' "that I have but just learned your name and lineage; the magic scene which you beheld at my house was intended to revive recollections of your early youth. As yet your father knows you not, nor has your gentle cousin any remembrance of you. I would fain advance your suit with the sweet girl; but, young, innocent, and guileless as she is, she has lately had cause to suspect that she was nearly in love without knowing it."

"Say you so!" exclaimed Marx, in a hurried and agitated voice; then affecting an air of calm indifference, he continued, "who is this favored mortal?"

"One, alas!" answered Oxenstiern, in a melancholy tone, "by whom such love as that of her warm heart can never be returned — one in whose bosom has for many long years been sealed up the memory of a deep and abiding passion — one who has never sought, and never can receive, the thrilling tribute of her affection— one, the companions of whose youth and manhood are equally numbered with the forgotten generations of the past; then steadily gazing on the wandering features of Marx, he added, "I am that lonely one! — But fear not, resumed the chevalier, in a more cheerful manner; "the damsel, methinks, hath reconsidered the subject; and January would be full loath to wed so fair a May, with such a Squire Damian as Marx Scheveling at hand."

Marx felt uneasy; the words of Oxenstiern, although apparently adapted to his consolation and encouragement, were calculated to convey an idea of control and influence over the object of his affections, which naturally aroused in the bosom of the young hunter emotions of mortification and wounded pride. What security had he (he mentally inquired of himself) that this mysterious individual might not change his intentions, and complete the fascination of the innocent girl, whom he had already admitted to have conceived for him, almost unconsciously, an incipient passion? And yet the views of the chevalier seemed fair and honorable; why else volunteer this information, and thereby ensure the vigilance of a young and jealous rival? — no bad motive could certainly induce a man of such extraordinary sagacity and acuteness to adopt such a line of conduct: and with a sudden revulsion of feeling, Marx determined to confide to Oxenstiern the history of his past life, and his plans for the future.

"Your noble frankness," commenced young Scheveling, "has inspired me with such entire confidence in the purity and friendliness of your intentions, that, if you feel any curiosity on such an unimportant subject, 1 will give you some account of the various scenes in which, either as actor or spectator, I have been interested since leaving my father's house at Amsterdam, when about twelve years of age."

"Nothing could give me greater pleasure," answered Oxenstiern, "than to listen to such a recital from your own lips."

Oxenstiern and the young hunter then seated themselves comfortably on a fallen tree, and the latter recited, as the former listened to,

THE TALE OF MARX SCHEVELING.

"It was, if I recollect aright, on the afternoon of a hot summer day in the year of grace 1720, that I persuaded, with much ado, the captain of the ship Santa Maria, bound for the Spanish Main, to consent that I should make my first voyage on board of his vessel, in the capacity of cabin-boy. This was sufficient; for although I suspected that he had no intention of taking me on board, from his naming the hour of three in the morning for my appearance ready equipped for the start, I was satisfied with having obtained his consent. About midnight I lowered myself with a rope from a window in the rear of the house, and with a beating heart hid myself on the quay behind some empty water-casks. The large town-bell chimed three; and ere the last stroke had ceased to echo through the dark and silent air, I was on board the Santa Maria. The crew were busy in getting up the anchor; the captain trod the deck with a bustling and active step; and I crouched down among some coiled and loose ropes — having some suspicion that the captain's promises were but intended to deceive me; and fearing that, if discovered, I might be put ashore without ceremony, I soon seized a favorable opportunity of gliding, unperceived, down into the cabin, whence I dropped quietly into the run, and soon fell asleep.

"In the morning I was aroused by one of the crew, who, in performing the functions of steward, having occasion to search for somewhat in the run, kicked me aside with an exclamation of surprise; and then, finding me wide awake, ordered me upstairs to report myself to the captain. On reaching deck I was struck with amazement at the scene around me. After weighing anchor, the wind had become fresh, and being favorable to our leaving port, the Santa Maria had cut through the waves like a dolphin, losing the low shores of Holland in a few hours, and now bearing on proudly in her rapid course over the free' ocean. The restless waves curling in endless succession, until they appeared to roll over the farthermost verge of the distant horizon — the bright sun glittering over the heaving mass of waters — the fresh land breeze blending with and driving along in its course the salt air of the sea — frolicsome flying-fish leaping from wave to wave — the straining of the cordage — the creaking of the masts — and the profane adjurations of the Spanish sailors, filled me, maugre the impending wrath of the captain, with tumultuous and rapturous delight.

"I was saluted by the captain with the complimentary epithets of scapegrace, devil's limb, and so forth; and after duly expatiating upon the enormity of my running off from my parents, during which he transferred me two or three times, by a tolerably vigorous application of the palm of his hand to my head, from one side of the deck to the other, he wound up by recommending me to make myself as useful as possible on board, and get 'the blind side of the doctor.'

"During the passage, I of course, at times, fell under the notice of all hands, from the captain to the cook's mate, — the latter a muscular dingy Ethiopian, by-the-by, who inspired me with more awe than any one on board: and I received the usual allowance of kicks and curses to which, *ex officio*, I was entitled. A little practice, however, taught me to dodge the former of my perquisites with much skill, and the latter I made it a point to return with interest; by which means I gradually became a general favorite on board, being, as I have since learned, for one so young, impudent and profane beyond example.

"Under such favorable auspices I commenced my career of active life; and was for some length of time, under such able instructors as the Spanish •marine never fails to furnish, employed in what they technically termed l sharpening my wits,' — in other words, acquiring a knowledge of, and perfecting myself in, all manner of vice and iniquity.

"I gradually acquired a reputation for hardihood, recklessness, enterprise, sagacity, and, above all, seamanship; and the consequence was, that at the. expiration of several voyages to Old Spain and back, I found myself stepping ahead of my Seniors rapidly, and at the age of eighteen, master's mate on board the brig Lealdad. I suppose I should have become a second Guzman d'Alfarache, had not an incident at that period totally changed the current of my ideas, and given a new turn to my prospects for the future.

"I was taking in cargo at Port au Prince for a Spanish market, standing as usual-on the quay to keep an eye on the crew, when I was struck with the singular appearance of a man, in whose uniform I recognized an officer in the British navy. His build indicated enormous strength, although of such low stature that his broad chest and massive shoulders bore gigantic disproportion to his dwarfish height; and a heavy jet-black beard, added to bushy locks of a similar hue, went to increase the. eccentricity of his general appearance. Upon inquiry I learned that he was in command of the armed brig Spitfire, bearing a commission from his majesty, and out upon a regular cruise against the pirates and buccaneers of the West Indies. He was then called Captain Teach, though he has since acquired no very enviable reputation as the notorious Blackbeard,

"Without knowing why, I regarded this officer with peculiar interest, and soon observed that he paid a marked attention to my movements. Our eyes often met, and 1 imagined that on such occasions he endeavored to throw into his countenance an expression of good-nature which his " rugged features were ill calculated to sustain. I had already a presentiment that our acquaintance would not be limited to this casual interchange of glances, and felt no surprise when the captain one day approached without ceremony and addressed me, —

"You are active, resolute, and a seaman!'

"I cannot recollect that my modesty was much disconcerted by this blunt and flattering assertion! for in those days I had no humble opinion of my own merits; I therefore coolly nodded an assent to his proposition.

"He continued, — 1 The lieutenant of the Spitfire was overhauled by the fever a few days since — take the vacancy — Spaniards abroad — hard knocks for hard dollars— tight craft — good Madeira — what say you?"

"I grasped his offered palm, and shook myself into a lieutenancy. The affair was not so easily settled with my owners as I anticipated; and no little demurrage took place before an amicable settlement was agreed upon. I provided a suitable mate for the Lealdad; and my captain filled my pockets with doubloons, that 1 might be suitably rigged out for a cruise.

"The Spitfire was a rakish brig, heavily sparred, flush deck, long and narrow, ten guns a side, and a complement of one hundred and forty men; mostly good-looking young fellows, though fifteen or twenty were considerably older, wearing grisly beards and a most truculent aspect.

"We took in water and fresh provisions, and stood out to sea, cruising about for more than a week, without meeting with anything worthy of being overhauled; when early one morning we discovered a strange sail, and gave chase. The stranger held her own pretty much through the -day, but towards nightfall it was evident that some change had occurred in her movements. She had now altered her course, and was bearing down upon us with all sail set. We prepared for action. As she came within hail we ran up the English flag and hailed her; her reply was a regular broadside, that peppered us severely; and then, amid the smoke that rolled up in clouds, the black flag, the banner of death, swung aloft.

"The buccaneers were commanded by a Spaniard, and principally of that nation — fought like devils, and gave no quarter — we gave them a Roland for their Oliver. When the action commenced, I experienced a thrill of nervous emotion that made me feel ashamed of myself; but as the enemy made an attempt to board, a cutlass swept so close by the tip of my nose that my wrath banished all nervous feeling, and I fought with a reckless hardihood that established my character on board the Spitfire.

"The result was, that we had but few prisoners to take on board, and lost the well-earned fruit of our exertions; before we could get out the treasure, the corsair went down, bow foremost, carrying with her eight of our own crew, who were busy in rummaging the hold, while I made my exit by the cabin window, and kept myself afloat until I was taken up by the Spitfire's jolly.

"Our prisoners were taken to Kingston and hung; and for some time this business was con " tinned, producing much honor, but no profit. The men grumbled, especially the grisly old ruffians, who generally messed together; and, somewhat to my surprise, the captain was evidently pleased with these symptoms of growing dissatisfaction.

"I hardly knew what to think of it, when Captain Teach showed the cloven foot. He had pressed me on a certain occasion to drink much more wine than usual, and when he perceived me fully charged with the grape, he abruptly proposed hoisting the black flag; the men, he observed, were ready for the change, and as to danger, he believed me to be no coward.

"I must have been delirious with intoxicating excitement, for I grasped his hand, and swore a most bitter oath to stand by him to the death.

"I stipulated, however, that none should be deprived of life— such as might be killed in attempting to repel us would be responsible for their foolhardiness; but mercy should always be shown, and women and children should not be so utterly plundered as other persons. Captain Teach smiled, but willingly took a solemn oath to respect my scruples; and filling up our glasses to the very brim, we drank success to free-traders, and I became unconscious of what followed.

"Many a galleon we took, and some well stored with platina; merchantmen supplied us with wines, spices, silks, and tobacco — a chase now and then from a British man-of-war, and a brush now and then with an English privateer, or a Spanish guardacosta. Ah! we led a right merry life in those days!

"It so fortuned that our harvest suddenly fell short — great dearth of vessels — the high seas yielded no increase; when 1 proposed what, though a novelty to me, was an ancient and well-established mode of levying contributions, — to wit, a descent upon the coast.

"Captain Teach honored the proposition with his approbation, and the plan was matured without delay. A populous village lying inland about three miles from a commodious harbor was selected; and, at my particular desire, orders were issued to sack the town with as little bloodshed as possible, and no women to be carried off but with their own consent.

"The arrangements were faultless. At the stated hour a hundred men, under my command nominally, but under the actual supervision and direction of a veteran buccaneer, whose familiarity with such forays, and knowledge of localities, entitled him to the privilege, surprised the town. A small garrison, whose military discipline, as well as their firelocks, had grown rusty for lack of use, fired upon the column, and were put to the sword, as well as others of the townsmen, whose valor got the better of discretion. The plunder was ample — great store of gold and silver. By some mistake, a noble mansion about the center of the town was fire" I, and the flames made rapid progress. As I approached the building I observed an old gentleman of most venerable appearance, struggling to disengage himself from the hands of some of my crew, who informed me that he was utterly bereft of reason, wishing to leap through the very midst of the fire, in hopes of saving a young and beautiful daughter, who had been unable, they presumed, to make tier way out through the smoke. Hardly had I ordered the men to release him, when, calling on his child in despairing accents, he leaped among the flames, tottered wildly for a few moments, and fell suffocated among the smoldering rains.

"Like an echo to his dying cry, a shrill shriek came, as it were, from the midst of the burning pile. Good God, sir! it was the young girl herself! It fell upon the ear a thrilling cry of supplication and anguish — I rushed forward, but the eddying smoke and hot ashes? blinded and nearly stifled me, and I staggered back into the open air. Refreshed, I hastily snatched a crape veil from the head of a Cartronne near me, and bound it over my face, when that cry came again— even the *'vieux routier,'* who had followed Morgan in many a bloody venture, was moved.

"Through clouds of whirling vapor, dashing against blackened walls and mounting the still uninjured stairway, 1 made my way into the upper apartments. There, in a room which, though surrounded by flames, remained almost unscathed by the conflagration, lay a young creature, molded in a form of surpassing loveliness. Taking off my veil, I bent over her to ascertain if life yet remained; when she unclosed her eyes, and gave a look of grateful confidence that I shall never forget She held firmly clasped to her bosom a casket of ebony curiously inlaid with plates of gold, which, as I afterward discovered, contained a lock of hair, and rich jewels of rare and almost incredible value. Lifting her gently in my arms, I conveyed her out of the burning edifice — protecting her person as much as possible, and taking advantage of a partial retreat of the fiery element to effect the passage without injury.

"She died four days out, leaving me the remembrance of her charms, and the casket to which I have already alluded, which latter bequest I committed to the charge of an old woman of St. Eustatia; who has doubtless transferred it, by this time, to more prudent hands, for she has left the island, and is supposed to have settled, with a little granddaughter of her own, somewhere in the Colonies."

"Do you recollect the granddaughter's name?" inquired Oxenstiern.

"Not exactly — but Sally or Susan; I think it was Susan.

"After this adventure," continued young Scheveling," we lost all discretion; and instead of showing a clean pair of heels to a Spanish frigate, that was descried one night by moonlight, standing her own course under easy sail, we clapped on canvass and made after her as if she were some rich carrack. She appeared to take no notice of us as we approached, and I believe that all hands and the cook were snoring in their hammocks — for upon our firing a gun we could distinctly observe an unusual stir and bustle on board. As we came within proper distance, the guns double-shotted and matches lighted, we let her have a broadside that did considerable execution; and we repeated the dose twice, much to her annoyance, before her preparations were completed to return the compliment. At last she got ready, and let drive at us. I thought the Spitfire actually trembled as she took it; our men fell before the iron shower, and splinters flew in all directions.

Finding her too heavy to give and take on anything like even terms, we ran aboard of her, grappled, yardarm to yard arm, made fast, and attempted to take her by boarding.

"The commander of the frigate was a fiery Castilian, and became absolutely furious at out presumption; shouting fiercely to his men, he at" tacked us, three' to one. Despite our desperation, we were forced, actually crowded back into the Spitfire. In this situation, I beheld Captain Teach in the utmost danger. He was alone on the frigate, and personally engaged with four determined men, who were resolutely bent on his destruction. Although he contended like a fiend incarnate, he was overmastered by their united strength; as he gave way I rushed forward to the rescue — they held down his arms and legs, knelt upon his breast, and a dagger gleamed aloft to send his soul to purgatory. Two pistols I fired at once — both balls did their errand — the dagger dropped harmlessly on deck with the hand that raised it, and Captain Teach felt his right arm suddenly freed. As the other two started to their feet Captain Teach did the same, and by dint of main force we made good our retreat. We then cast off our grappling irons, and the engagement ceased as by mutual consent. We had ascertained that nothing could be done with the frigate, and she was willing to be quietly rid of such a troublesome customer.

"Captain Teach said not a word about the assistance which I had rendered him, although I afterward discovered that he had never forgotten it.

"About a month after this engagement an incident occurred, the result of which was my total separation from the buccaneers, and a solemn vow of vengeance against Captain Teach, or Blackbeard, as he then began to be denominated, which, by the holy Apostles! I am yet to accomplish.

"I had observed, for some time, a growing disposition among the crew to indulge in cruel and wanton barbarity towards the individuals who now and then fell into their power. I had, in fact, become in a measure disgusted with the system of indiscriminate plunder which we exercised, as habit wore off the pleasure of novelty; and although in nowise scrupulous myself in regard to the distinction between *meum* and *tuum*, I discouraged at all times the propensity to add insult to misfortune. My interference on several such occasions created no little dissatisfaction; but my authority had never been openly disputed, and I eared little that it was privately murmured at.

"We captured a Spanish merchantman, bound to Cadiz, which had been chartered by a Marquis Santa Flor to convey himself and lady to Spain. The crew made no resistance, but the marquis, driven to desperation at the probable fate that awaited his young and lovely wife, was determined to die in her defense. He stood at the head of the companion-way, pale, calm, and resolute.

He was summoned to surrender, and smiled bitterly — they closed upon him, but before he was cut down, four of our best men lay dead before him. As he lay weltering in his gore, a beautiful young creature rushed upon deck, and beholding her husband dead, fell upon his body with exclamations of heart-piercing anguish. When she arose, she lifted her fair hands towards heaven, and invoked the curse of the Almighty on his murderers. I shrank back instinctively as she pronounced the solemn adjuration; but Blackbeard, approaching with an air of sneering levity, whispered in her pure ear some villainous ribaldry, at which she drew back with a most sovereign contempt and defiance depicted in her noble features. "You shall smile anon!" said Blackbeard.

"Here, Garcias! Manuel, if she will not walk, carry her into my cabin."

"Touch her not!' said I, as the men approached to seize her; "Captain Teach," I continued, confronting Black beard, I claim to protect this lady from violence and insult, and I beg, as a particular favor to myself, that she be allowed to continue her voyage without further molestation."

"The lady gazed on me as I spoke with an incredulous air, as if surprised to meet with a man among so many demons.

"So ho, youngster! you would be merciful, would you?" and Blackbeard knitted his brows into a terrific frown, as he added, "Remember! mutiny is death!"

"He nodded to the men with a significant gesture towards the lady, and they seized her without more ado. She, poor lady, turned upon me an imploring glance, that might have moved anyone but a buccaneer; and I acknowledged its power by darting forward, striking down Garcias with my clenched hand, and flinging Manuel, who was a slight-made youth of about my own years, to the distance of ten feet from the spot.

"At this Blackbeard let drive a horrible oath, whirled out his cutlass, and attacked me. I was not backward, and what I lacked in strength 1 fully made up for in activity— in short, I evidently had the advantage, when his myrmidons pressed on to his assistance — a handspike felled me from behind, and in a moment I was handcuffed at the mercy of my opponent. They raised me, and Blackbeard approached, cocked a pistol, and pressed the muzzle against my forehead. His appearance was truly horrible — his eyes glaring with savage ferocity, and a deep cut on his left cheek from my cutlass streaming with blood. He observed something, I believe, of a haughty defiance in my countenance, and, withdrawing the pistol, issued some orders in a low chuckling tone. These were instantly obeyed f and I must confess, that when I beheld the preparations for running me up to the yardarm, I felt, for the first time, the fear of death: a ball burying itself in your brain, or a sabre cleaving you to the chine, are actual luxuries, compared to the sensations produced by the fitting of a rope around your neck, and the peculiarly scientific adaptation of the knot under your left ear.

"Blackbeard looked on with vindictive exultation, while some older buccaneers, with right goodwill, led me to the proper position, and garnished my ankles with a thirty-two pound shot, to give due efficacy to the swing. All was ready, the rope manned, and drawn taught for the signal, and my neck beginning to twist from the tension of the cord, when Blackbeard directed the ministers of his vengeance to slacken the line, and cast off the tackling. He then addressed me.

"'c You did me service, young man, on board that Spanish frigate — that saves you from a hempen neckcloth; but, lest we disagree hereafter, let us part company.'

"With these sneering remarks, he had the longboat of the merchantman lowered, untied -my arms, and bade me jump aboard. I had no choice, and obeyed, after cursing the villain to his face in the most energetic forms of imprecation, which only excited his laughter, without in the least degree awaking his angry feelings.

"As if willing to prove his grateful remembrance of my services, by affording me some prospect of escape, Blackbeard supplied the boat with a barrel of pilot-bread and a keg of water; and as she parted from the ship, some benevolent individual hove after me a cutlass, which I contemplated with great satisfaction.

"A current of about two knots drifted me slowly away; and when at a considerable distance, I imagined that I could distinguish coming over the rolling: waters the plaintive cries and agonizing shrieks of a female. This was, perhaps, naught but the workings of a distempered fancy, for my brain was heated almost to delirium; and although it now appears as a dream, I can recollect that I grasped my cutlass, raved wildly and madly for revenge, and finally sunk, in a state of complete exhaustion and insensibility, into the bottom of the boat.

"How long I slept I know not, but I awoke just as the sun rose on the waters, bathing the east in a flood of golden light. I was alone upon the ocean; yet the fresh morning breeze came gently over the waves, the billows sparkled in the sun, and my heart felt free and buoyant.

"For three days and nights my bark pursued her solitary course on the deep, and on the morning of the fourth day I discovered land far to the west."

Here the speaker suddenly ceased, and listened attentively; he grasped his rifle — Oxenstiern did the same – a noble buck came bounding through the forest — both levelled — fired — and a single report echoed through the woods; for a moment the stag stood perfectly still — bounded high into the air, and fell dead on the spot.

"A good shot you have made," said Marx.

"Your rifle did the deed," returned the chevalier; "I aimed for the eye."

"And I," continued Marx, "under the fore-shoulder.

The distance was considerable; and when the hunters examined the deer, both shots were found to have taken effect, in the very parts indicated by the respective marksmen.

To settle the question of property, Oxenstiern proposed that young Scheveling should dine with him on the venison in question; and this being readily acceded to, it was concluded that the remainder of Scheveling's history should be deferred until a more convenient season, the chevalier professing to take exceeding interest in the story and, shouldering their game, they departed.

CHAPTER XVII.

**"One that is sick o' th" pout had rather
Groan so in perplexity, than be cured
By the sure physician Death."**
Cymbeline.

Major Scheveling began to find that long-continued indulgence in Madeira and Burgundy produced its usual effect, the gout: twinges of this aristocratic affection became more frequent, and the old gentleman somewhat testy. On such occasions, Barbara felt for his sufferings, — consoled, soothed, and sympathized with him. She would read to him some pleasant book by the hour, talk to him, sing for him, and beguile his pain by her very best music.

Then, as he got better, she would lead him into the garden, cull the prettiest and sweetest flowers for a nosegay, choose the driest paths, shelter him from the high wind and hot sun, and hurry him into the house ere the heavy dew of evening fell upon the earth. Let her uncle, under the influence of a violent paroxysm, be ever so petulant and hasty, or ever so crusty and querulous, her kind and gentle forbearance never for a moment gave way, but with a light step and cheerful voice she moved around his couch a "ministering angel."

An unusually severe attack had driven the major to his elbow-chair; confinement he ever disliked, and it rendered him irritated and splenetic. He was scolding the servants in no measured language: this they bore with all consideration — for, the fit past, a kinder and more indulgent master never was. He was finding fault also with Barbara, whom in his heart he loved so dearly that his soul wrapped itself op in her existence.

It may appear strange, that an old soldier, familiar with battles and death, should be so driven from his equanimity by mere personal suffering; but the fact is constant, that gout and nervous irritability cannot be parted. Sir Thomas More, who laid down his head so calmly on the block, is said to have thrashed his wife and children all around whenever he had a fit of the toothache; and we are informed, upon the authority of Geoffrey of Monmouth, that the "venerable Bede," being "seized with a vehement pain in the face" (probably a species of tic douloureux), "which endured for three days and three nights, became, in that space, as it were, utterly dement, enacting such things as may not readily be spoken of."

This and other testimony have we to this effect Oxenstiern called to see the major, and found him as above described. "My dear sir," inquired the chevalier, approaching the sufferer very tenderly, and modulating his usually cheerful voice to a tone of commiseration and sympathy, "how are you today? Anything I can do for you? what would you like?"

"Damnation!" exclaimed the veteran, the application being intended, not for the chevalier, but elicited by a momentary and most piquant twinge.

Barbara blushed, not for herself, but for her uncle; such energetic expression she had never before heard him make use of: in fact, although an old soldier, he always carefully eschewed aught approaching to profanity in the presence of his niece — the word slipped out in extreme pain.

"Barbara, my dear girl," continued the major, as the pain subsided, "you must overlook my impoliteness — I will not repeat it."

The beautiful creature, in token of her willingness to forgive this involuntary breach of decorum, gently passed her arm around the old soldier's neck, and kissed him. This time she felt no confusion as she met the eye of Oxenstiern, — she wondered why she had ever done so; and the chevalier, as if pleased with the change, met her glance with a benevolent, meaning smile of satisfaction, that told Barbara, as plain as words could convey it, that she had done well in correcting the error of her imagination.

"Now, my child, arrange the chessboard; and tf the chevalier purposes nothing of a more agreeable nature for his amusement, I challenge him to essay whether the gout hath or hath not left me totally void of vigor."

Thus spoke the veteran; and Oxenstiern professing his readiness for a contest with his ancient antagonist, Barbara produced the chessboard, drew the table up to her uncle's couch, placed a chair for Oxenstiern, and seated herself hard-by to watch the progress of the combat.

"Methinks, my good sir," said Oxenstiern, "that in consideration of the disadvantage under which you labor at present, I can afford you the queen's pawn."

"Gout or no gout, chevalier," exclaimed the major, "I warrant me that I give you a checkmate in less than — eh! eh!"— and the old gentleman drew in his breath, and gritted his teeth amazingly.

The game became interesting, and Barbara —who usually identified herself with the play of the chevalier, rejoiced in his success and lamented his defeat — now, by a natural sympathy with the afflicted, took sides with her uncle, and observed, with much pleasure, that his judgment, instead of being at all impaired by confinement, was actually more acute, discriminating, and comprehensive than usual He pressed the chevalier with irresistible vigor, forced him to act altogether upon the defensive, and completed his triumph by a brilliant coup de main.

Oxenstiern threw himself back in his chair, passed his hand over his brow (the day was warm), looked away from the chessboard, and observed, — "That wild son of yours, major? have you heard of him since his elopement?"

"Poor boy!" mournfully replied the major, "I fear he is dead; the little rogue used to call Barbara here his sweetheart, and I always intended her for his wife— wouldst have him, girl?"

"Certainly, uncle, an he would ask me!" exclaimed Barbara, with a smiling air, being nowise disposed to dampen her uncle's cheerful feelings.

"It is a match!" exclaimed the veteran, with much more gravity than his niece thought suitable to the occasion, adding, "I will answer for Marx, that he fulfills his part of the contract; and I take you, Chevalier Oxenstiern, as sponsor to my fair niece — would to God that Marx knew of this!"

"Marx may claim his bride sooner than you imagine," replied Oxenstiern; "I have consulted the aspect of the planetary intelligences, and if they deceive me not, Marx Scheveling is alive at this moment, and will ere long meet his father."

As Oxenstiern uttered these prophetic word, Major Scheveling covered his face with his hands, and after he had finished, remained for a short time in the same position. He then raised his eyes to heaven with an expression of grateful feeling, that drew tears into the eyes of Barbara, and told the chevalier that his words had poured balm into the wounded heart of a forsaken father.

Barbara had at first regarded the conversation as a piece of harmless levity. Then, as it became more serious, she experienced unwonted embarrassment — her imaginary acceptance of a cousin, who seemed to her equally imaginary, had been construed, with equal seriousness by her uncle and the chevalier, as a solemn plighting of her troth to the son of Major Scheveling; who, according to the declaration of the chevalier, would, tn propriA perosond shortly make his appearance.

She might like him, and -she might not; perhaps he might not fancy her — there was some consolation in that idea: perhaps he was already married in some foreign country to some dark-eyed Spanish beauty, it might be, or graceful French girl; or, if wandering to more distant climes, a mandarin's daughter, or a Mexican princess, or an Indian squaw might claim Marx as husband. Any of r these probabilities would settle the matter comfortably, and leave her at liberty to accept the devotion of any admirer who might please her fancy. To do this, he must needs be young, bold, active, good-looking, and accomplished. (The image of the young hunter rose before her imagination, and she blushed at the treachery of her own conscious fancy.)

As if Oxenstiern divined the subject of her thoughts, he suddenly turned to Barbara, and observed, —

"Our young friend, the nameless hunter, to whom we are all under such obligations, turns out to be a Mr. Sylvan; and as he has consented to divide his time equally between me and his hermitage, I hope that your uncle and yourself may find his acquaintance as agreeable as I think it likely to prove to myself."

Barbara replied with becoming grace and modesty; hoping that her uncle might find in Mr. Sylvan an agreeable companion, and acknowledging her obligations to the hunter in expressions so unaffectedly sincere and grateful, that Oxenstiern was exceedingly pleased thereat.

The chevalier did observe, however, that as he mentioned the name of the hunter, a scarcely perceptible blush tinged the features of Miss Scheveling, which he took for granted prognosticated nothing unfavorable to Mr. Sylvan; the more a? she became somewhat absent, and answered to her uncle's remarks in a manner that indicated the feet of her mind being too much pre-occupied to gather the exact purport of his observations.

"Barbara, my love, who went to the city, Fritz or the gardener?"

"Yes, sir, about an hour since."

"I cannot bear very distinctly, my dear; did you say the gardener?"

"He is very well to-day, sir" but his wife is complaining."

Barbara looked full into her uncle's face as die delivered these answers to his inquiries, and seemed nevertheless unobservant of the surprise which was now clearly depicted on his visage. Oxenstiern with difficulty repressed his laughter.

"I would crave to be informed, Miss Scheveling, whether you are awake or asleep."

The tone of measured rigidity in which the major requested this information fully aroused his niece from her partial reverie. She started, blushed, and stole a glance at the chevalier, which, happily for her, he did not meet, as she replied,

—

"My dear uncle, I believe I was dreaming."

"Dreaming about your cousin Marx, I warrant me."

"Not so, indeed, dear uncle;" and she shook her head as if in defiance of his attempt to fathom her thoughts, while

Oxenstiern shrewdly divined that the major was right and his niece wrong, unwittingly to both.

The major never doubted for a moment the correctness of his own conjecture; and, pleased with the plan of matrimonial happiness that he had now so satisfactorily arranged between his son Marx and his well-beloved niece, and also much consoled and cheered bv the prediction of the chevalier, whose words had always merited the utmost confidence" he proposed gayly that Oxenstiern, in fault of his own services, should escort Barbara to town, where she proposed making a few visits and some purchases.

Barbara disclaimed any intention of doing so, -while her uncle was still so disabled as to require her assistance; but the old gentleman, at the moment rendered more energetic by a gouty twinge, overcame her scruples by a few laconic observations, of so terse and decided a quality that, fearing lest further opposition might lead to some indecorous exclamation, she prudently acquiesced.

The chevalier and Miss Scheveling entered town together, admiring the beauties of nature with no lack of entertaining and rational conversation; and passing up Penn Street, received a bow of infinite gravity from Asterley's factotum Nero, who failed not to present himself in his usual guise of a white apron.

In Front Street they were saluted in passing by Doctor Eastlake and his trusty comrade Bob Asterley; the latter of whom could not refrain from turning back several times, to admire the exquisite form of Miss Scheveling.

"I must marry that girl, Eastlake," ejaculated Bob; M by all that is lovely 1 I never met with such a voluptuous figure. Take care, my lad, you'll break your neck I"

The little urchin to whom the latter portion of Bob's apostrophe applied was making vigorous efforts to stand upon his head; and stopping for a moment to survey the philanthropic individual, made no reply, but resumed his labors.

"I would marry her myself," observed Eastlake, M sooner than suffer her to fall into the hands of that reckless libertine Robert Asterley; but happily there is no necessity for the sacrifice— she would never have you, Bob!"

To this savage remark, Bob, who was thinking •f something else, which at the moment attracted his entire attention, made no reply.

At the bridge over Dock-water, Barbara stopped to look at the anglers, who were patiently abiding the biting of the fish; and Oxenstiern pointed out the various species as they were drawn from their native element on the deceitful hook.

The sport was not then, as in our degenerate days, confined to that specific class of idlers who now frequent our wharves and steamboat-landings; but the old substantial citizens of those days deemed it in nowise derogatory to their characters to participate therein. At the moment that Barbara looked over the parapet, Thomas Hasell " (Mayor of Philadelphia), who was sitting on a log projecting a few feet from the southern pier, was pulling up a large sized mullet

"You have good sport to-day, friend Hasell."

cried the chevalier, looking with some envy at the large fish which Thomas deliberately unhooked.

"Nine such as this within the hour," returned the major, putting on, as he spoke, fresh bait, and heaving to the extent of his rod.

Why is it that angling has been condemned as a cruel and barbarous amusement, and yet ever hath been the best solace, the favorite pastime of mild, inoffensive, gentle, quiet, peaceable, just, and good men? Was ever a better neighbor, a truer Christian, a meeker man, a steadier friend, than Izaak Walton? and what shall we say of that excellent scholar, that upright judge, that courteous knight. Sir Charles Cotton? Ever have the disciples of the piscatory art been known by their courteous learning, their gentle demeanor, their noble liberality, their Job-like patience. Their hooks humanely pierce the insensible bodies of factitious flies, and even worms are put on. with tender consideration.

Their diet is frugal — their drink water — their imaginations pure — their souls untainted; they sin but little, for they care neither for wine nor women. An they, catch fish, they are content — an they catch them not, there is more for to-morrow. Every month in the year hath its appropriate delight. January affordeth its tench, its grayling, or umber. February the same. The pike, the salmon, and the trout reward the angler who braves the blustering winds of March. April yieldeth its bream, its barbel, and its tiny smelts. From merry May to cold December the angler hath his chub, his roach, his gudgeon, his perch, his carp, his dace, his Weak, and store of other fish. Truly, it is a wholesome and a pleasant science, and may not be compared with the boisterous, rude, and noisy sports of hawking, hunting, and the like.

Leaving for a short time the fair Barbara to profit by the instructions of the chevalier in the art of angling, we must now transfer the reader to the mansion of Madam Christine Markham, which, as has been already stated, stood in Second Street, a little way beyond Christ Church.

There, in a back room handsomely furnished, on a sofa which would not be considered highly luxurious at the present day, although covered with rich chintz, sat the beauteous widow, armed with an enormous India fan, which served coquetishly at times to conceal her countenance from the gaze of Captain Solgard, who sat at the other extremity of the sofa.

The gallant captain had sat out scores of visitors with admirable endurance, and had marveled much at the refined tact with which the widow paid her compliments to her various guests. He had viewed with pleasure the measured and courteous ceremony with which Doctor Eastlake tempered his visit; but beheld with something like a pang of jealous feeling a little flirtation into which the inconstant bat fascinating Christine entered with the indefatigable Asterley. But as Bob departed eventually without farther notice from the fair enslaver than she bestowed upon other guests, Solgard's jealousy diminished sensibly, and an expressive glance from his mistress re-established her empire.

When the last visitor departed, Christine and her lover remained for some time silent: he gazing upon her with a mute devotion, that, however flattering to a lady, performs fewer miracles than voice and eloquent gesture; and she, with bashful hesitation, every now and then stealing a modest glance, as if she were actually afraid to break the silence.

This singular behavior of Madam Markham had such an effect upon Solgard, that he found much uncertainty in his mind in regard to the most appropriate mode of renewing the conversation; and after balancing for some time the comparative merits of gayety and sentiment, he decided that the latter was 9 better adapted to the present humor of his mistress: so, composing his visage to a serious and passionate earnestness, he kneeled before the lovely widow, and had commenced a most plaintive declaration of his despairing love, when he was completely interrupted by her dropping the fan, leaning back upon the sofa, clapping her hands together with delight, and making the saloon absolutely ring with the music of her mirth.

"Pardon me, captain," cried she, as soon as she had recovered sufficient breath to speak; "but I will absolutely die with laughter, if you enact the sentimental and despairing inamorato any longer. Prithee resume that air of modest assurance, that so well becomes a son of Mars. I had rather be taken by storm than be blockaded and starved into surrender"

The gay, nonchalant air of Madam Markham relieved Captain Solgard wonderfully from his embarrassment; and improving on the hint she kindly gave, he pushed the courtship with martial vigor — poured forth his vows of passion and adoration in bold and energetic language; and, not content with the little hand which was abandoned to his kisses, sought the ruby lips of the struggling beauty, and clasping her pretty form in his arms, swore by all the bright gods of Olympus that she should remain thus imprisoned until she consented to become his bride.

"Will you not release me!" exclaimed she with an affectation of indignation, which she did not actually feel, and a well-feigned struggle, which her jailer punished by a shower of kisses.

u I care not, dear Christine, if you refuse me, for then I hold you thus forever; these arms thy prison cage, and these lips thy punishment."

As he spoke, he suited the action to the word; and his prisoner, pouting her pretty lip in affected disdain, acceded to the ternis of enlargement.

Solgard was so enraptured when his mistress finally consented to be his, that he forgot to relinquish his beloved captive, and uttered such a tor" rent of grateful nonsense, that it was some time before she could get an opportunity of reminding her lover of the terms of the compact.

At this moment Oxenstiern and Miss Scheveling, whom we left superintending the operations of the fishermen on Dockwater, entered the room. Neither Madam Markham nor Solgard heard the door opened (which, however, can excite no surprise), and the chevalier and Barbara even reached the centre of the apartment; and guessing at the state of affairs, were on the point of retiring, when the widow observed them, and disengaging herself with a deep blush from the arms of, Solgard, constrained herself to receive them with an appearance of great cordiality, although an embarrassment, widely differing from that excited by an agreeable surprise " wu plainly enough to be seen in her .flushed features.

Solgard, on the contrary, made no effort to appear polite; but, utterly absorbed in the contemplation of hit own happiness, remained precisely in the position which he had occupied when the widow sprang from his arms, noticing neither Oxenstiern nor Miss Scheveling, but watching, with a countenance of smiling delight, the confusion, the blushes, and the graceful movements of his mistress.

At length he arose, and approaching the party who were now calmed down into the discussion of some trifling topic, such as by a general and acknowledged want of interest always produces a proper equanimity in the minds of the interlocutors, he grasped Oxenstiern by the hand, and exclaimed, —

"Give me joy, chevalier! perseverance has conquered the long indomitable Christine; she has fairly consented to be mine 1"

"Not so, forsooth," cried the lovely widow; u my life was threatened by this desperado, so that in fact no consent of mine, but sheer compulsion, has brought me to such a pass; however, as promises must be kept, I shall marry him, and torment him as much as possible for his treachery."

Solgard looked more pleased than ever as she thus threatened his future comfort; and Barbara, instinctively judging that the lovers might have some subjects to discuss which were more agreeably spoken of without the intervention of a third person, withdrew, in company with the chevalier; and meeting on the way home Miss Rachel Curtis, the whole town, in the course of an hour, rang with the interesting intelligence that Madam Markham, who had received so many hearts without returning them to their owners, ^as to be carried off at last by the gallant commander of the *Greyhound*,

CHAPTER XVIII.

"In eastern climes they talk in flowers,
And tell in a garland their loves and cares — '
Each blossom that blooms in their garden bowers
On its leaves a mystic language bears.'"
Percival.

The townsmen thought It rather singular that the *Greyhound*, having been sent out expressly to capture the notorious Blackbeard, had remained so long in port without any apparent efforts to accomplish this desirable object. But more circumstances than one conspired to produce this state of repose. In the first place, it proved a matter of far more difficulty than Solgard had anticipated to procure any information touching the movements of the buccaneer; and secondly, those sources from which intelligence seemed most likely to be obtained proved so fallacious, that he was led strongly to suspect the existence in many quarters of a disposition not unfavorable to these outlaws.

Another cause, and perhaps, although the feast ostensible, yet the most effective one, of his inactivity, was the ardent and really sincere passion which he had conceived for the beautiful Madam Markham. Accustomed, as he had ever been, to meet with favor from those beauties to whom, in the gay spirit of universal gallantry, he had hitherto paid his vows of homage and adoration, he became interested in a beauty who, like himself, considered love as a pretty amusement, and suffered not her heart to take an interest in the game.

So long had the lovely widow been in the habit of trifling with Dan Cupid, that she was unconscious of the growing tenderness of her feelings towards the gallant captain, until an invariable degree of uneasiness, almost approaching to jealous fear, of which she was conscious whenever Solgard endeavored to render himself particularly agreeable to Miss Scheveling, warned her of her own danger.

Then, as if to punish her for her previous indifference to the sufferings of her admirers, love took absolute possession of her heart; and as Solgard was ever gay, lively, and disposed to an agreeable flirtation under all and any circumstances, she had many an opportunity of paying the penalty due to her past misdeeds.

The interest which Solgard began to take in the fascinating coquette also grew more powerful every day; his adoration became less complimentary, but more real — his happy despair was converted into an apprehensive hope — his eyes became more, and his lips less, eloquent — never doubting, however, of his final success, as he contemplated his address, his rank, and his person. His pride, for the most part, guarded him against jealousy; although at times, as we have seen in the case of Doctor Eastlake, it could suffer great excitement.

Hardly had the widow accepted Solgard, and plighted to him her solemn troth, when the happy man became restless and uneasy. The purport of his visit to the shores of America started up, with all the vividness of a long-forgotten idea, before him; and although it had been nearly lost sight of during the ardor of his courtship, yet, now that the piquancy of the chase was diminished by the game being finally run down, his mind reverted to his primary intentions; and without more ado he directed Lieutenant Curt to make preparation for a cruise.

All was life and activity on board the *Greyhound*; and precisely one week from the day when Madam Markham entered into terms of capitulation, she put to sea.

As matters of more importance are likely to press upon us shortly, we purposely pretermit a detailed account of her passage down the river — a very singular quarrel of Captain Solgard with the pilot, and the last view of the capes, which gave rise, in Solgard's bosom, to sentimental feelings.

We must also in brief relate, that after being out for a week, and coming in sight of the Hole in the Wall, the *Greyhound* fell in with two pirates. That upon being summoned to surrender, the "Merry Christmas," commanded by the well-known Sprigg, opened her fire upon the *Greyhound*; and that her consort, of which it was afterward ascertained that Blackbeard himself had the command, followed up the attack by assuming a raking position athwart the bows of the British man-of-war. A desperate engagement ensued, in which the "Merry Christmas" was taken; but, owing to the rigging of the *Greyhound* having been so much shot away, her consort escaped. The loss of the *Greyhound* in killed and wounded was severe; and after repairing damages, she bore away for the capes, with Sprigg and fifteen of his men in irons.

The citizens of Philadelphia awaited with no inconsiderable degree of interest the return of the *Greyhound*; some indulging the hope that her cruise would be successful, and others shaking their heads doubtfully, as fearing that Blackbeard might be too much for the British captain.

Madam Markham was of that class who indulged in sanguine anticipations. She had heard, it is true, of the desperate valor of Blackbeard, — but her lover was equally brave, his crew was better disciplined, they fought in a better cause, and their guns were two to one. These considerations she urged in conversation with Barbara Scheveling, who, having learned from Oxenstiern more of the character of the buccaneer, stated it as her belief that Blackbeard never would be taken alive, and horrified the fair widow with the probability of her lover being blown up as soon as he boarded the pirate, in which case the desperate rover had threatened to fire his own magazine.

Marx Scheveling was standing hard by as Barbara spoke, and the widow appealed to him for consolation.

"Pray, Mr. Sylvan, is Blackbeard such a desperado? "You have seen him, have you not?"

"Is he a short man?" inquired Marx.

"Very short," replied the widow, — "very broad, and a huge beard."

"I rather think," resumed Marx, "that I must have seen the man once in Porto Rico; and his appearance, if I recollect aright, would fully confirm the impressions entertained by Miss Scheveling touching his character."

There was nothing like consolation in these remarks, and the widow's confidence in the success of her lover suffered considerable abatement

At this moment Master Nicolas Salomen entered the house of Madam Markham, in which this consultation had been held, and approached the party, holding in each hand a cat by the nape of the neck.

"Prithee, Master Salomen!" cried the two ladies simultaneously, "what are you doing with those poor cats?"

"Curious! curious! curious!" responded Nicolas; and he looked first at one and then at the other of the animals in his clutch, with something of that paternal pride which a father feels when his child gives indications of precocious talent.

"This cat," continued Master Salomen, holding forward a venerable mouser in his right hand, "neglected, peradventure a week since, its accustomed nutriment; wandering hither and thither with a melancholy and uneasy aspect. At times also it would look me in the face, methought, with a supplicating glance. Thus it held for a space of two days, during which Jeroboam ate nothing; but on the third day, even as I craved a blessing at table, Jeroboam sprang upon my left shoulder, and opening his mouth as wide as possible, lo! a cork sticking fast in his gullet! *Haud mora, nee requies.* I immediately extracted the same, and without more ado he fell to and ate. This morning Jeroboam scratched at my chamber-door, brought in this kitten by the neck, end laying it on the floor, set upon his haunches to await my proceedings. Certes, the poor creature needed aid, for a large fish-bone had got entangled in the swallowing thereof. *Quid nultis?* I drew out the bone — *in cujus rei testimonium*, here be the witnesses themselves — curious! curious!" And, nodding his head to confirm the story, Master Nicolas departed to make known more extensively the marvelous sagacity of Jeroboam.

"He is a worthy man, but somewhat eccentric," observed Madam Markham, smiling on the retreating figure of the pedagogue. "But hark!" added she, "what is that ?"as the voice of a deep-mouthed cannon came booming up the river.

Her color went and came, and her bosom heaved tumultuously as gun after gun echoed along the shore.

"'Tis the *Greyhound*!'" exclaimed Marx.

"'Tis Solgard!" whispered Christine to herself.

"Have they taken Blackbeard, Mr. Sylvan?" inquired Barbara.

"I will ascertain, Miss Scheveling, as soon as possible, for your information" replied Marx; adding, in a voice inaudible to Barbara, "Holy Virgin! no! not for a Spanish galleon should be escape me thus!"

"Shall we to the river, fair ladies?" continued Marx.

"I think," responded the lovely widow, tossing back her head with a show of affected reserve, "that I shall wait until he — that is to say, until Captain Solgard — I mean that — don't you think it too warm to go just now?"

"Nay," replied Marx, "it needeth not — for here is one that hath advised himself touching the natter, I warrant roe."

As he spoke, the Chevalier Oxenstiern entered and verified his prognostic.

"I give you much joy, fair dames," said he, on the return of our gallant protector Captain Solgard; and albeit he hath not yet laid hands upon Blackbeard,"— here Oxenstiern noticed the eyes of Marx to sparkle with undisguised pleasure, — "yet hath he compassed the well-known Sprigg, and of his crew some fifteen."

Something like a shout of triumph was heard in the streets as Oxenstiern concluded; and Madam Markham, being now particularly on the alert, ran to the porch, followed by Miss Scheveling and the two cavaliers, the latter proceeding at a more sober pace, in proportion to their curiosity.

Just as they all got to the door, the pirates, chained two and two, crossed Second Street, on their way to the jail, guarded by a detachment of marines from the *Greyhound*, and accompanied by a cortege of sailors, idlers, negroes, and Indian boys, shouting over their fallen enemies.

It was singular to observe how suddenly the shout ceased whenever Sprigg, whose truculent features garnished with but one eye, gave him a very Polypheme aspect, turned his petrifying gaze upon his exulting followers.

The other fifteen were men whose very appearance sufficiently indicated their profession — some cracking profane jokes with each other as they passed along, others ruminating enormous quids of tobacco which the marines, knowing they would shortly be hung, indulged them in; and some with their hands and heads bound with bloody handkerchiefs, scowling vindictive defiance.

As soon as his prisoners were securely housed, Solgard made no further delay, but hurried to greet his affianced bride. Both Miss Scheveling and her cousin Marx witnessed the first salutations; in which the widow endeavored to conceal her joy under a pretended amazement at her lover's sudden return, and Solgard made no secret of his satisfactions, to which Christine's lips bore testimony.

When Miss Scheveling arose to take her leave, Marx gallantly begged her to accept him as her squire; and as she had neither fallen in love with Mr. Sylvan, nor suspected him of falling in love with her, she acceded to his proposition with ” out any difficulty; and they passed along Mulberry Street, until they reached Lloyd's garden. Here they stopped to admire its beauty, when a venerable old lady, plainly attired in a dress of drab silk, and a snow-white cap that seemed purity itself, approached them from the garden, and said, —

"Come in, Barbara! and thy friend with thee; 'tis wonderful, the roses and tulips since thy last visit!”

Barbara and her cousin entered; and the old lady, after subjecting Mr. Sylvan to a tolerably rigid scrutiny, which he bore like a hero, concluded to enter him in her books as a probable favorite; and having accompanied the young” folks for a short distance, she felt so tired as to take a seat with her knitting in a well-shaded arbor, permitting Barbara and Marx to roam onward through the "wilderness of sweets,” and bidding them be sure to select pretty nosegays.

Her behest they obeyed, gathering great store of splendid and fragrant flowers, framing most brilliant and odoriferous bouquets; in the formation of which, Barbara, who was extravagantly fond of flowers, found much cause to admire the zeal and activity of her confederate.

"Prithee, Mr. Sylvan, get me an amaryllis for Mrs. Lloyd! and a campanula for my uncle. I am so delighted with your being a botanist!”

"So am I!" whispered Marx to himself; "I believe those lessons of Professor Linkendorf *will* be of some service to me, as he always maintained."

I "Bless me, Mr. Sylvan! you have brought mean amaryllis — would you accuse Mrs. Lloyd of coquetry?"

"Nay, I thought you sent me to procure this flower; but as it is an emblem of coquetry, suppose I bestow it on Madam — "

"Fy, Mr. Sylvan! you are too uncharitable! I told you to get me an amaranthus. How could you make such a mistake!"

Marx very well remembered what she had said at first; but perceiving her mind to be made up on the subject, he concluded that contradicting the lady would in no degree further his views: accordingly, he acknowledged his error with hypocritical penitence, and plucked an amaranthus.

"And here, Mr. Sylvan," said Barbara, with a smile of peculiar meaning, "is an evening primrose for yourself. Man's love, you know, is like the changing moon; but, not to be too merciless, I must even give you this bachelor's button."

"Of a truth. Miss Scheveling, you alarmed me not a little with the evening primrose; but the bachelor's button reviveth me so that 1 may say, with Crashaw, —

"Sweet hope! kind cheat! fair fallacy I by thee We are not where or what we be; But where and what we would be — thus art thou Our absent presence, and our future now."

And now, Miss Scheveling, take this sprig of veronica, and construe it when convenient— or perhaps you would listen to the interpretation thereof."

"Nay! it matters not," quoth Barbara; and her blush betrayed that she knew well enough what it symbolled.

Farther they strolled along, Barbara well pleased in her innocent heart with the admiration of her young and handsome squire; and Marx fearing to venture too rashly, but inwardly delighted that she blushed not with anger at his presumption, and swearing to himself that he had never seen his cousin look so beautiful as when he presented the last flower"

"Here is a flower," said Marx, "that has given occasion to no little innocent Action among the poets. If you permit me, Miss Scheveling, I will venture upon a quotation."

"At your own risk, Mr. Sylvan," quoth Barbara, holding up her finger with a warning gesture; "perhaps I can quote as well."

"Methinks," said Marx, "it runs somewhat thus; —

"Oh! there are looks and tones that dart
An instant sunshine through the heart.
At if the soul that moment caught
Some treasure it through life had sought"

As Marx uttered this rhapsody, he gazed upon his pretty cousin with so much meaning, that, after a momentary glance, she ventured not to look up again until he got through; and then, endeavoring to hide her agitation under a semblance of gayety, she exclaimed, as she held up a pink larkspur in her trembling fingers, — "Now, Mr. Sylvan, listen to my quotation:
—

"Men's fancies are more giddy and infirm,
More longing, wavering, sooner lost and won,
Than women's are."

This was repeated with peculiar archness; and then the graceful girl tripped lightly under the trees to where Mrs. Lloyd had taken her seat, and displaying to the kind old lady her collection of flowers, presented her with the amaranthine bouquet, kissed her, and bade her good-day, telling Mr. Sylvan that her uncle would wonder what could have become of her.

"Prithee, Barbara," exclaimed the old lady, "couldst thou find nothing prettier than that sprig of speedwell to carry in thine own bosom?"

It was the veronica which Marx had given her to which the old lady alluded; and Barbara was as much surprised as Mrs. Lloyd, to find it in such a situation — most probably it occurred from want of thought.

Marx took Miss Scheveling home, and conversed only upon such subjects as might occasion no embarrassment, imagining, perhaps, that what had already occurred would be sufficient for the damsel to cogitate upon for the present, and rather disposed to take encouragement than otherwise from what had taken place during the day.

BLACKBEARD

CHAPTER XIX.

"I am a man of war and might,
And know thus much, that I can fight,
Whether I am in the wrong or the right,
Devoutly."
Sir John Suckling.

Towards two of the morning, not long; after the moon had gone down, Nero, who was sitting up for his master, was aroused from a cat-nap, into which he had insensibly fallen, by a subdued murmur of rough voices, and a heavy tramp of many men passing along Penn Street through the darkness; upon which he suddenly got wide awake, and, with curiosity strongly excited, stealthily crept out to reconnoiter.

He could distinguish nothing for the obscurity of the night, which was so intense that he could barely see his own apron; but, listening attentively, he could hear a heavy tread of many feet, becoming more and more indistinct in the distance, from which he concluded that a large body of men had passed up into the city.

Nero's imagination was active, and this mysterious circumstance gave rise to a vast number of fanciful conjectures; until, by dint of hard thinking, he fell asleep, and dreamed incontinently that the town was sacked and burned by the Dutch.

At the same hour a single lamp shed its rays over Doctor Eastlake's office; and before the table on which it stood sat the doctor himself, with the light full upon his sallow features as he pored over an ancient volume that lay open before him. With his finger resting upon the book, as if pointing to a. particular sentence, he leaned back in his chair, musingly, unconsciously giving utterance to his thoughts in these words:

—

"If it *was* publicly taught in Padua, as Oxenstiern maintains — and yet Sennertus favors it not — now, in case —
"

A gentle tap at the window put a stop to the soliloquy and leisurely closing the volume, Eastlake opened the door, and Bob Asterley walked in.

"Eastlake, my boy! I was on my way home, when I espied a glimmering through the chinks of your window, and recollecting that *'Nocturnd versate manu"* was one of your favorite mottoes, and the ' midnight oil*"* spoke for itself, I concluded to overhaul your lucubrations."

"You will undermine the fair fabric of your constitution, I fear me, Bob; nay, you look chilly now" observed the doctor, as he stepped to a crypt behind his bookcase, from whence he returned with a dusty bottle and a couple of wineglasses.

"Hear you that?" exclaimed Bob.

Eastlake stood, with the bottle in one hand and the glasses in the other, and listened; and both heard a heavy trampling of feet on the outside, which gradually passed on, waxing less and less, until all was again quiet

"That reminds me," said Eastlake, filling the glasses, "of an old*"* Spanish ballad, which tells, that Grenada being besieged by the Moors, and reduced to great straits, dead warriors arose at night, headed by Bernardo del Carpio, or some such worthy, tramped through the silent streets, sallied forth, utterly routed the pagans, and were back and in their graves before daybreak."

Bob shook his head doubtingly, emptied his glass, and replenished. Much the two friends talked on philosophical as well as more trifling subjects, until the office became murky with aromatic clouds of smoke, and their forms, indistinctly seen around the table at that silent hour of night, might have been taken for incarnations of evil spirits, the effect heightened by the demoniac laugh that at times rang through the vapor.

Bob rose to depart: his step was not remarkably steady. Eastlake accompanied him to the door: not a single star to diminish the pitchy darkness.

"By all that's lovely, Eastlake! you must see me home.";

"The skies forbid the seeing of anything at present," replied the doctor; "but I will undertake to deliver you into the custody of Nero — there! hold fast."

It was well for the merry little man that his friend was at hand to uphold him through the darkness, for his irregular motions put the constancy of the doctor sorely to the test — pitching and rolling hither and thither like a ship in a shortsea — singing fragments of bacchanalian glees — blundering, with a species of elective affinity, over every obstacle that lay in the path — and finally reaching his domicile with vacillating and uncertain movements, where Nero gently conveying his oblivious master to his couch, Eastlake set forth on his return.

On reaching the foot of Society Hill, Eastlake was aware of the approach of two individuals, moving at a rapid pace down Pine Street. Having become by this time tolerably well familiarized to the darkness, he was enabled to perceive them at some distance, and to observe that they were moving in a direction that would shortly bring them within hailing distance.

The doctor was sufficiently well charged with the Tuscan grape, and when the strangers were within thirty feet of him, he sung out, in a stentorian voice,

"'Whither away, ye prowlers of the night? stand, an ye be true men!"

"Well met! most learned doctor!" responded a voice, which Eastlake had no difficulty in recognizing to be that of Oxenstiern; "gird up thy loins, and get thee ready for a fight My friend here, Mr. Sylvan, and myself intend pressing all able-bodied men for this night's service."

"What service mean ye, gentlemen?" quoth Eastlake.

"Follow us," answered Marx, "and you shall know anon." Eastlake observed that both of his companions were well armed with cutlass, dirk, and pistol; and presuming something serious to be in the wind, he stopped for a few moments at his official sanctuary, to garnish his person with the weapons of war; after accoutring himself in which, and dipping his head into a basin of cold water, he sallied forth, as he observed, ripe for any frolic.

Just as they turned the corner of the London Coffee-house into High Street, several pistol-shots rang upon their ears in quick succession — then scattering peals of musketry — and presently the alarm bell in the Guild belfry could be heard tolling with sharp startling strokes, that echoed far and wide over the silent city.

"Now!" cried Oxenstiern, unsheathing his cutlass, and turning to Eastlake, who became wonderfully alert as appearances of danger manifested themselves; "now, Eastlake, strike for your city! the pirates have attacked the prison, and Blackbeard has made a solemn oath that Sprigg shall be brought off. Nay, Sylvan!" continued he, turning to Marx, who began to show symptoms of impatience at this long harangue, "*you* need not to press onward so fast to-night; I tell you his time is not yet come."

As the alarm-bell continued to ring, the citizens began to turn out in all directions; some thinking that the Indians were upon them — others that the town was attacked by the pirates, and getting sacked and plundered. The bold and the young, furnished with such implements of war as were at hand, rushed towards the Guildhall, forming on their route bodies of eight or ten, and increasing in numbers as their forces converged to a common center.

The old and wary set about fortifying, every man his own domicile, in the most approved and substantial manner, much to the consolation and encouragement of their wives and daughters, who, being too seriously alarmed to think of fainting, lent them a ready assistance: so that in a very short time every householder had converted his mansion into a fortalice of no inconsiderable strength.

Had it not been for the prompt succour thus afforded by the turning out of the citizens, it hath been doubted whether Solgard, prepared and forewarned as he had been by the chevalier in relation to the nocturnal attack, would have been able, of his own force, to repel the savage and determined onslaught made by Blackbeard and his followers.

The pirates, under this formidable leader fought with a determined valor worthy of a better cause. Twice they reached the door of the prison, and twice the disciplined mass of marines bore them back at the point of the bayonet.

The more bold and active of the townsmen soon mingled in the fray. Oxenstiern led the way, and, as if satisfied with having set the example, withdrew from any active participation in the conflict further than to rush in, when he beheld any of his friends in great danger; and after extricating them with a reckless hardihood that defied with impunity cutlass, dirk, or pistol, he would resume his post of observation, as if it had been expressly appointed for him to watch the progress of the combat "

Doctor Eastlake chivalrously made an onset on the buccaneers; for which he received a blow on the bead, that put him immediately *hors de combat*, and rang in his ears for a week after. The chevalier succeeded in clearing a space around his fallen body, and, dragging him from the *melee*, carried him into a house near the scene of action, where the doctor lay insensible until after daylight. For a time, Marx Scheveling was more fortunate, though as rashly precipitate as the doctor: he was accustomed to the buccaneer mode of fighting, and annoyed his ancient allies exceedingly; felling his man here and there, and dodging by instinct the blows that his quondam associates, with right goodwill, levelled at his pericranium. But his evil genius prompted him, maugre the express injunctions of Oxenstiern, to have a bout with his ancient captain.

This grim leader had observed that his *ci-devant* lieutenant, Marx, was doing more mischief among his myrmidons than any one man had a right to do; and being chafed at the prospect of retiring without accomplishing his purpose, and disposed to give Marx a salutary lesson, he advanced with a grim smile to meet him.

Marx sprang upon him with a true buccaneer yell, that startled the townsmen — his cutlass flashing in the air like lightning, and his bounding leaps like those of a young tiger. But Blackbeard's blood was up, and he was not now to be trifled with. He pressed upon his foe with a degree of activity that surprised his own men: in strength he was superior beyond comparison. Marx at length succeeded in giving Blackboard a gash in the chest that most men would have been satisfied to retire with; but he took in return a cut on the left shoulder, so well applied that he went down, helpless as an infant: upon which Blackbeard, shouting for the encouragement of his men, began to cast about for a retreat from the field of battle; searching for the weakest point in the enemy's ranks, being now hard pressed by the mayor himself, a strong and lusty man, who was too scrupulous to use firearms or any such implements of war, but limited himself to a huge club, with which, as opportunity served, he would essay to keep the peace by knocking down such of the buccaneers as came within his reach.

Marx was taken by the chevalier to a place of safety, and, as he was very severely wounded, he was indebted to the surgical skill of Oxenstiern, who stanched the blood, bound up his wound, and read him a tolerably serious lecture on his imprudent conduct in spite of the most solemn warnings.

To his benefactor's excellent advice Marx listened with an impatient and vexed spirit. He panted to be revenged on Blackbeard, who had just added another to his former list of injuries; and now, disabled and unfit for fight, he was forced to listen to a dull lecture from a man to whom he felt himself under obligation for past kindness, and whom he could not silence without disrespect. These considerations threw Marx into a fever, which only made the matter worse. A high delirium succeeded: but, as he had lost an immense quantity of blood, he was too weak to overcome the force of his attendants, and his extravagance vented itself in a whimsical combination of the most passionate terms of endearment addressed to his "sweet cousin," and a torrent of most profane maledictions and threats of vengeance upon Blackbeard, that caused the female part of the household to turn pale with dismay.

Thus far the attempt made by Blackbeard to effect the liberation of Sprigg and his confederates had been signally defeated; and, so far from obtaining this desirable object, they found themselves in a situation of extreme peril, being environed and hemmed in by the force under command of Solgard on one side, and the irregular body of citizens on the other. Under these circumstances, Captain Teach deemed it expedient to make good his retreat, which he commenced in a movement down Second Street, breaking through the force that formed that portion of the blockading circle with much ease.

Save a few parting shots, their retreat was unmolested, the townsmen well satisfied to get rid of such ugly customers, and Solgard's detachment having been too severely handled during the engagement to undertake any serious annoyance. A mass of irregulars, however, hovered on their skirts as a body of observation until they issued from the town; and on their embarking in a number of boats that lay ready to receive them, they replied to the valedictory, triumphant shout of the townsmen with an ominous yell, that produced no very agreeable effect upon their pursuers.

The result of this nocturnal attack was matter both for regret and consolation. Of Solgard's marines, who received Blackbeard's first furious onset, seven were left dead in front of the Guildhall, and eighteen carried off the field of battle severely wounded. Solgard himself received a scratch from cutlass, which afforded him an excellent opportunity of exciting the tender sympathy of his betrothed, by wearing his left arm in a sling for two weeks afterward. Eastlake experienced no ulterior bad effects from the concussion he had suffered on his headpiece, save a partial and occasional lightheadedness during twenty-four hours after receiving the blow. None of the townsmen received any material injury; and those whose faces were much blackened by the priming of their own or their neighbors' guns, were asperged by their careful wives with proud and tender solicitude.

Marx Scheveling continued delirious for some hours, but gradually became composed; and, on recovering his sober senses, found himself so seriously wounded, and so weak from loss of blood, that he submitted, without any opposition, to the arrangements of Oxenstiern, who recommended repose, and delivered him up to the medical care of Doctor Eastlake.

On the other hand, three of the pirates lay stark and stiff at the corner of Second and High Street, and two had been captured after having been successively felled by the club of Thomas Hasell, not a little amazed on recovering their senses to find themselves in bondage.

MATHILDA DOUGLAS

With a commendable alacrity, the *Greyhound* immediately gave chase to the buccaneers, but without success. Not a vestige of the pirate was to be met with, although a most diligent and persevering search was made in every direction; and it might have been supposed that no such disturbers of the peace were in existence as long as the *Greyhound* was on the quest; but no sooner had she returned into port, than the indefatigable Blackbeard was heard of in every direction. Inflamed by his recent discomfiture, and rendered, if possible, ten times more ferocious than before, his cruelties were perpetrated, not only on the high seas, but inside of the capes, and, as if in mockery of his Britannic majesty's man-of-war, to a considerable distance up the Delaware itself.

These outrages called forth new exertions on the part of Solgard, but all attended with the same result — disappointment; which, however, served but to stimulate the captain to renewed efforts, that may be in some measure accounted for by the fact, that to his duty as a naval commander was added the necessary fulfilment of a vow, which in his pride he had made at the feet of his fair mistress, — to wit, that until Blackbeard was captured" he would not consider himself at liberty to call upon her for the performance of that promise by which she had pledged to him her lovely person.

Madam Markham found her confidence in the all-sufficiency of the *Greyhound* much impaired: Blackbeard had twice escaped when he seemed within the very grasp of her lover. Destiny perhaps protected this man of blood; and if he had sold his soul to the Evil One, as some ventured to affirm, then Solgard might give up all hopes of accomplishing his capture, and that vow — why, that vow could be forgotten by mutual consent.

Thus thought the lovely widow; but she was careful not to give utterance to such sentiments, at least the concluding portion of them. She hinted to her lover that his search for the rover might never be successful; at which he only pressed his lips firmly together, and said nothing — acknowledging, nevertheless, in his own mind, that her observation was by no means unjust, and repenting him, like Jeptha, of his rash and unreasonable vow.

BLACKBEARD

Major Scheveling, when, in due course, he received an account of the nocturnal onslaught made by Blackbeard, and further full and interesting details from the lips of his trusty friend the chevalier, lamented most bitterly his crippled condition; cursing the gout (Barbara was not within hearing) in the choicest Dutch epithets of malediction. Such an opportunity, he swore, might never occur again — he was always an unlucky man — he missed that great day at Gravelles, from having received a sabre-cut the day before in a petty skirmish that let nearly all the blood out of his body.

"And there I lay," exclaimed the major, "heard the firing that made the earth tremble beneath me, and had not even strength to crawl to the door 4f the tent! Think what I must have suffered!"

"Could not your attendant carry you to see the fight?"

"He, indeed! as soon as the firing got pretty brisk he left me to take care of myself, and soon provided himself with a good place in the Walloons. There, Barbara, my dear girl, take away this pillow. So three of the pirates, you tell me, were killed, and how many on our side?"

"Seven of Solgard's marines," replied Oxenstiern, "were killed on the spot, and our young friend Mr. Sylvan" (Barbara became pale as death) "was severely wounded" (her color returned a little); "but with good nursing he will soon recover. He is a noble fellow, full of spirit" (Barbara blushed as if the chevalier intended the compliment to herself), "with a little too much hot blood in him yet. Nothing would serve him but a bout with Blackbeard himself, and he fought beautifully before he went down, I assure you."

"Have him brought here directly," cried the major; "I like him, by the holy pipe of St. Nicolas! And thou, Barbara, wilt nurse him, there's a good girl, to oblige thy old uncle?"

Miss Scheveling cast down her eyes as she promised to take charge of the wounded stranger, else the old gentleman might have observed those beautiful blue orbs suffused with bashful pleasure, which " if he had traced to its proper source, would have given the veteran cause for apprehension that he was not acting very prudently in bringing into daily intercourse, under circumstances so well calculated to excite sympathizing pity on the one part, and grateful admiration on the other, the destined bride of his son Marx and the young and handsome hunter.

Where the parties also are favorably predisposed towards each other, sympathy deceives itself, gratitude becomes warmer, and both are by degrees blended in more tender and thrilling emotions. But of all these very probable contingencies the major never for a moment thought, in making his hospitable arrangements.

The chevalier promptly obeyed the suggestions of his warm-hearted old friend, and Marx, much to his surprise, was conveyed to the house of his father; who welcomed him with soldier-like frankness, and informed him that Miss Scheveling was a good nurse in the main, "although," he whispered to Marx, "a little whimsical in her notions at times."

This information Marx received with most profound respect, exposing his grateful feelings to the major for his kindness and hospitality, and taking especial care not to betray the satisfaction be experienced at the prospect of being nursed by his charming cousin.

It may appear somewhat singular that an old soldier, like the major, should so far forget his cautious principles as to admit to the familiarity of his domicile one almost a stranger. But the fact is constant — the major took a decided fancy to one so brave, ardent, and impetuous, — it seemed to remind him of his own youthful days, -— the impulse was strong, and the major did not at the moment recollect that sudden impulses often prove dangerous"

"He threw temptation in the way of his niece, and she must have been more than woman (she was not) to have withstood it.

THE END

www.ingramcontent.com/pod-product-compliance
Lightning Source LLC
Chambersburg PA
CBHW020636110726
47899CB00002B/786